Inheriting Fear

Sandy Vaile

CRIMSON
ROMANCE
F+W Media, Inc.

Published by
Crimson Romance
an imprint of F+W Media, Inc.
10151 Carver Road, Suite 200
Blue Ash, OH 45242. U.S.A.
www.crimsonromance.com

ISBN 10: 1-4405-8992-5
ISBN 13: 978-1-4405-8992-8
eISBN 10: 1-4405-8993-3
eISBN 13: 978-1-4405-8993-5

Cover art ©*moji1980*/123RF;© iStockphoto.com/Ljupco

*In memory of Fay,
an exceptional Aussie battler,
whose imprint remains on kindred hearts.*

Miss me, but let me go.

Acknowledgments

The art of creating a fantastical story and turning it into a saleable manuscript is a process that not only involves the creator but a collection of support people. It is these people who generously impart life wisdom, inspire me, provide moral support, participate in brainstorming sessions over cups of tea, and encourage me to never give up, whom I wish to thank here.

First and foremost I have to thank my family for their unwavering belief in me. My beautiful sons keep me on my toes by sharing their spirit of inquiry and discovery, but have yet to fathom why anyone would want to read a book without pictures.

My husband is my sounding board for new ideas and does his best to play it cool when I'm researching the best way to poison someone, or testing fight scenes on him—naturally, I wait until we're walking the dog, so I have a captive audience. Most of all I appreciate his acceptance of the peculiarities that come with living with an author. His firm confidence in my success sustains me when I reach the inevitable point of self-doubt.

My key technical guide was the esteemed Senior Sergeant Steve Hammond of the South Australia Police. He generously explained police procedures in layman's terms and helped bring into focus the indistinct line between realism and artistic license. You can be sure that Mya's story is fictional and, where I have strayed from the path of accuracy, the culpability lies with me alone.

A special mention to Lynn Wallace, who reads my *very* rough drafts, and Jamie Crannage. The remaining members of my support network are so numerous that I must mention them in general terms. They include literary colleagues from the Novelist's

Circle (past and present), Seaside Writers and Romance Writers of Australia, and my friends who listen to me ramble about my characters or plot twists.

All of these people have kept me motivated and, whether they know it or not, are experts on something I'm not, be it their job, hobby, or life experience.

And of course, I must thank Crimson Romance for providing the opportunity for me to realize a lifelong dream.

Chapter 1

Her brown combat boots pounded the bike track as her eyes searched the shadows on either side. Mya had made the same short journey five days a week for eleven years, but at night it still made the back of her neck prickle. She could buy a car and live in fear. Not a chance. Fear could go to hell.

Intermittent puddles of lamplight dripped onto the tarmac. Laughter and evening TV programs carried through the open windows of weatherboard houses along the railway track, and she inhaled a waft of grilled chops with the rail grease. She pushed her chef's skull-cap into the back pocket of her jeans and wrapped an elastic band around her long hair. On the other side of the tracks, the Croydon Hotel emitted a bass beat that vibrated in the viscous humidity.

She glanced at her watch and picked up the pace. It was supposed to be her night off work, but the sous-chef wanted to leave early for a party, and it was Mya's responsibility to make sure the kitchen ran smoothly. It wasn't like she had a social life anyway.

An androgynous shadow ambled from the bushes ahead, hands shoved deep into the pockets of a hooded jacket. She moved to the opposite side of the track. As the shadow solidified it looked taller, broader, with a hairy chin protruding from the obscurity of the hood. A flickering fluorescent streetlight alternated the image of a man and an ominous silhouette.

They passed one another and he looked up. Red, glassy eyes devoured her from head to toe. A shiver ran up the back of Mya's legs to her scalp. One side of his mouth lifted in a half-smile, so she nodded a greeting but kept walking.

With her eyes ahead and ears trained on his retreating footsteps, she breathed easier as each second passed. Walking the bike track at night certainly had its hazards, but it just wasn't worth getting the motorbike out of the shed and donning all the gear to go a few hundred metres. Besides, she had as much right as anyone to be there, and she'd made herself a promise a long time ago to never let anything or anyone stop her from doing what she wanted. Fear was just an emotion and she could overcome those with steely resolve.

The footsteps behind her ceased and her heart flip-flopped into her throat.

Mya turned around slowly. The hood guy had turned around too, and his left hand held a beer stubby, but not at the base like he was about to take a swig. His long fingers were wrapped around the neck of the bottle, making it look more like a weapon.

A lump of panic stuck in her throat. Best to get the hell out of there, but it went against her training to leave her back unprotected. Her kick-boxing mentor, Ned, would clip her around the ear if she let anyone get the upper hand on her. When the thug finally took a long draught from the stubby, she hurried in the direction of the Croydon Hotel again.

"Whocha doin' out 'ere in the dark, Mya?" he slurred.

She spun around and narrowed her eyes at the blackness beneath his hood. "Do I know you?"

He swayed closer. "Nah, but I know you."

"Look, I'm going to work. I don't want any trouble."

"Oh, you're in a lotta trouble, love."

Something glinted in the faltering light; his other hand strangled the hilt of a long blade. Her pulse thundered in her ears, drowning out the crickets in the grass. The hood slid back as they sized each other up. He looked a bit older than her, maybe mid-thirties, half a foot taller and beefy—although height and weight didn't always mean much in a fight.

After a deep, calming breath, she drew on the long hours spent in the gym facing her demons. She wasn't the angry teenager Ned had taken under his wing all those years ago. Learning how to kickbox had given her courage. No longer a victim, but in control. Another deep breath. Her pulse slowed fractionally. She *was* in control.

The thug leered with a mouthful of mangled teeth. She'd seen that look before, and it meant trouble. Whether it was trouble for him or her remained to be seen.

"I've gotta deliver a message." He tapped the corner of a white envelope that protruded from his pocket, sloshing beer down the side of his jeans. "She says it doesn't matter if I mess you up a bit, s'long as you're alive enough to read it."

"What? Who says?" Maybe he was hallucinating from drugs. Unpredictable, but she'd been taught to deal with that. A long time ago she decided no man was going to beat her the way she'd watched her mother get beaten. She summoned an inner calm, relaxed her stance, and held his gaze. "You know, alcohol slows your reflexes. Be careful with that knife."

A crease formed between his brows, but any doubts he had appeared to pass because he clenched the knife tighter and took a step toward her. She took a step backward and waited with feet shoulder-width apart, knees soft. The rumble of a train built in the distance.

Hood-man lunged, but his depth perception must have been distorted, because the blade was half a metre shy. He looked at it with a confused expression.

It was probably a waste of breath, but... "You *could* just give me the letter."

"And leave a fine piece of tail like you alone?" He lunged again.

This time she lifted onto her toes, raised a knee, and snapped the ball of her foot into his gut. He grunted and dropped the stubby in preference of clutching his stomach. Brown glass shattered and latte-looking foam pooled on the tarmac, circulating a yeasty smell. She was relieved to see the knife had slumped downward with his shoulders.

"I told you it was hard to concentrate when you're under the influence." With one finger she hooked her undie elastic out of her arse. Jeans weren't ideal for kickboxing, but her boots were solid. Old faithfuls, with years of stains slopped over them and frayed stitching.

"You're gonna be sorry for that, bitch."

"I doubt it," she muttered.

She'd spent too many years living in fear as a child. Now she was in charge of her own destiny, and no man was going to dictate to her. His eyes were wider now, and the whites were yellow with red capillaries tangled like a mess of string around the irises. Definitely drugs. Dark hair flopped across his face, and he pushed it back with a twitch. His weight shifted left and he feinted right.

Mya stood her ground.

"Why don't you give me the letter and we can call it a night?"

The sounds of crickets and a baby crying were swallowed by the rumble of the passing train. As he thrust the knife again, she pinned his wrist in her armpit, and elbowed him in the gut. He hunched over, and she snapped her arm back. Knuckles connected with his nose. *Crunch*.

He yowled and stumbled back, dropped the blade to better clutch his bleeding nose. Quickly, she snatched up the knife—cheap army disposals crap—and tucked it through a belt loop.

"Message delivered," she told him as she grabbed the envelope from his pocket.

He remained bent over, nursing his nose, as she jogged along a strip of moonlit track to the footpath. The envelope felt like a hot coal in her hand. She glanced over her shoulder. No hood-man, so she slid the blade up her sleeve, cupping the hilt in her palm, and crossed the railway track.

It looked like local band Shamrock had pulled a big Saturday-night crowd. Windows vibrated in time with the thud of the bass. Party-goers leaned against the faded blue pub front, and she held her breath to pass through the haze of smoke drifting in the warm air. She stepped through the back door of the pub and … breathed. It felt safe here, almost like home. She'd worked her way from apprentice to head chef at the Croydon and was practically part of the furniture.

At the back of the store room, she stashed the knife behind a sack of rice, then wiggled a finger into the back of the envelope and split it open. Inside there was a lined page with a jagged edge, like it had been torn from a spiral-bound pad. The handwriting had a backward slant, but the note wasn't signed.

She could just throw the letter in the bin and pretend she'd never seen it, but whoever this woman was, she had gone to the trouble of paying off a druggie to deliver it, maybe hoping Mya would get roughed up some. The guy had said "she," and he didn't look in any position to improvise, so the author must be a woman.

More worrying, the woman knew her by name. That took motivation, and Mya needed to know what kind of person would go to those lengths. Sure, she'd pissed off a few people over the years—especially in the boxing ring—but an enemy? She couldn't think of anyone who hated her enough to bother.

After a fortifying breath, she read the letter.

You're good at running and hiding, aren't you, Mya? But I know who you are. I bet you thought I'd forgotten about you and your retarded mother. Thought you could hide from me, but I'm coming for you, bitch.

I'll be watching … sleep well.

Something slimy slid down her throat and into her gut: familiarity. There was no way it could be who she thought it was, but the note gave her a sense of panic from a long time ago. It felt like when she was eighteen, standing in front of her government-appointed housing with a thirty-something redhead yelling at her.

The conversation had started civilly. The woman wanted to know about Jack Roach, but Mya's father had been dead a year by then, and good riddance to him. But carrot-top wouldn't leave her alone, insisting Jack had another family, and wanting to know things about Mya. Things she wasn't ready to share.

Bloody Jack had been the one who tore apart everything she knew and devastated the only person she cared about, her mum. There were only tatters of her life left, but they were hers and no sham relative was going to turn up for a hand-out and stop her from taking care of her mum.

It couldn't be possible for Rhonda to have tracked her down. Mya had changed her name and moved. It wasn't feasible. She forced short breaths out of her tight lungs. A shudder started at the crown of her head and made its way down her spine. She glanced at the darkness beyond the hotel's back door and then hurried to the bright kitchen. Service was in full swing and the din of the exhaust fan, crockery, and sizzling food soothed her raw nerves.

She'd left Jack behind, but the prick was still tormenting her a decade after he died.

"Hey, Mya, you look like you saw a ghost." Jilly tucked a pen behind her ear and dropped an order pad into the pocket on the front of her apron.

"You okay?" Marion, the sous-chef, stepped away from the grill.

Even the dish pig had stopped feeding greasy plates into the commercial dishwasher to stare.

"I-I'm fine. Just had a run in with a punk on the bike track, that's all."

Marion nodded knowingly. "Why you insist on walking along there in the dark is beyond me. It's not safe for a woman."

"I'm not scared of any man," Mya snapped a little too forcefully to be convincing.

Marion shrugged. "Well, thanks for covering for me tonight. I just put a medium-well rump on the grill and a salmon in the oven."

"Sure. You're still okay to work tomorrow?"

"Don't worry, I won't get smashed at the party. I'll be here at ten a.m. Enjoy your day off." Marion tossed her tea towel at Mya and circled her hand at the kitchen. "Have fun, peeps."

"Enjoy the party," everyone called.

With a shake to clear her head, Mya tucked the tea towel into the front pocket of her jeans, slid the white skull-cap onto her head, and familiarised herself with the dockets clipped beside the grill.

Worrying about the letter would have to wait until after service. God knew she'd lived through enough bad news to last a life time, but she wasn't the same girl now. Whoever sent the threat would have to wait their turn and, when the time came, she'd face them head on.

Chapter 2

Mya sat on an upside-down milk crate by the back door of the pub. Jilly sat beside her, waving a hand in front of her face to fend off the cloud of flying bugs. She used both hands to readjust her bosoms in the tight white shirt whose buttons strained dangerously in the middle.

"Damn, there's something swimming in my drink," she complained, using a long pink nail to retrieve the winged intruder.

Mya swigged orange juice and shifted on the milk crate so it wouldn't leave a pattern on her butt.

"I don't suppose there's vodka in that?" Jilly motioned toward the juice.

"You know there isn't."

Jilly made a distasteful face. "Need a good, stiff drink after a Saturday night shift." Ice swirled around the tumbler of dark amber liquid in her hand. "Got any plans?"

"Nah, it's late."

Jilly glanced at her watch. "Five past midnight is *not* late on a Saturday."

They turned to the sound of footsteps, and Flynn Murphy's sun-beaten face appeared in the doorway, lips grinning around a mouthful of yellowed teeth. Flynn was the hotel's publican and one of only three men Mya had ever trusted.

"Mya, love, I heard you had some trouble on the way here." He smoothed the gray hair at his temples and scanned the car park. His Gaelic accent was so slight most people wouldn't pick it. "Would you like a lift home?"

It was nice of him to offer, and it would be nice to avoid a repeat performance on the bike track. Then again, she'd set the creep straight. Face my fears. It was a mantra that had got her this far. "Nah, it's nothing I can't handle. Thanks, Flynn."

"I know." He sighed. "At least Daylight Savings starts tomorrow. See you in a couple of days."

"Good night," the girls chorused.

"Flynn's a good bloke," Jilly declared. "Speaking of which, you oughta find yourself one."

Mya clenched her teeth. "Not this again. I told you, I don't need a man in my life."

"It's not a matter of *need*. It's nice to have someone take care of you."

"I take care of myself."

"There are plenty of other reasons: someone to come home to at night, to take out the garbage, sex on tap. Take your pick. Don't you get sick of one-night stands?"

Mya took a deliberately long drink of juice. Jilly knew her stance: *her* house, *her* life, no sharing.

Jilly shrugged. "Anyway, you should come shopping with me tomorrow. Dave and I are going to a friend's wedding in a couple of weeks, so I need to get a new dress, maybe shoes."

"As fun as that sounds"—she grimaced—"I don't need anything."

"You don't actually have to buy anything. It's a girl's day out. Besides, I bet you don't even own a dress." Mya shook her head and Jilly grunted in disgust. "All you do is cook and work out in that grimy gym." She drained her brandy and went back inside.

Mya wasn't about to tell her friend it was the gym that had given her power over her own life for the first time, or that she owed Ned the world. Without him she didn't like to think where she'd have ended up. She stacked the crates by the wall and retrieved the knife from the back of the store room.

"See ya," she called to the dish pig as he waved a mop back and forth over the tiles.

She walked home along the bike track, shoulders tense and eyes scanning for trouble. It might have been a good idea to take

Flynn up on that lift. Then again, she never was one to back down from anything that scared her. It was the only way she'd survived a childhood with Jack.

Most of the streetlights had been stoned, leaving long, sinister shadows across the track. She clenched the knife tighter when she saw the dark stain of drying blood under the flickering light. A trail of spatter went in the opposite direction, but there was no sign of hood-man.

Railway Terrace followed the train track, and century-old terraced houses lined one side. Mya had bought number twenty-one cheap, because apparently the fumes and noise from the trains put a lot of people off. It wasn't one of Adelaide's sought-after suburbs, but it held a certain appeal for her. When she was a kid she had spent plenty of time riding trains. The click-clack sound and rocking motion was soothing, and it kept her out of the house for hours at a time. Besides, she had more important things to spend her money on than herself.

The houses shared common walls and picket fences. Most of them had paved paths to heritage-green front doors, rust-red bricks, and fruit trees sheltering rows of petunias. Someone with more money than sense had built a second story on the house at the end, and it now loftily surveyed the street from frosted windows. A real-estate sign in the front yard had a red SOLD sticker slapped on it at an angle.

Mya sidled through her front gate as it drooped on broken hinges. Hers was the only yard with wild alyssum rambling through knee-high grass. She smiled at the thought of old Bert next door complaining it was high enough to hide snakes. He invariably waited until she went out before trimming it.

A fistful of envelopes were jammed into the letterbox. She held her breath and turned each one over, scanning for a backward slanting script, and then puffed it out when she realized they were all regular mail.

The front door stuck in the warm weather, so she pushed with her shoulder. Once inside, she flicked on lights and pushed two slide bolts into place. She tossed the knife into a bowl half full of confiscated weapons. If the police raided the place, they'd think they'd hit the jackpot and hooked themselves a serial killer.

Reclining in her favourite red-leather chair, she re-read the threatening note. It didn't make sense for Rhonda to have tracked her down after all these years, but who else could it be?

After Cockroach—that was what she called Jack Roach—died, Mya had applied to Deed Poll to change both her and her mum's names. She needed a fresh start—something she couldn't do traversing the streets of her childhood or being recognised as a drunk's daughter. Until tonight, she was sure moving to the opposite side of Adelaide had been far enough to leave her previous life as Lara Roach behind.

Lara. The name sounded alien now. There was only one thing she missed about Lara the victim, and that was having her mum whole.

But the likelihood of a regular person tracking a name change was too slim to consider. So that meant the author must be someone from her present life. After all, they had used her new name.

The real question was, what did this person want? Whoever was gunning for her obviously wanted to toy with her, make her sweat. Which left only one motivation.

Revenge.

Chapter 3

Mya buried her face deeper in the pillow and ignored the alarm. The threat from the note had leaked into the recesses of her mind, like oil into the cracks of wet cement. She'd tossed all night, but no amount of calming breaths could stop her worrying about her mum. She needed to see and touch her. Know she was safe.

After a quick shower and toast, Mya pushed her Triumph Speed Triple motorcycle out of the backyard shed and into the access alley—Railway Lane, some bright spark had named it. The bike was her one luxury with its red tank, silver pipe, and hulking black 1050cc engine. She swung a leg over and turned the key in the ignition. Hopefully none of the neighbours were trying to sleep in this morning. The three cylinders growled as she twisted the throttle and then gurgled and spluttered as she coasted away from her house.

A moving van almost blocked the end of the lane, behind number twenty-five—the two-story monstrosity—but there was just enough space to squeeze the bike between it and the fence without taking off a mirror. She nearly lost her balance when a tall bloke with shoulder-length blond hair appeared in front of her.

His smile pulled the left side of his mouth up crookedly around a thin scar on his top lip, but it didn't detract from his rugged good looks. In fact, it added character and maybe made him look older—she guessed he was a few years older than her, which would make him about thirty. A white tank top clung to his chest and his tracksuit pants hung low on his hips.

"Sorry. Do you want me to move the van?" he asked.

She dragged her gaze up to meet his powder-blue one. "Nah, you're 'right." She knocked the bike's gear pedal into neutral and flipped up her visor.

"I'm Luca, by the way. Just bought this place." He held out a hand.

She pressed her palm against it and watched long fingers wrap around her leather glove, mesmerised by the way his tanned bicep contracted as he shook her hand.

Won't mind having him for a neighbour at all. "Mya from number twenty-one. Are you moving in with your family?" She cringed internally, not really interested in hearing about Mrs. Luca.

"Nah, just me." He flashed another crooked smile and disappeared inside the van. With a box in hand he said, "Come by for a housewarming drink later if you're free."

"Sure."

She nodded a farewell and coasted the bike down the alley. What a shame she had no intention of having that drink with him. No sense getting chummy with a bloke who knew where she lived.

Sunday morning traffic was light as she wound back and forth through the side streets, dodging morning joggers and a couple of drunks sprawled half on the road. Even the throaty reverberation of the engine and warm summer air couldn't diminish her desperate need to lay eyes on her mum. With a brief glance around to make sure no cops were nearby, she took the sweeping right-hand intersection on Port Road at 120 kilometres an hour.

Richmond Hill was on the other side of Adelaide city, where the houses all had an attic or second story, manicured gardens with topiary pittosporum and pastel roses in neat lines. Huge jacarandas sprinkled wide streets with purple petals. A mother wearing a designer pantsuit, full makeup, and immaculate hairstyle pushed a Rolls Royce pram. A pot-bellied man buffed a silver BMW on a paved driveway. A gang of children on shiny bikes waved, tassels streaming from their handlebars.

Hard to believe she was only a few kilometres from Croydon, where the soup kitchen regularly turned people away.

The Speed Triple pulled up the incline at the back of the suburb to Rich Haven—Mya loved the play on words—Aged Care Facility, for the rich. There were annoyingly spaced speed humps along the kilometre of driveway, so she stood on the foot pegs to ease over them. Lawns sprawled on either side, dotted with park benches and rose gardens, shaded by vast gums, ash, and beech. The groundsman made deliberate arcs on a ride-on mower, throwing up the crisp scent of cut grass.

The grand Victorian building looked a lot like a castle with three stories of weathered stone and arched verandas with filigree rails and spires. On either side of the central building were large wings. With a see-saw motion, she walked the motorbike back into a parking space and left her helmet on the ground. No need to lock anything at Rich Haven. The mental image of a primped old lady taking off on the Triumph like a Hells Angel cracked her up.

She was still giggling as she climbed the wide slate staircase and passed through half-metre-thick walls into the reception.

"Hi, Mya." Beverly Aldridge had been the bubbly receptionist for all of the nine years Mya's mum had been there.

"G'day, Bev."

Beverly pushed the guest register across the counter for her to sign. She tested the pen, secured to a silver chain, and signed *Mya Jensen, visiting Rosalie Jensen.*

Neither of them had used Jack's surname after *that* day. The day their lives changed for the better and worse.

It had been SWOT Vac week at school, so Mya had been studying at home when Jack Roach—now Cockroach to her—returned from the pub. He swaggered through the front door and clipped her across the head by way of a greeting. She ignored him, like she always did when he was tanked.

Her mum was in the kitchen, rushing to heat a plate of food, but she wasn't fast enough and there was a slap, followed by crockery clattering to the floor. Her mum didn't cry right away, but as each blow landed, Mya's intestines knotted tighter and tighter. She closed her books with a wallop and shoved them into a backpack. It was time to ride the trains.

That was more than a decade ago. She shook her head to clear the acidic thoughts on her way down the cream-coloured hallway. At door number thirty-two, she knocked gently and let herself in. A petite brunette nurse was writing on a clipboard.

"Hi, Anne."

Anne flashed a brilliant-white smile. "Good morning, Mya. It's a beautiful day today."

"Yeah, I think we'll go for a walk."

"Give me a minute and I'll help you move her into the wheelchair."

"How is she?" Mya held her breath, the way she did every time she asked. Her mum was the only person left in the world that she cared about, and the thought of losing her was unimaginable.

"No change. I'll let you know if the doctor finds anything at her weekly check-up tomorrow."

"Thanks."

Anne pulled a flat-folded wheelchair from a nook beside the wardrobe. "What are you reading at the moment?"

"Oh, I just finished a wicked suspense by Helene Young, but I'm into *The Girl with the Dragon Tattoo* now and can't put it down. You'll have to borrow it afterward."

"I'd like that. A couple of friends said it's a good story."

Rosalie Jensen looked small in her floral-print recliner. She didn't turn to the sound of Mya's voice, but stared peacefully through multi-paned French doors to the garden. The natural light made her soft skin glow. Mya had paid an exorbitant amount of money to get a room on the ground floor in the high-dependency wing, and it was worth every penny. Of course, she wouldn't be able to afford Rich Haven if it weren't for Cockroach. Irony was a bitch.

"Hi, Mum."

Rosalie moved her head slightly and her brown eyes flickered sideways, but her face remained blank, gaze vacant. Deep down Mya believed her mum was still in there, somewhere. Believed she recognised her only daughter.

Anne unfolded a wheelchair beside Rosalie and Mya bent to lock the wheels in place and swing the footrests out of the way. They slid her mum to the edge of her armchair, and she put her arms around Mya's neck.

"Hold tight, Mum."

Rosalie was cooperative, but still a dead weight as Mya lifted from under her armpits and Anne supported her thighs. They stepped sideways and lowered her into the wheelchair. Rosalie's left arm spasmed and her hand automatically tucked under her chin. Mya straightened it.

There wasn't a lot she could do for her mum these days, but she took pleasure in the little things. She'd failed to protect Rosalie all those years ago, but she wouldn't fail her again. Tender care was the best she could do now. This was all she had left.

"Thanks, Anne."

"You're welcome. Enjoy the walk." She flicked dark hair over her shoulder and picked up a tray of tiny plastic cups holding multi-coloured pills.

Mya flung open the French doors and wheeled her mum onto the patio. Rosalie's head tilted toward the sky and she closed her eyes. Maybe it was because of the dazzling light, but Mya preferred to believe her mum enjoyed the warmth on her face.

Footpaths criss-crossed the fourteen-hectare property, and today there were lots of people pushing wheelchairs or sitting on benches and watching grandchildren scamper across lawns. Mya made a loop around the lake and paused on a PermaPine boardwalk. She liked to keep her mum up to date with her life, even if it was a monologue.

"Can you believe the corner store got an ATM? I guess it was too far for people to walk another 200 metres to the supermarket."

She reached into a plastic bread bag and tossed crumbs in an arc across the water. A raft of speckled-brown native ducks glided from the bank to squabble over the tidbits.

A raised voice—male, of course—disturbed the tranquility. Mya grabbed the handles of the wheelchair in an automatic flight reflex, and her limbs tingled with a surge of adrenaline.

I'm safe. Mum is safe.

"Sorry, Mum. Now where was I? Oh, yes, we were flat-chat at the hotel last night, which is why I slept in a bit today. Met my new neighbour this morning, too. Mighty fine," she added under her breath.

Rosalie stared across the lake, not even flinching when an overzealous duck took flight and flicked water onto her face. Mya used her sleeve to wipe it off, and her mum held eye contact for a few seconds longer than usual—a fleeting glimpse of lucidity.

"I know you're in there, Mum," Mya whispered. She pressed her lips to Rosalie's velvet-soft cheek. "You're too young to be in this place." Her mum was only forty-nine and surrounded by the elderly, but there wasn't any other option. "Nothing but the best for you."

Shoes clip-clopped along the path and she heard the angry male voice again, followed by the hushed disagreement of a female. A man and woman rounded a violet honey-myrtle bush and glanced in her direction. The woman wore the Rich Haven uniform: navy skirt and pale blue pin-striped shirt. Mya didn't recognise her, so she wasn't from the high-dependency wing, but there was something familiar about her walk, the way she dragged the toes of her left foot with each step. She couldn't place it.

A tall blond man in an orderly's outfit had thick fingers wrapped tightly around the woman's bicep and was propelling her forward. His gaze flicked in Mya's direction, and he released the arm. Mya's instincts told her the woman needed help, but the couple kept their eyes on the footpath and disappeared around the next bend. What people needed and wanted weren't always the same.

Mya wheeled Rosalie back to her room, settled her in the recliner chair, and left the doors open to let the breeze in. She tossed a tartan blanket over her mum's knees and retrieved a glossy, black jewelry box from the bedside drawer. It had been a birthday present for her mum, bought in a secondhand shop when Mya was in primary school. The menagerie of African animals painted on the lid had attracted her. Rosalie had often talked about taking Mya to Africa one day, to stand so close to a lion that the hairs on the back of their necks would stand up, or look at a strange giraffe with its long lips, doe eyes, and not-quite horns.

There was an assortment of trinkets inside the box, but only two were valuable to Mya. The first was a wedding ring with a small diamond caught inside a golden web, handed down from her grandma to her mum. Pity Mya would never use it, because she had no intention of ever letting a man control her.

Nestled beside the ring was a long silver chain with a tiny cylinder pendant and a crystal bauble on the lid. She lifted it out, surprised that it didn't feel as cool or heavy as usual, but that was probably because of the warm weather.

It might just be her memory playing tricks, but she could swear the jewelry still smelt like her Grandma's floral perfume, intermingled with the mothballs from her clothes.

She sat on the arm of her mum's chair and dangled the necklace high, so the crystal caught the light and sent a rainbow of refracted light across the room.

"Do you remember the story Grandma used to tell us? She said Grandpa scrimped and saved for weeks to get enough silver to make the necklace. Then he drew the metal over a stake to form the cylinder and embossed the pattern on the outside. When he made the secret chamber, even the master silversmith was impressed.

"Grandpa was so nervous when he proposed that his voice shook, but Grandma already knew he was a special man and said yes right away." She sighed deeply at the memory. "I wonder if he was the last decent man on the planet."

Rosalie's eyes swayed back and forth in time with the pendulum motion of the suspended necklace. Mya twisted the crystal bauble between thumb and forefinger, to pop the hidden chamber. It was stiff, so she tried again. The necklace was old, but it usually turned easily, so she wiped her hands down the front of her jeans and tried again. It would not twist.

With her cheeks suddenly hot, she hurried to the jewelry box, snatched the gold ring out, and flicked on the bedside lamp. She tilted the ring.

"No!" There was no inscription inside. She'd seen it a hundred times before. *Ádh na nÉireannach*: luck of the Irish. Her gaze tracked from the necklace to the ring and back again. A fist of dread sat heavily in her gut, and she toppled onto the bed as her legs gave way.

She picked up the bedside phone. "Beverly, someone's stolen Mum's jewelry."

Chapter 4

Luca Patterson lay on his brown three-seater lounge with bare feet hanging over one end and surveyed his new house. It looked pretty good, despite the boxes stacked in corners. Sure, you had to stop talking when a train passed every half hour, but it was far enough away from his old home to start anew.

"Well, you finally did it," Quinton said.

His big brother had been harping on for ages about Luca moving house. It wasn't the only "moving on" his family had encouraged either. Apparently seven years was long enough to mourn a wife.

It wasn't really about mourning though. Luca had given Olivia his heart, and it wasn't his to re-gift. Selling the house they'd shared had seemed like a betrayal, but the real clincher had been when his younger brother, Gabe, proposed to Bree. They looked so damned happy. It reminded him of what he used to have, and he wanted it again—even if he didn't deserve it. Not that Olivia had blamed him for spending time at work instead of with her, not ever.

Too late to dwell on the past though, because there were no do-overs in life.

Quinton tossed a beer stubby to him and flopped onto the chair opposite.

"Thanks for helping." Luca raised the cold bottle in appreciation.

"Anything for a beer, but I don't know why you need such a big house."

Luca shrugged and stared down the amber neck of his stubby. Although his optimism was low, he'd bought the house to someday accommodate a family.

"Hey, who was the chick on the motorbike earlier?" Quinton grinned teasingly.

Luca raised an eyebrow in response.

"Oh, you thought I didn't see. There *are* windows on the top floor, you know. Did you invite her over?"

"Yeah, but only to be neighbourly." Although he wouldn't admit it to Quinton, Luca hadn't stopped thinking about his neighbour all afternoon. She had long, slender legs and a cute face—even squished into a helmet. Gleaming hair the colour of liquid caramel spilled down her back and, although he couldn't see the rest of her under the leather jacket and gloves, there was something seriously hot about a chick on a motorbike.

"Well, send her my way," Quinton said.

"Geez, arrogant much? You're supposed to be a pillar of society."

"I'm a lawyer, not a saint."

Luca grabbed a cleaning cloth and tossed it at his brother, who ducked, tipping the characteristic Patterson hair over his eyes. All three of the brothers had the same blond hair, blue eyes, and tanned skin, but the similarities were only skin deep. Luca was a typical middle child. He didn't have the leadership drive of Quinton, and he wasn't quite as laid-back as Gabe. No, Luca had to find a way to stand out in a family of academics. What better way to capture his parents' attention than to follow a dangerous and dirty career in law enforcement?

A song about being on the edge, screamed from Luca's top pocket, indicating a work call—his idea of a joke.

"Detective Patterson." He shrugged an apology at Quinton, who waved his indifference and headed to the kitchen, opening and shutting cupboards.

"Luca, it's Kate. Sorry to phone during your holiday, but I've got a lead on the nursing home case."

"You have? I could do with some good news on that front."

"Well, I cross-referenced the staff from Happy Vale Nursing Home with all the other aged-care facilities in the metro area and I got a hit. Two hits, in fact."

"Two coincidences?" He put his beer on the dining table and pulled a pad of paper and pen closer.

"It gets better. Both staff members left Happy Vale at the same time, nine months ago."

He chewed the end of the pen. Nine months ago he'd investigated reports of jewelry thefts at the nursing home and overheard staff discussing the sudden increase in deaths. He dug a little deeper and confirmed an increase compared to previous years, but the deaths weren't suspicious enough to warrant autopsies.

The same resident doctor had signed each death certificate, so Luca had investigated him. No evidence of anything untoward, but something didn't sit right in his gut. There was a pattern of ladies without relatives dying, which meant no one to ask questions. Of course, once Luca started snooping around, it all went quiet.

Quinton reappeared, put an unopened stubby on the table in front of him, and dropped onto a chair with a bag of chips.

"They're both working across town now, at Rich Haven Aged Care Facility," Kate said.

"Hell. That place is the Ritz of nursing homes. Sounds like they're moving on to bigger and better things. See if their contact details are current and speak to the director at Rich Haven. Find out how they got their jobs. Were the staff they replaced sacked, pushed, or did they quit?"

"I'm onto it, but I can tell you both phones are disconnected. I'm on my way to check out the addresses now."

"You're a gem, Kate, but be careful. You're just looking, okay? And keep me updated." He balanced the phone between his ear and shoulder to use both hands to crack the seal on the new beer. *Kssst.* "You know what happened last time."

"Yeah, the boss told you to leave it the hell alone."

"Right. Without evidence we haven't got a case, so tread lightly."

"Talk to you tomorrow."

"Thanks, Kate." He snapped the mobile shut and dropped it back into his pocket.

"Good news?" Quinton sat sideways on an armchair, drawing a moisture trail on his forearm with the bottom of his stubby.

Luca nodded. "Yeah, real good. Shall we order pizza?"

"I could kill a pizza right now." Quinton grinned. "We should see if the biker chick wants in."

The thought of him ogling Mya created a strange, tight feeling in Luca's chest. "If she turns up for a drink, then she's all yours, but I'm not chasing her so you can disgrace yourself." He punched Quinton on the shoulder and flipped his phone open again to Google a local pizza delivery joint.

• • •

Mya sat in the wicker chair on her front porch, enjoying the evening breeze across her face. The porch light was off—not because she enjoyed sitting in the dark, but because she believed in facing her fears. Besides, it deterred the bugs. She had one of those blue zapper lights once, but the sound of frying insects put her on edge, so she gave it to Jilly at the Croydon Hotel.

This morning she had gone to the police station to make a statement about her mum's jewelry. They took the fakes as evidence, but the young constable with cropped hair, had a dull look in his eyes that told her he'd already taken too many statements without fruitful outcomes.

The smell of warm tarmac wafted on the breeze, along with the delicate perfume from the jasmine on Mr. Reiner's porch next door. Some of the nails holding together the rain-stained wicker chair she was sitting on had worked loose. She pushed one down with the bottom of her tea mug.

A pizza delivery car stopped at Luca's house. Maybe she should take him up on his offer of a drink. But that wouldn't be a good idea; she preferred her men random, so they couldn't find her afterward. Besides, there was laughter coming through his open windows, so he obviously had company and didn't need an awkward neighbour hanging around.

Pity, because he was mighty fine to look at. Not department store brochure good-looking, but he had a jovial face that promised entertainment. There was something special in his eyes too. They were guarded by feathered lines, as though they'd seen things they didn't want to, but when she looked deeper still, they were open and honest. Eyes she wouldn't mind staring into again sometime.

The three-quarters moon provided enough light for Mya to see four shadows skulk along the footpath. There had been a lot of late-night skulking since the Mason family took a six-month rental at number eleven. The elderly residents living on Railway Terrace had been complaining about rubbish tossed in their yards, drunken parties, and revving cars. Mya sat still and watched.

Mrs. Mason wandered into the middle of the road. She had an unnatural-looking potbelly, like there was a tumour under her belt. The face of Paula, her teenage daughter, was half-hidden by a long fringe, the glow of a cigarette swinging at her side. Padding barefoot behind them was Paula's little sister—almost as wide as she was high. An unfortunate-looking lot.

Where's the fourth shadow? Mya leaned forward and the wicker squeaked. There was movement in the front yard of number seventeen. Paula's boyfriend waddled out with his pants down around his ankles. Classy.

The Masons laughed and jostled one another on their way past. They didn't see Mya sitting in the dark, but she watched them until they were out of sight.

Seeing ferals stroll the streets got Mya's back up, but there was no point calling the cops, because they wouldn't bother chasing after petty criminals, just like they didn't bother doing anything about Cockroach all those years ago. Her neighbours back then had called the cops plenty of times when he went on a bender, and sometimes the cops held him overnight to sober up, but never long enough. He always came home.

Yep, the cops were unreliable, so tomorrow *she'd* start scouring the pawnshops for her mum's jewelry. Whoever stole it went to the trouble of making replicas, so they wanted to sell it somewhere and she was going to find it, and them.

Chapter 5

Bright and early Monday morning, Luca perched on the edge of his wood-laminate desk and read Melanie Lane's and Kevin Barnes's résumés. Constable Kate Derman sat with her pen poised.

"So," she began, "the director assured me the staff Melanie and Kevin replaced at Rich Haven resigned of their own accord. Um … I haven't told the inspector I'm working on this yet." Kate doodled arrows along the top of her paper.

The last time Luca had been on the trail of suspicious deaths in a nursing home, the inspector had told him that no evidence meant no case. Luca sighed and smoothed his hair into the rubber band at the nape of his neck.

Kate's mouse-brown hair was cut into a utilitarian bob and her face was makeup free. Her pale blue shirt had a crease pressed into each sleeve, likewise down the front of her navy slacks, finishing with polished black lace-ups. She was the picture of enthusiasm and diligence. He shouldn't involve her in his obsession, but he couldn't do it without her. "Thanks, constable. Leave the inspector to me. What happened after I spoke to you yesterday?"

Kate flicked through a spiral-bound book. "The address for Melanie was vacated around the time she left Happy Vale Nursing Home. Kevin's turned out to be bogus."

Through his office window Luca watched his boss, Inspector Brian Moss, stop to get updates from three officers on his way from the coffee machine to his desk. He'd soon want to know why Luca was hanging around the station during his annual leave.

Luca started pacing in front of his desk. "Their identities are probably fabricated, so I'm guessing these glowing résumés are too." He waved the faxes in his hand. "The question is *how* did they get these jobs? I want you to get me the contact details for the staff Kevin and Melanie replaced at Rich Haven and send them to my phone. We're going to talk to them."

"Should I run down the references on their résumés, just in case?" Kate stood and smoothed her slacks.

"Good idea." He gathered his suit jacket and unearthed his car keys from a fresh pile of internal mail. When he turned toward the door, he almost bumped into Kate. "Is there something else?"

"What should I tell the inspector if he asks what I'm working on?"

"I appreciate your help, constable. Just tell him the truth. I'll deal with Moss. In the meantime, you'd better keep working on our current case, too. It was an anonymous tip-off about stolen jewelry being resold, which could be just someone dicking us around, but head over to Pete's Pawn Shop and then Junk 'n Stuff. Review their records for the last couple of weeks. If we keep the pressure up, we're bound to find something."

Kate scowled. "Dirtbags. I'm sure there's stolen merchandise going through those places. We just have to catch them at it."

"Pay a visit to Southern Second Hand too."

She nodded and disappeared with purpose in her step.

Best to avoid Moss and head home. Luca needed time to process this new information about the nursing home enigma and figure out how it all fit together.

• • •

Mya ground her teeth together while mulling over an unproductive morning. Four pawn shops and no sign of her mum's jewelry. Knowing her luck, the stuff was interstate by now, but she wouldn't give up yet. There were more shops on the list to visit, but with an empty fridge and just over an hour before she had to be at work, she figured she ought to do the domestic thing and go shopping.

She regretted leaving the motorbike at home in favour of exercise and sunshine, because she'd bought too much at the supermarket. Re-adjusting her grip on the green cloth bags, she cursed herself for not bringing a backpack. She took a well-worn track through the park and stopped halfway along to put the bags on the dry grass and shake out her aching shoulders.

Three young women sat atop the monkey bars, fags hung loosely from painted lips. It was difficult to tell their ages with all the black kohl on their eyes, but she recognised Paula Mason from 11 Railway Terrace, who she guesstimated to be in her late teens. Their skirts were hitched up to reveal three sets of pale legs—two chubby and one skinny—and they giggled as a younger boy walked past.

His hands were pushed into pockets, shoulders hunched, head down. Scruffy hair hid his face, and he made a wide berth around the girls.

One of Paula's friends had cropped hair that stuck up at every angle and a ruby stud on the side of her nose. She called to the boy, "Can we bum a smoke off ya?"

He ignored her. The girls jumped to the ground and jostled him. Paula pushed him from behind and his hands jerked out of the pockets in an effort to keep his balance.

"Leave me alone." He walked faster.

Mya picked up her shopping bags and continued along the track, which happened to take her in the same direction as the young boy. With one eye on him on and the other the girls, she saw the one with spiked hair move in behind him and give her friends a sideways glance.

"Give us a fag," she said as she shoved his shoulder.

He stumbled and turned to face them. "I don't smoke."

Mya sighed deeply. These girls were old enough to know better, and she *really* hated bullies.

"He's got nothing. Let's bail," said the tallest girl, a willowy blond with hair to her waist and a rainbow of streaks through the top. She was dressed more modestly than the others, in a skirt that reached her knees and colour-coordinated shirt. Multi-coloured bangles jangled on her wrist as she crushed the butt of a cigarette into the ground. Mya had seen her coming and going from the Mason house now and then.

When the boy turned away again, Paula hooked her toes in front of his ankle and sent him sprawling. She grinned with hot-pink lips while the boy sat on the dirt, rubbing bloody knees.

"Hi, Paula," Mya called.

The girls flinched and turned to eye her. She strode over and offered a hand to help the boy to his feet.

"Hey, you live down the road from me," Paula accused.

Mya ignored her. Well, she was telling, not asking. She smiled at the boy as he backed away, and something hit her shoulder from behind. The handle of one shopping bag slipped through her fingers, and she growled as green pears and glossy Royal Gala apples rolled out, leaving scuff marks in the dirt. When she turned, Spike was grinning.

Paula picked up an apple. "Guess I'll have this one, seeing as you don't want it." She rubbed it on the front of her T-shirt and took a bite. It sounded crisp, and juice squirted far enough to land on Mya's face. Spike giggled.

Mya wiped her cheek with the back of her hand. "You like messing with people, don't you, Paula?"

"Yeah, I do. What you going to do about it?" Paula straightened her back and Spike moved to her side.

Blondie hesitated behind them. "Come on. Let's see who's hanging at the shops."

"Don't you ever worry you'll mess with the wrong person?" Mya narrowed her eyes a tad, hoping to make them think twice about what they were about to do. The last thing she wanted was to get into it with a couple of teenagers, even if they did need to be taught a lesson.

Paula spat. Mya looked at the frothy blob on her boot and felt pain run up her temple as she clenched her jaw hard. She took a deep breath and drew on her reserves of calm. People who were put in bad situations could go either way. *She'd* chosen the right path and made a decent life for herself. Paula, on the other hand, was headed in the wrong direction.

In a steady voice, Mya said, "Hey, girls, you've had your fun. No one's got a cigarette for you, so let's all be on our way."

"Where you goin'?" Paula lurched at the retreating boy and backhanded him across the face.

He whimpered and held his palm to his cheek.

Bully! Anger boiled inside Mya. Paula drew her arm back with a clenched fist, aimed at the wide-eyed boy and—Mya stepped forward at the last second. She took the impact in her open hand, wrapped her fingers around Paula's fist, and used momentum to yank the girl forward. Paula lost her balance and ran a few steps with her face a foot from the ground, before putting her hands out to break her fall.

Mya automatically turned to face the other girls. Spike's eyes were wild. Mya had automatically adjusted her stance so she was side on to the teenager, elbows pulled close to her body. Spike poked her fingers at Mya's chest, but Mya grabbed them and pushed back until the girl's eyes and mouth widened—enough to hurt, but not enough to break them. A quick jab in the ribs made Spike stumble backward.

"That's my last warning, girls. Can I go home and put my groceries away now?"

Paula was on her feet again. Her nostrils flared and her teeth grated audibly.

Guess not.

A solid blow landed on Mya's upper arm, and she turned to see Spike holding a wrist-thick tree branch.

"No. One. Hits. Me." Cockroach used to wield a similar weapon.

The anger Mya kept locked inside leaked from its vault. A deep breath wasn't enough to stop the flow this time.

She rolled under Spike's next swing and knocked the chubby legs out from under her. While the girl was on her back, Mya stomped on her arm. Her hand spasmed open and the branch rolled out. Mya was tempted to hook a nail under the ruby nose-stud and rip it out of that cute button nose, but her training kicked in. Reason returned.

Mya was stronger and more skillful than these girls. They didn't deserve years of fury aimed at them.

The boy's eyes met hers and he nodded a thank you, then turned and ran. Spike was still on the ground, looking considerably less sure of herself. Mya gathered her grocery bags and picked up the scattered fruit.

A snarl caught her attention, and she pivoted in time to see Paula's foot aimed at her crotch, but Mya's leg was already in motion. Paula looked up at the last second. Bad move. One of the old faithful combat boots connected with Paula's face, sending a spray of spittle and blood in an arc through the air. Another stain on the leather.

She could stomp on the girl's head for good measure, but Paula's nose was already broken and Mya wasn't a total bitch.

Both of Paula's hands covered her nose and bright blood ran between the fingers, smudging her pink mouth. The long brown fringe stuck to one side of her face and tears streamed down the other side.

Mya drew her foot back and feinted a kick. Paula squealed. Okay, maybe she was a little bit of a bitch. She gave Blondie one last look, but the girl's eyes were wide and her feet were moving backward. Wise.

The early summer heat had turned the grass crispy, and Mya's boots kicked up little puffs of powdery dust as she walked from the park along Roger Street and onto Railway Terrace, her ears trained behind her. She didn't hear anyone following.

"Howdy, neighbour."

"Shit!" Mya nearly dropped her groceries when Luca appeared from behind a hibiscus bush, secateurs in one hand and a red flower in the other.

"Sorry." A huge smile pulled his mouth up unevenly. "You want a hand with those?" He stepped forward, pointing toward the bags.

A quick appraisal sent her heart racing. He was decidedly tempting in faded jeans that showed off the arc of his thighs and hair combed into a ponytail. Being clean-shaven made him look younger—cuter.

"No, thanks, but they *are* heavy, so I won't stop. Catch you later."

His smile disappeared and his eyes narrowed in the general direction of her chest.

Geez, he could be a little *discreet.* Automatically, she looked down to make sure she hadn't forgotten her bra or something and saw the blood spatter. *Ah.*

"You're not working today?" Luca queried.

Her arms felt stretched like an ape's, so she put the shopping bags on the footpath and inhaled the sweet hibiscus scent. "I work split shifts at the pub, if you must know." Her hands were on hips to show annoyance. "Why the hell aren't *you* at work?"

"I'm *supposed* to be on holidays." He shrugged and his tight white T-shirt clung to tanned biceps.

She had trouble concentrating. "Supposed to be?"

"I worked this morning. Did you have an accident?" He waved a hand in her general direction and glanced at her bloodied hand.

"You could say that. Living in Croydon can be hazardous." She glanced at her watch—only an hour to put the shopping away and clean up for her next shift at the pub. Time to end the inquisition, so she collected her bags again.

"Is that someone else's blood?" Luca stepped forward.

She tensed as he breached her personal space. "You're bloody nosy for someone who just moved in."

Her lips tightened and they glared in a Mexican stand-off. His pale blue gaze searched hers and the thin white line of the scar above his lip twitched, but he didn't make another move, so she turned her back on him and headed for her house.

Bullies and an overly observant neighbour were not what she needed in her life right now. It was complicated enough with the menacing letter and missing jewelry. Her attraction to Luca was stronger than just an appreciation of eye candy though, and that was adding another tier to the difficulty-gateau, but it wouldn't deviate her from her goal.

Chapter 6

Luca swapped his T-shirt and shorts for a police-issue shirt and navy slacks, smoothed his hair into a ponytail, and grabbed the car keys. When he had one hand on the back door, his mobile phone rang.

Crap.

His mind was on the case right now, not a chit-chat, but if he didn't pick up, he'd never hear the end of it. Instead he sighed and accepted the call.

"Hi, Mum."

"Hello, darling. I just wanted to see if you're still alive, because I haven't heard from you in a while. How did the move go yesterday?"

"Without a hitch. You'll have to come over and see the new place this weekend."

"Oh, I'd love to, darling. Quinton tells me it's a bit noisy, though. I don't know why you bought something so close to the railway. There are plenty of suitable properties closer to us."

"It's only fifteen minutes, Mum, and you know why I had to get away."

"Yes, darling, I know. Now, when you get time, could you drop by and take a look at Dad's new TV? He can't seem to program the digital channels."

Luca smiled. His dad was a genius in a courtroom but completely clueless with electronic gadgetry. "Sure thing. I'm just on my way out the door."

"Oh, I won't keep you. Be safe. I love you, darling."

"Love you too, Mum."

He slipped the mobile back into his shirt pocket and headed to the garage. Today he intended to find out how Kevin Barnes and

Melanie Lane came to work at Rich Haven, but in order to follow the lead, he'd had to get permission from Moss to interview the staff they'd replaced. That had been an uncomfortable conversation. Moss might have mentioned time wasting, and Luca might have pulled the little-old-ladies-in-danger card, but in the end they agreed that if he kept the hours he worked while he was supposed to be on holiday to a minimum, he could take time off at a later date.

What the hell else did Luca have to do with his time? He didn't have a wife waiting at home for him anymore.

He turned the car radio to an easy listening station and ran the gauntlet of peak-hour traffic. His new neighbour, Mya, was worth keeping an eye on and not just because she looked a lot hotter with her motorbike helmet off. That was definitely blood on her T-shirt this afternoon, and she was evasive about how it got there, even hostile. He needed to make a few inquiries when he had time.

He turned off at Millswood and followed wide, tree-lined streets past houses with formal gardens. As he moved through the suburb, the houses shrunk and the gardens were unkempt. Amazing how quickly the financial demographic changed nearer the railway line.

Now that Daylight Savings time had kicked in, there were only short shadows at five thirty, when he parked behind a police Commodore out front of Agosto Cali's house. Kate climbed out of the Commodore and waited for him on the footpath.

"Hi, Kate. Sorry for diverting you on your way home from work."

"It's fine." She read from a background check he had asked her to do. "Agosto Cali was a cleaner at Rich Haven. He emigrated from Italy twenty years ago. No convictions, no red flags. I couldn't find any information about why he left the job, but it seems strange, because he didn't have another one to go to at the time."

He pushed through a low chainmail gate and almost tripped on the cement path that had been lifted by a gum tree root. The front lawn was sparse; vegetables grew in the garden beds on Agosto's half of the cream-brick maisonette.

A man wearing overalls opened the door and a powerful smell of frying onions and garlic made saliva pool in Luca's mouth, reminding him it was dinnertime. Agosto was head and shoulders shorter than Luca.

"*Si?*"

"Good evening, I'm Detective Patterson. You spoke with Constable Derman here on the phone." Luca held his right hand out and shook Agosto's hand.

"*Buon giorno.* Come in." Agosto bounced his head up and down and ushered them into a tiny lounge room with mustard-coloured carpet and a threadbare two-seater couch. "Can I get you a drink?"

Luca perched on one edge of the couch, so his height wouldn't be intimidating. "No, thank you, Mr. Cali. We won't take up too much of your time. We just want to ask you a few questions."

Kate crossed her legs at the other end of the couch, winning smile in place.

Luca used the low, measured voice he reserved for citizens from whom he wanted to extract information. "I want to ask you about the circumstances under which you left Rich Haven Aged Care Facility."

Agosto pursed his lips and roughed up the jet black hair over his ear. "I dona understand. That was eight months ago and I didna make any trouble." He glanced at Luca's gun.

Glad he left his police cap and jacket in the car, Luca leaned back to appear more relaxed, and smiled. He should've taken the drink. "You're not in any kind of trouble, Mr. Cali. I'm just following a lead on a case. I wonder if you could tell me about your decision to leave Rich Haven."

"Okay, but I feel a bit embarrassed. There wosa fat guy who come to my 'ouse and tell me I should quit, or bad things will happen, like maybe security guards will find something *illegale* in my locker. I think he is bluffing, but two days later my boss calls me to his office and say I leave the door to the high-dependency wing open. I know I don't, but I quit right away, because I know what will come next."

Luca cut in. "You think this man had something to do with you getting in trouble with your boss?"

"*Si.*"

"Why is that?"

"I very careful at work, especially to make sure security is good. Mostly so the residents can't get out, but also so bad people can't get in. I don't leave the door open!"

"I'm sure you were vigilant, Mr. Cali, but how do you think this man got into the nursing home and set you up?"

"I dona know how he did it. Maybe he have accomplice, maybe he's friends with the boss, so they make it up."

Agosto's face and ears flushed as he wriggled uneasily on his chair. Luca needed to placate him before he fixated on proving his innocence and clammed up.

"I understand how you came to that conclusion. Would you mind explaining what you thought would happen next, if you *didn't* leave Rich Haven?"

"He say security would find something in my locker. He wouldn't say that unless it was something bad, and I dona want to find out how bad. I dona like working there much anyway." Agosto wrung his hands in his lap.

Luca suspected the man needed the job more than he was letting on. "Do you have work now, Mr Cali?"

"*Si*. I collect trolleys and pack shelves at the Foodland supermarket."

"Okay. Can you give me a description of the man who threatened you?"

"He only come here once. He wosa same height as you, but really wide, with dark hair and expensive suit. Plenty of hair on the back of his hands, like me." He laughed.

A fluffy white cat strolled into the room, sniffed Luca's shoes, and wrapped its body around his leg. *Cat hair on navy pants. Excellent.*

"And how do you think he found out where you live?" Luca asked.

"I guess he knows someone at Rich Haven."

"Or maybe he worked there." *Crap. Did I say that aloud?*

Agosto gasped and withdrew into his seat. "I never think of that, but I never seen him before."

"Thank you so much for talking to us, Mr. Cali." Luca was half out of his seat when Kate interrupted.

"Actually, I have a question, if you don't mind. Is there any reason you didn't call the police after the man threatened you?"

Agosto shrugged. "It's not a good idea for someone like me to make trouble."

She tilted her head to the side. "How do you mean?"

"I dona speak good English and I just want to keep my job."

"We understand that, Mr. Cali. You've been a huge help. Thank you for your time." Luca got to his feet, effectively concluding the interview.

So, Agosto being forced out of his job seemed to support a connection to the arrival of new staff, Kevin Barnes and Melanie Lane. Whether it equated to jewelry thefts or was linked to Happy Vale Nursing Home remained to be seen.

He offered Agosto his hand again. "Here's my card if you think of anything else."

• • •

Out front of Linda Morgan's modest house, in a typical middle-class Adelaidian suburb, Luca sat in the passenger seat of the police Commodore and read Kate's notes. It was a comfy portable office, and it smelled better than his car, filled with Kate's perfume.

"Well, they both gave a similar description of this wide, hairy man and they were both worried for their safety. I wonder how the two are connected."

"Maybe they're not." Kate leaned across the console to look at the file, too.

Her shoulder touched Luca's and they both flinched away.

"Sorry," she mumbled.

Luca ignored it, but the discomfort from the incident at the Christmas party a few years back remained. The booze had flowed freely and music vibrated up through their feet while sweaty bodies gyrated. One minute they were dancing together and the next Kate had kissed him. It wasn't until he saw the horror register on her face that he realised he'd taken a step backward.

At that stage it hadn't been long since Olivia had passed away, and a new relationship was the last thing on his mind. They'd talked about it later and agreed not to ruin their working relationship, but it had still been awkward for a while. What a relief when Danny had swept Kate off her feet.

Luca tapped a finger on the dash. "They were both threatened, but the threat to Linda was different."

"Yes, but it had the same effect. Linda would do anything to protect her daughter." Kate said. "So what's next?"

"Well, we can't directly link Melanie Lane and Kevin Barnes to forcing Agosto and Linda from their jobs, but the timing is right. At least them leaving Happy Vale Nursing Home and moving to Rich Haven explains why the trail of jewelry thefts dead-ended nine months ago. I'd bet money on the fact they're resetting the scam. We should ask the Rich Haven director if there have been any jewelry thefts reported, but we'll have to tread lightly. We can't make unfounded accusations. Perhaps try to get some current information about Melanie Lane and Kevin Barnes, contact details, friends and family, anything you can find to build a picture. At the moment we have precious little to work with. It couldn't hurt to find out if the death rate has changed, either."

"Will do."

Kate grabbed a packet of chewing gum from the console and offered him one. He shook his head, so she unwrapped one for herself.

"Are you going to be in the office tomorrow?"

"No. I'm spending time with Gabriel."

"The brother who got engaged?"

"Yeah." Luca stared through the windscreen at a pair of sparrows flying through a grevillea bush as though playing hide-and-seek.

"You don't sound too happy. Don't you like the girl?"

Whoa, how had she come to that conclusion? He didn't realise he sounded so down. He needed to snap out of it before seeing Gabe tomorrow.

"No, I'm happy for them. She's really nice. It just … reminds me of Olivia, that's all."

"Oh, of course." Kate wrung her hands, looking uncomfortable.

He glanced at his watch. "It's late. Do you want to grab a bite to eat somewhere?"

"No, I can't. Danny's expecting me home. He's been kinda pissed at the amount of time I've been spending at work lately."

"Oh, sure. Family comes first. You can reach me on my mobile if anything comes up tomorrow. See ya." Luca levered himself from the passenger seat.

"Bye." Kate locked the doors behind him and waved as she pulled away from the curb.

In his own car, Luca followed the railway line in the direction of Croydon, his stomach rumbling. He slipped a Seal CD into the stereo and chilled to the mellow tunes—background music always helped him mull ideas over during a case.

Late commuters alighted from oily trains, and a couple of kids, no older than six or seven, dragged a reluctant fox terrier along the footpath in the long evening shadows. He tutted. If he had kids he wouldn't let them out of the yard. He'd seen too many bad things happen to good people, but it was a moot point, because fate had robbed him of the chance to have his own children by taking Olivia before her time, and he didn't believe he'd be lucky enough to get a second chance.

The western skyline glowed orange and some of the streetlights blinked, so he turned on the car headlights. As he approached the railway crossing, bells clanged, the red disc lights flashed, and the boom gates lowered. He braked and a green neon sign caught his eye to the left: the Croydon Hotel. It was as good a place as any to stop for dinner, and he might be able to find out something about Mya while he was at it, so he swung the car into the potholed car park.

Yes, his neighbour sure was an enigma. She was almost as tall as him, with a slender body and nice rack. When he'd seen her earlier today, she appeared to have been shopping, which was a normal enough thing to do, but there was definitely blood spatter on her hands and chest. Bloody nose? Could be, but he doubted it. Whatever it was, he sure as hell wanted to know the truth.

He glanced around the car park to make sure it was deserted, and then yanked his blue work shirt over his head and replaced it with the spare black one he carried in the car—for the same reason he drove an old Toyota Corolla instead of a police sedan: obscurity. It was amazing how much more information people were willing to give when he wasn't dressed like a cop, and the baggy black shirt hid the bulge of his weapon nicely.

There were two youths leaning against the flaking cobalt-blue facade of the building, dragging on rollies. Luca got a whiff of pungent smoke as he passed and frowned. Marijuana for sure, but it wasn't worth spoiling his dinner for two rollies. He smiled at the thought of the reaction he'd get if he was still in uniform.

A sign above the front door read The Track. A fancy name for a front bar, by the looks of it. The door squeaked as he pushed it and walked into a blast of beer-tainted air-conditioning. He nodded at the inquisitive glances from the regulars lined up on barstools.

"One?" A young waitress with huge tits squashed into a low-cut bodice pointed to a table by a window.

He took the seat and she placed serviette-rolled cutlery on his right side. Her gaze scoured him.

"You wanna drink?"

"A lager, thanks."

"Sure."

She disappeared through saloon doors and almost immediately returned carrying three plates to another table. He watched three men with salt-and-pepper hair ogle her as she delivered a curry, thick stew, and battered fish. The aromas made his mouth water, and he had to admit the meals looked more impressive than the pub's exterior suggested.

The waitress trotted behind the bar to pull beer from a ceramic-handled tap. The table he sat at was dark wood, covered with clear plastic, and glass condiment containers huddled by the window ledge, propping up a laminated menu. Outside, a steady procession of headlights slowed for the railway crossing. A young couple in surf logo gear jogged along the footpath.

Returning his attention to the single-sided menu, he'd decided what he wanted to eat by the time the waitress placed a dripping schooner glass on the table.

"What'll it be?"

"I'll have the Croydon Burger, thanks."

She scribbled on her order pad and tucked the pen behind her ear. He felt her eyes on him again, and it made his skin crawl.

"Hey, can you tell me if someone I know works here? Her name is Mya."

The waitress narrowed her eyes and looked him up and down. "Yeah, she works here."

Luca shot her his best smile. "Is she working tonight?"

"Who wants to know?" She blatantly adjusted her bosoms and drummed long pink fingernails with silver stars on the tips, on the order pad.

"I'm her neighbour."

"Humph. I'll tell her you're here." She watched him from over her shoulder on her way into the kitchen.

"If a bloke ogled like that, he'd be dealt a serve of insults," Luca mumbled under his breath.

Just as well Mya wasn't as obvious when she checked him out. In fact, she went to great lengths to hide any interest, but he'd definitely seen hunger in her eyes. It didn't matter, because the right woman for him would need to be less complicated, and she'd actually have to fancy him, too.

Chapter 7

"Order up." Jilly slapped a docket on the stainless steel bench.

Mya flipped a plate-sized rump steak on the grill and looked up to read the new order. Jilly stood on the other side of the servery with a playful smile on her lips.

"What?" Mya frowned.

"There's a hot bloke in the dining room asking for you." Jilly jiggled her eyebrows suggestively.

"Not that skinny bloke I picked up at the servo last month?" Mya moaned, standing on tiptoes to look over the doors, but she had a limited view of the dining room.

"Not skinny. Buff, blond ponytail. Says he's your neighbour."

"Shit!" Her teeth clenched. That was all she needed. A guy following her around.

"Did you get into his pants yet?" Jilly ducked her head to look Mya in the eye between stainless-steel shelves.

She shook her head. "No, and I don't intend to. He lives two doors up from me," she said as though it was an explanation. She preferred men she wouldn't see again. No strings. "Tell him I said hi, but I'm too busy to come out."

"What*ever*." Jilly looked disappointed as she disappeared back into the dining room.

It shouldn't have surprised Mya that Luca was eating at the Croydon, seeing as it was his local pub too now, but she had a sneaking suspicion it wasn't just a coincidence. After prodding the rump steak with an index finger, she determined it was medium and served it with golden chips. She turned on the heat lights above the plate and hit the bell to get Jilly's attention. Then she grabbed the empty chip bucket and headed for the freezer.

There was a milk crate outside—*Mya's crate*, the other staff called it—to prop the door open with. She flicked the light on and stepped inside. A shudder ran the length of her spine, but it wasn't from the cold. Her heart rate increased and she wrapped her arms around her torso in a protective gesture. It was a stupid reaction, but the big metal room reminded her too much of the box Cockroach used to lock her in when she was a kid. His was a tool chest, so it was a tight squeeze and didn't have a light, but she'd spent enough hours in it to never want to be trapped in anything like it again.

She refilled the chip bucket and rushed back to the kitchen.

"Here's another order," Jilly called. "Hey, your neighbour's asking questions about how long you've worked here and what days."

"Tell him to piss off." Mya slapped a tea towel against the bench, nearly upending a jar of parsley. "What I do is none of his business."

Jilly shook her head and adjusted her boobs so they were pushed half out of her top. "You've got some serious issues, Mya. More for me."

It was a quiet night in the dining room, so at seven thirty she wiped down the benches and turned off half the char grill. At eight o'clock on the dot she turned off the other side of the grill and the deep fryers, wrapped containers of garnish, packed everything into the cool room, and turned off the massive exhaust fan. Blissful silence.

The dish pig was scraping plates and feeding trays of dirty crockery into the commercial dishwasher. Mya felt sorry for him. He probably didn't dream of dishwashing at the Croydon fresh out of high school. They all had to their fair share of hard yards at the sink, though.

"You good to finish the floors?" she asked.

He grunted in her general direction, which she took as a yes. She signed her timebook and stepped through the back door into the humid night, mouth shut until she was through the cloud of flying things jostling around the light.

"Can I walk you home?"

Her arm flew up to protect her face and her legs tensed for an attack. Then she squinted at the man who stepped from the shadows.

"Luca? Jesus, you scared me."

"Sorry, I didn't mean to. So, can I walk you home?"

In the warm, still air with him only a metre away, she could smell a sweet, woody-cinnamon cologne—and beer. He wore a loose black shirt, exposing sinewy forearms. A dusting of blond hair gleamed in the fluorescent light. He was strong, but confident enough not to have to build himself up to rock-ape proportions.

She met his steady gaze and held her breath under the force of candour in those powder-blue eyes. After a few moments she had to turn away. The car park was too dark to see what was in it, but she wondered aloud, "Don't you have a car?"

"It's a nice night for a walk." He shifted from foot to foot.

"Look, you seem like a nice guy, but I want to get something straight. I don't need a bloke stalking me. I can walk myself home."

Luca frowned and his lips thinned a little. "I stopped here for dinner because it was handy, and I thought, seeing as we're neighbours, we may as well walk home together. Safety in numbers. But you go right ahead." He waved his arm to the side and took a step back.

Great, now she felt like a heel. Still, the message had been received. She shook her head and stomped into the night.

It wasn't until she had crossed the railway line and was away from the noise of the pub that she heard quiet footsteps behind. She sighed. Well, he did live two doors from her, so she would have to get used to seeing him around the place. Just so long as he didn't get any ideas about taking a neighbourly friendship to any other level. Cuteness didn't equate to trustworthiness in her book.

She turned around.

Luca looked up and stopped too. "I'm not stalking you. I'm walking home."

He moved past her, eyes ahead. Mya fell into step beside him. A train squealed as it pulled into Croydon station and half a dozen passengers spilled from the sliding doors and down the cement ramp. A lady pushed a sleeping toddler in a stroller; the child's head bobbed on one side, pacifier adhered between soft lips. A couple of suits in a hurry strode past and a group of teenagers laughed at a private joke.

"Have you lived on Railway Terrace long?" Luca looked sideways at her.

As they passed under a streetlight, the shadow of stubble along his jaw was highlighted, and his pale eyes looked as cold as the steel benches at work. The yeasty scent of beer on his breath made her turn her face away.

"Nine years."

"Wow."

She wasn't sure if he was impressed or appalled.

"Most of the neighbours seem nice," he commented, "except number eleven. They're a bit rough."

"Ha!" Didn't take him long to peg the Masons. "Yeah, they're a real pain in the arse."

They walked in silence for a few minutes. Mya led the way along the dirt track to the street and, although it looked quiet, paused, her gaze on number eleven for a few seconds. She kind of expected Paula to pay a visit after what she did to her face today. She could feel Luca watching her, and his eyes followed her line of sight.

When they reached her front gate he said, "Goodnight, Mya. Hey, I enjoyed my burger tonight. You're a good cook."

"Thanks." She shrugged.

"I ... er ... wanted to ask you something."

Her breath caught as she stood halfway through the garden gate.

"Whose blood did you have on you earlier today? *You* don't look hurt."

Heat flushed through her body. "You really are a nosy bastard, aren't you?"

She stepped quickly toward him, intending to intimidate, but he didn't flinch. Only the definition of a tendon down the side of his neck hinted that he'd tensed his body, and now their faces were a ruler-length apart.

A vaguely cinnamon-infused scent emanated from him, and brown curls peeked from the V of his shirt front. His chest had a nice shape, from what she remembered seeing of him in a tight T-shirt, and she wondered how warm and solid it would feel under her hand.

Luca's Adam's apple bobbed up and down and their gazes met. He stared with a strangely hungry look in his eyes, and it took all of her willpower to remind herself that she didn't need this complication in her life.

She tried to blow him off with venom in her voice, but it came out a whisper. "When I'm looking for a new BFF, I'll let you know."

Chapter 8

Later that evening, Luca sat in a black leather armchair by the window of his second-story bedroom in silk boxer shorts, with a laptop balanced on his knees. The glow from the screen was enough to work by. The dark was soothing. Somehow, being crowded by shadows made his home feel less empty. The whir of the laptop motor and creaks from the cooling corrugated iron roof were his only company in the three-bedroom house. A house that was meant for a family: noise, laughter, and clutter.

Somewhere deep inside of him there must still be hope.

With eyes accustomed to the dark, he easily spotted three members of the Mason family as they strolled along Railway Terrace, peeking inside letterboxes and swiping the tops off flowers as they went. He might have to do something about them soon.

As he typed "Mya Jensen" into the police database and hit search, he ran his tongue over his teeth to appreciate the lingering flavours from his Croydon Burger. Mya could certainly cook. The homemade patty, piles of fresh salad, slightly runny egg, bacon, chips that were crisp on the outside and soft inside—they were all delicious—but it was the Moroccan chutney that really gave it zing.

Her cooking wasn't the only reason he was interested in her, though. She was stunning, with long legs and curves in all the right places. He felt a little guilty using his police clearance to access this information, but he had a gut feeling about his hot-bodied neighbour and it wasn't good. Something about her just didn't sit right. She had a low-paying job, lived in a low-income neighbourhood, but rode an expensive motorcycle, came home with blood on her T-shirt in the middle of the day, and was hostile when asked personal questions. Her defense reflexes were way faster than a regular person's—he thought she was going to take his head off when he surprised her at the back of the hotel.

Returning his attention to the results of his search, he jotted in his notebook and underlined keywords as he read.

> Mya Jensen
> Father: Jack Roach 1958-2000.
> Mother: born Jean Donaldson 1962, married Jack Roach 1987, traumatic brain injury 1999, resident of Rich Haven Aged Care Facility.

What the hell? Her mother was at Rich Haven? The same week he moved onto her street, he got new information on a cold case that led him to Rich Haven. No way could this be a mere coincidence.

So, she had a deceased father and hospitalised mother. More interestingly, who was paying to keep the mother at a retirement home? Places like that cost a fortune just to get into, let alone the ongoing fees. He doubted Mya could afford it on a pub chef's wage.

He read on.

> Mya Jensen: Certificate IV in Hospitality (Commercial Cookery) 2003, 1 property at 21 Railway Terrace, Croydon, South Australia.

Where was her date of birth? His fingers stabbed at the keyboard as he dug a little deeper and found a Deed Poll application. Could be in the witness protection scheme. Not many people changed their names legally, and even fewer who weren't hiding from something. The data took a while to load, but when it did he had to read it twice.

She was born Lara Roach on November 25, 1984. There was confirmation that she was awarded guardianship of her mother, Jean Roach, and then changed both of their names so they were now Rosalie and Mya Jensen.

Who are you, Lara? There had to be something significant to make her change names and drag her mother along for the ride.

The database referenced a police report. Out of curiosity, he dialed the original case manager.

"Kaufman," the abrupt greeting came.

"Detective Patterson from the Adelaide Police Station. Sorry to trouble you so late, but I was wondering if you could give me some information about an old case. Jack Roach—"

"Scumbag. What's your interest? He's deceased."

Okay, this could be like getting blood from a stone. "Yes, well, I'm interested in his daughter, Lara Roach."

"Nasty incident all around. Pull the file and you'll see what I mean."

"Would you mind giving me an overview?"

There was silence. Was Kaufman considering telling him to go to hell?

"Jean Roach sustained a serious head injury, and I suspected Jack Roach inflicted it. I accompanied her to the hospital, and by the time I had enough evidence to come back and arrest the bastard, he'd fled. Just got in his car and drove away. Left the teenage girl alone in the house.

"He was on the run for a year, so I suspect he had help. A patrol eventually caught up with him when he ran a red light. They engaged in a high-speed chase, during which Roach wrapped his car around a tree. Died on the scene."

"I'm especially interested in what happened to Lara." Luca sat with pen poised.

"The girl was only sixteen, no living relatives, so she became a ward of the state. She got into a bit of trouble at first but seemed to settle down. Her mother was put into a government-run nursing home. The ironic part was that Jack left everything to his wife in his will, so the estate was held in trust."

"Anyone else make a claim for the estate?"

"Not that I'm aware."

"Was it large?"

"Not especially. The house was sold, but he had life insurance."

"Interesting." So, Mya had been a troubled teenager with a mother who couldn't provide for her and no other family.

"Well, that's the sum of it. Why're you dragging this up now? I'd hate to see the girl in trouble."

He hadn't planned for that question and couldn't tell Kaufman he was just being nosy. "Nothing specific. She's just a person of interest at this stage."

"Sure. Let me know if I can help. I always felt bad about the cards the girl was dealt."

"She's doing all right. Thanks for the chat."

Why had Mya changed her name? It wasn't like she had any other relatives who were after the estate, and if it was purely a matter of starting over, she could have just moved. What else had Lara Roach been running from? He was digging himself in deeper. Still, there was nothing he liked more than a puzzle to solve.

Chapter 9

Luca leaned against the sink and spooned soggy Corn Flakes into his mouth. He needed to walk to the Croydon Hotel to retrieve his car. If it was still there. When he went to the hotel for dinner, he hadn't planned on leaving his car in the parking lot. Hadn't planned on walking Mya home either, but the opportunity presented and there was something about the woman that drew him in, like an arithmetician to a sudoku.

What he'd find under his neighbour's brash exterior was anyone's guess. Maybe a feminine softness. Maybe something he didn't want to find.

He studied the photo in the silver frame on the kitchen window sill, even though he could describe it with his eyes closed. Olivia's face was etched into his mind. He remembered when Gabe took the photo. Olivia wore a cheeky grin, because she'd stolen Luca's cupcake and he was chasing her around the backyard. Her wide mouth had the most contagious, melodic laugh, her blue eyes sparkled at him, and her short, dark hair stuck out in a fun, elfish style. He grinned hugely. He couldn't help himself. With one finger, he traced the blush of her lips—how yielding they'd been when kissed. He closed his eyes and imagined the feel of her silken cheek against his.

Linkin Park's *One Step Closer* emitted from his mobile phone on the kitchen bench and he flipped it open. "Kate."

"Hi, Luca. Hope it's not too early to call you."

"You'd think I'd get the hang of sleeping in after two weeks on holiday, but no such luck."

"You could try actually not working."

"Very funny. You sound like my family."

"I've been in touch with the Rich Haven director this morning, and there has only been one reported theft. However, he did confirm there have been sixteen deaths in the past nine months, which is higher than usual."

"Hmm." Luca clamped the phone between his ear and shoulder, tipped milk down the sink, and washed his bowl.

"Eight of them had no living relatives."

"*Very* interesting." His gut constricted. It had been the same at Happy Vale Nursing Home. No relatives and no suspicious circumstances meant no autopsy, but he didn't believe it meant no foul play.

"Any suspicions raised?" he asked.

"No. I also asked the director about Kevin's and Melanie's résumés, and he assured me he called their references. So I decided to call too—just for the hell of it—and the numbers are all disconnected."

"Kate, that's excellent work, but don't forget about looking for pawn shops that are moving stolen goods, too." Luca sighed; Moss would put a foot up his arse when he found out Kate was working on his obsession instead of their current case.

"I'm not, sir, just doing my job. Anyway, my theory is someone manned pre-paid phones especially to get Kevin and Melanie these jobs."

"Did you find out anything about the type of jewelry stolen, or from whom?"

"No, sir. I'll look into it tomorrow."

"Okay, talk to you then."

Luca tucked his mobile into his top pocket. There was some legwork to do tomorrow, to find out who the hell Melanie Lane and Kevin Barnes really were, but today was family time.

•••

Mya walked her motorbike back on tiptoes until the rear tire bumped the curb and then kicked the stand down and turned off the ignition. She threaded her forearm through the face of the helmet and took it with her. Yesterday she went to four second-hand shops, and this was the fifth one she'd been to during her split-shift today. It was a long shot that her mum's jewelry would be sold so close to home, but worth a try. She checked her watch. Half an hour before she had to be back at work.

Pete's Pawn Shop was squeezed between a laundromat and a news agency on Blewitt Boulevard. A bell jingled above the door when she pushed it and a potbellied man with white hair looked up from a *Post* magazine. His gaze traveled from Mya's head, lingered on her chest, moved down to her stained combat boots, and then brought his attention back to the magazine.

She wasn't interested in the trash or treasure he was selling, only her mum's jewelry, so she marched straight to the counter. Pete—she presumed—dragged his eyes from the page to her face with a sour look, like she'd interrupted the most riveting article he'd ever read. Yeah, right.

"I'm looking for a necklace and ring," she told him.

"The jewelry's over there." He flicked a thumb over his left shoulder and raised the magazine in front of his face again.

"Look, Pete." Mya tapped the cover and leaned forward. "I'm looking for very specific stuff. It would have been pawned in the last month."

Pete slapped his magazine on the counter and folded his arms. On closer inspection, his eyes narrowed. "What's it look like?"

"A silver chain with a little bottle pendant on it and a gold solitaire ring with a *real* diamond."

Pete put both hands on the counter to lever his hefty frame off the stool and grunted his way over to the jewelry section. He scanned the glass cabinets and finally pulled a tangle of keys from his pocket to unlock one.

"Here." His chubby fingers fumbled a delicate item from the cabinet and dropped it into her open palm.

Her heart skipped a beat as a long silver chain spilled between her fingers, leaving a cool, heavy, silver vial behind. Trying not to look too excited, she twisted the tiny crystal ball on the lid. *Click.* Holding her breath, she turned it over. A breath of relief whooshed out. She tapped the vial on the side of her hand and a central cylinder slid out, dropping a sliver of paper into her palm. Using only the slightest pressure of one finger, she unrolled the paper to reveal a sepia photograph of her Grandma and Grandpa on their wedding day.

"Shit, didn't know that was in there." Pete edged closer, and Mya scrunched her nose at the odour of stale smoke.

"And the ring?"

Pete shrugged. "I've got lots of solitaire rings. Knock yourself out." He waved a plump hand towards the next cabinet.

The glass looked like it had never been cleaned, but she peered inside at the rows of gold rings, skipping anything that wasn't a solitaire. It only took a few minutes to locate Rosalie's. It was the only one with a delicate web of gold cradling the stone.

"That one." She pointed.

He shuffled over, flipped through his handful of keys again, and unlocked the cabinet.

"Thanks." She loaded her gratitude with as much sarcasm as she could muster and turned the ring over to check for the engraving. "*Ádh na nÉireannach*," she mumbled. Without another glance at Pete, she headed for the door.

"Hey, wait a minute." A quick shuffle, accompanied by rhythmic grunts followed.

She turned to meet him head on, watching a bead of sweat roll down his temple.

"You have to pay for those."

"Now that's where you're wrong, Pete." She sidestepped to the counter, placed her helmet on it, and then tucked the jewelry into her pocket. "You see, these are already mine."

Pete shifted his weight from foot to foot, looking uncomfortable, and she doubted it was just because his arse had a permanent imprint of the stool in it. A growl rumbled in the back of his throat as he sidled behind the counter and rested his belly on it.

"Look, missy, if you want the jewelry, you gotta pay for it. If you think it's stolen, then you gotta go to the police."

"I went to the police, but they're too lazy to do the legwork. I, on the other hand, am highly motivated. Now, you're gonna let me take the jewelry *and* tell me who sold it to you."

"Ha! Like hell I am." Pete's arm appeared from behind the counter, a long iron bar grasped in his hand.

She jumped back instinctively, but he was bulky and slow. She slid one foot back and softened her knees while Pete came around the counter, slapping the iron bar on his open hand for effect. The only effect it had was to piss her off. Big men who thought they could bully women were *not* high on her sympathy list.

"Why don't you tell me where you got this stuff from, and I won't have to get blood on my T-shirt. It's not due for a wash until tomorrow." She tugged at the cuffs of her leather jacket, slid it off, and threw it on the nearest cupboard. It was her rule to never start a fight, but she had kind of thought it might go like this.

There was a film of sweat on Pete's upper lip as he swung the bar like he was bowling over-arm. Mya sidestepped and it whistled past her shoulder and smashed a sideboard, sending splinters of china 360 degrees. A fragment lodged in the back of her hand and left a pinprick in her skin when she pulled it out. Pete sniggered. He lowered the bar, maybe expecting her to turn and run.

Sorry to disappoint.

She didn't wait for him to put the bar in motion again, but leapt at him fist first. It connected with his left eye and he staggered backward.

"You bitch!" With his left hand covering the watering organ, he pointed the iron bar at her again. It was useless if not in motion.

"So, how about you 'fess up who sold the stuff, and I'll get out of your shop before anything else gets broken."

His neck turned red, sweat dripped from his face, and he looked like he might boil and blow his top any minute. With a hand still over one eye, he lunged and raised the bar at the same time. It sideswiped Mya's elbow and hurt like hell. He kept it moving and it was all she could do to raise her arm and deflect the next blow. She yelped as pain sliced down her forearm and snatched the breath from her lungs.

Now wasn't the time to act like a weakling, so she mentally repeated the mantra she saved for difficult times.

I am strong and in control of my destiny. I am strong and in control of my destiny.

This time when Pete circled the iron bar in her direction, she jumped back and clenched her abdominal muscles as it almost hooked the fabric of her T-shirt, but didn't catch.

The momentum of the swing threw Pete off balance, so she made her move. She stepped back with one foot, and then brought it forward and high. The ball connected with Pete's solar plexus, spittle sprayed from his mouth, and he slumped forward with a satisfying grunt. The bar clanged to the floor. It was a bad move to leave himself unprotected in a fight he started.

"Where did you get this stuff from?"

"Piss off," Pete gasped.

She jabbed her fist into his right eye. A puff of dust came up from the rug as he dropped to his knees, both hands cupped over his face. She stepped back and relaxed.

"It's a guy brings a lotta stuff in here," he mumbled. "A regular."

"No good without a name. I'm gonna trash your shop next." She tipped the nearest tea cup onto the floor to back up the promise. He flinched as it shattered on the floor.

"If I tell you, I won't get his business anymore. He brings me real quality stuff."

His nose and eyes were leaking down his ruddy face and the stench of fearful sweat was strong. A guttural growl rumbled in Mya's throat; it was time to take a few deep breaths. Even Pete didn't deserve the full force of her anger unleashed on him.

With an edge to her voice, she spelled out his options. "If you don't tell me his name, you won't be doing *any* business anymore. You understand me?"

The man swallowed hard and rubbed his eyes tenderly. "Will you piss off if I give you a name?"

"Yep."

"And never come back?" He was pushing his luck.

"Maybe. Unless the name you give me is no good."

"It's Willy Mason, and I don't wanna see you near here again."

Her mouth dropped open, wide enough to fit a whole coconut macaroon in. She hadn't thought her sorry neighbour was smart enough to tie his own shoelaces, let alone flog expensive jewelry from a closed facility and on-sell it. She snatched her leather jacket and helmet from the counter and got the hell out of there, confident that Pete wouldn't follow, because he couldn't see shit.

Chapter 10

"Gabe?" Luca called as he opened the gate at the side of his brother's house. He made his way past a tool shed and into the cool climate of a lush shade house along the length of the carport.

"Down here." Gabriel Patterson's voice came from behind the house.

Luca followed a path encroached by delicate baby tears, passed a trickling pond, pushed aside the perforated leaves of a monstera, and re-emerged into bright sunlight. On the other side of an expanse of mowed lawn, a dolomite trail curved like a grey snake beside the back fence, ending at a pallet of beige keystone blocks. From behind it protruded two dusty legs and a pair of work boots.

Gabe knelt in the dirt, hands down a shallow hole, mumbling curse words. Straight blond hair that was short at the back and long in the fringe hung over his eyes. His skin was darkly tanned from years working outdoors.

"You couldn't make it straight?" Luca motioned to the serpentine base for the retaining wall he'd come to help build.

"The missus likes curves. Besides, I've got *you* to cut the blocks." Gabe laughed and pushed loose soil into the hole before jumping lithely to his feet to hug Luca. He might be younger, but was several centimetres taller. "'Bout time you got here. I was worried I'd have to build this thing myself. Hey, I hired you a brick saw." He pointed to a big yellow contraption on the footpath.

"I would've thought you'd get enough of working in other people's gardens," Luca gibed.

The family horticulturalist had his own landscaping business and was a genius at converting dead garden space.

"Let's get this show on the road." Luca grabbed a keystone block, knelt beside the dolomite base, and banged it into place with a rubber-headed mallet. He rested a spirit level on top and tapped one edge to adjust the block. "And where's Quinton?"

"Big brother's too important to build retaining walls, mate. He's kicking some corporate arse in court today." Gabe dropped the next block in place and let Luca bang it down.

"How are the wedding plans coming along?"

Gabe shook his head. "It's all colour coordination and money, man. Bree gets stressed out, but I know how to relax her." He wiggled his eyebrows suggestively.

Luca jabbed an elbow in Gabe's side, leaving a grey smudge on his T-shirt, but his brother raved on.

"Auntie May is driving me crazy worrying about the seating arrangement. She doesn't want to be near Uncle Ralph, because he's 'loud and obnoxious' when he drinks." Gabe used his fingers to quote her. "And she can't sit next to the in-laws because she 'just wouldn't feel right.' There's a lot to be said for eloping."

"You wouldn't dare. Mum would never forgive you and Quinton's already planning the buck's night, you know."

"Should I be worried?" Gabe rested a dusty hand on his hip.

"Hell, yes, but I'll make sure he doesn't shave anything or leave you in another state."

"Hey, how's the holiday going?"

Luca made a small clicking sound in the roof of his mouth.

"You haven't." Gabe glared at him.

Luca shrugged and banged another block down. "I got a lead on the nursing home case, so I've been doing a bit of work here and there."

"That's not the idea of a holiday. Besides, I thought that case was dead in the water. In fact, I remember you being pissed when the inspector told you to drop it."

"Yeah, well, I've mostly got Kate doing the legwork, so he can't complain."

He ignored Gabe's deep sigh, threw a pair of earmuffs at him, and put another pair over his own ears. With goggles and leather gloves in place, he turned on the brick saw. Gabe twisted the tap and water trickled over the diamond blade as it spun. In a smooth motion, Luca fed a thick block into the saw at an angle and pulled it back out. The angled cut would start the curve of the retaining wall.

As the brick saw slowed, Gabe placed a dusty hand on Luca's forearm. "You're not going against the grain again, are you?"

Luca shrugged the hand off.

"Luca, I'm only asking because I care."

"I know. Look, I let Moss know what I'm doing. I'm just following a lead, nothing risky. Okay?"

Gabe nodded, his lips twisted into an unconvincing grimace.

Luca knelt to place the cut block and changed the subject. "I've got a good-looking neighbour that Quinton's interested in."

"Quinton's interested in anything with tits," Gabe mumbled. He took a swig from a water bottle and wiped the back of his hand across his forehead, leaving a cement-coloured streak. "Maybe you should chase her? Not far to go when you want some." He sniggered.

"Too close for comfort." Luca adjusted the level of the block.

"Yeah, and you're not the one-night-stand type, are you? Maybe Bree can set you up with one of her girlfriends."

"I don't think I'll be that lucky twice."

Gabe put his tools down. With a hand on Luca's shoulder, he looked him in the eye. "You deserve to find love again, but it won't happen if you don't put yourself out there." Quietly he added, "It doesn't mean you love Olivia less."

"I took her for granted." Something strangled the breath in Luca's throat as he admitted it aloud. Sure, he'd punished himself for years about not doing enough for his wife, but this was the first time he'd verbalised it.

"Enough self-loathing already!"

That wasn't the response Luca expected. Pity maybe, sympathy definitely, but not a rebuke. He stayed on his knees and stared at the ground. After a minute Gabe offered a hand to pull him to his feet.

"Let's have a beer before we start the second row," his brother suggested gently.

Chapter 11

The night air was hot and humid as Mya walked home from the Croydon Hotel and, according to the Bureau of Meteorology, there was no rain in sight. Her legs ached after a particularly busy shift. The usual Tuesday crowd had been boosted by a darts tournament.

It was midnight, but a full moon lit the bike track. All she wanted was to ditch her work clothes and jump in the shower. The stench of deep fryers had a way of getting in so deep that it took a double shampoo to get it out of her hair.

She counted each boot clomp to keep her mind from the shadows. She liked it better when she was kept busy because it didn't give her time to stew over the letter or think about what had happened at Pete's Pawn Shop earlier today. She had considered, for a millisecond, telling the cops. Not much point now, because they'd only ask a lot of questions about how she got the stuff back.

Then there was the problem of Willy Mason being the one to sell her mum's ring and necklace. If she hadn't already had a run-in with his daughter, Paula, she might bang on their front door and have it out right now. No, better to mull this one over and come up with a proper plan.

As soon she stepped from the curb onto Railway Terrace, she noticed shadows moving in her front yard. She contemplated doing a lap around the block to suss out the situation, but then recognised Paula's pale figure sitting on the porch, and was surprised it had taken the teenager a whole day to rally an angry mob after the beating she'd been handed in the park.

Pity Paula hadn't waited until tomorrow though, because Mya really didn't have the energy for this.

As she approached, four other figures emerged from the shadows. This was going to hurt. Pete from the pawn shop might have told Willy that someone was onto him. Even if he did, surely Willy wouldn't realise it was her. Unless Pete specifically mentioned her motorbike. There weren't many locals with Triumph Speed Triples.

As she stood on the broken white line in the middle of the road, the streetlight blinded her and put her at a distinct disadvantage, so she moved back to the shadows. It took a moment for her eyes to refocus, during which her other senses worked overtime. Cheap cologne and floral body products were caught in the humid air and clung to her skin. Heat radiated up from the tarmac. Crickets were going nuts in the moist grass.

The whole Mason family was there: Mum and Dad, Paula and her skinny boyfriend, and the chubby little sister. Ferals were always brave in packs.

Willy Mason stepped forward first. His shoulders were as wide as Mya's front door and his fists looked as big as her head. The delicate wings of a butterfly trembled in the pit of her stomach. The weedy boyfriend shadowed Willy, leering with a mouthful of teeth that looked like they had been knocked out and stuffed back in any which way.

Paula laughed from her seat by the front door and slung her fringe aside. "Not so brave now, are you, bitch?"

"Does your nose hurt much?" Mya snipped.

Paula snarled.

It would be easy to take on a couple of them, but there were too many, and she had no desire to hurt teenagers or the younger sister. It wasn't her fault she was born into a family of deadbeats.

Willy took another step and she looked up into his eyes. She didn't like what she saw. Cockroach used to look at her like that a long time ago—eager to inflict pain. Well, if they wanted her, they could come get her, because she wasn't taking another step.

There were no lights on in the houses along Railway Terrace. Good. She didn't want to involve the neighbours.

"Hey, Willy, what say I buy you a carton of beer and we call it a night?"

Willy sidestepped through her sagging picket gate. Although the footpath gave him only a couple of inches of height advantage, she had to lean back to see his stubble-shadowed mug. A black T-shirt strained over his chest and swollen biceps.

"What say I pummel you into the ground."

"Come on. I'm sure we can work something out."

He inched forward, fingers splayed and at the ready. There was no way he was getting those hands on her.

Finally he lunged—nimble for a big bastard—and she felt the heat from his enormous fist as it whistled past. He looked from her face to his fist and back, as though he didn't understand how it hadn't connected. Peripheral movement made her jump, expecting a surprise attack. Then she recognised the tousled blond hair and round face.

"Luca?" Great, the odds just kept getting worse. It wasn't going to be easy to keep an eye on all of them.

Straight white teeth glinted as Luca stepped into the bright streetlight. His hair hung loose, brushing the top of his T-shirt and softening his face.

"You look like you could use some help." His grin widened.

Hell, he was on her side. What she really wanted was to tell him she didn't need any man's help, but it'd be complete bullshit and he'd know it, so she nodded. Still, it didn't feel right to drag him into her mess.

"What's going on here?" Luca asked Willy.

"She messed up my kid, so now I'm gonna mess her up."

Luca raised an eyebrow at Mya. She shrugged.

"I'm sure we can resolve this without bloodshed," he insisted.

Willy's fist hurtled toward Mya again. She rolled and landed on her feet behind him. Using the forward momentum to her advantage, she brought her knee up to her chest and slammed her foot into the skinny boyfriend. He stumbled back and Paula squealed like a stuck pig in sympathy.

Mya might not have started this fight, but she wasn't taking any chances on who was going to finish it. Her mentor, Ned, had always said to avoid fights like the plague, but if she got into something she couldn't get out of, to make sure every strike counted. No sparring.

She extended her hand and her fist contacted the boyfriend's nose with an audible crunch.

"Ow! Fuck, you broke my nose."

The little sister and mother both screamed and lights went on in nearby houses.

Paula ran to his aid, and under the streetlight Mya noticed Paula's two black eyes, care of her handiwork in the park. The lovebirds matched now.

She heard Luca curse behind her and turned to see Willy's whopping fist lift Luca off the ground and hurl him several metres. Air expelled from his lungs with a hollow grunt. She couldn't let him get hurt on account of her, so she took a running leap and kicked the back of Willy's left knee. It gave way, but he didn't go down. She spun in a circle and kicked the back of his right leg. His thick knees hit the tarmac with a dull thud.

Luca was on his hands and knees, struggling to catch his breath, but he'd survive. She spun 180 degrees and connected the top of her boot with Willy's rubbery cheek. There was a moment of satisfaction before his vast hand wrapped around her ankle and tipped her backward.

The impact of landing flat on her back punched the air from her lungs. A pain as sharp as the slice of a knife slid from the back of her head down her spine. Not good. For a moment she stared into the bare bulb of the streetlight and sucked short gasps of warm air. Her head felt like an axe had been driven into the skull.

Shit, I can't move my legs. Was this how mum felt, lying on the kitchen floor when Cockroach beat her? I can't end up like that, at the hands of a halfwit gorilla. Move, legs, move!

Suddenly Willy's moon-shaped head eclipsed the streetlight's glare and she couldn't even tense for a blow. He toppled forward—oh, God, he was going to body slam her—but then spittle sprayed from his lips. He staggered and the ground shook as he hit it face first, next to her.

Wildly searching with her gaze, Mya hoped like hell Willy wouldn't get up again, and then Luca's face came into view. There was someone beside him, holding up a bloodied cricket bat for her inspection. Luca glanced in the direction of approaching sirens.

"Breathe," he coached her.

Finally, she managed to fill her lungs and wriggle her toes.

He knelt beside her. "You all right? Your eyes are bugging out of your head."

She did her best to scowl and rolled onto one side, but with hook and eye joints that wouldn't cooperate, she felt like a marionette.

"Mya, you might have a concussion. Stay down until an ambulance gets here."

She struggled harder to sit, using the ground for support as the scenery lurched. Willy was face down in the middle of the street, blood pooling beneath him as his wife tried to shake him awake. The little sister stamped her feet on the footpath, screaming at the top of her lungs that they'd killed her daddy.

Geez, I hope not.

Paula comforted her boyfriend as blood poured from his crooked nose. A bunch of neighbours were leaning on picket fences, clutching the fronts of dressing gowns, watching the show.

A blue light flickered across the road and reflected in house windows. The siren was off as the cop car approached. Mya held onto the fence and pulled.

"Perhaps you'd better stay there," Luca said.

She continued to struggle, and he extended a hand and hauled her to her feet. When she staggered, he held her elbows with strong but gentle hands. The world spun worse than after she'd ridden the Gravitron at the show grounds, but she could do this. She jerked her arms free and leaned on the fence. He sighed.

Two cops got out of the car. One had a hand on the butt of his gun and, when he saw Willy lying on the road, pulled the two-way radio from his utility belt.

"Car thirty-two requesting back up and an ambulance at twenty-one Railway Terrace, Croydon. I have an unconscious adult male and multiple minor injuries." He paused to do a head count. "Seven possible victims."

"What's going on here?" the female officer asked Luca. "Hey, you're—"

In the dim light, with still blurred vision, Mya wasn't positive, but she thought she saw Luca shake his head. He stepped closer to the officer and said something in a low voice. When he backed up, he looked at the name badge on her pocket.

He raised his voice. "I heard voices in the street, Officer Herd, and when I looked outside I could see this young woman needed help."

Mya nearly snorted as he pointed at her. Young woman?

"This family was threatening her, and when I came to her aid, they attacked me too."

"Both of you go stand on the footpath. And keep your hands where I can see them," the officer instructed.

The youngest Mason was still screaming, and Mya really wished someone would shut her up. Her head felt like she'd stuck it into the subwoofer at the pub. She sat on the cement footpath, letting the radiant heat soothe her thighs. White flakes peeled from the picket fence she was propped against. It would need repainting after summer. Luca sat beside her.

While the male officer checked Willy's vital signs and provided more information to the call centre, the female subtly checked the little sister for injuries. Finally the girl toned it down to a sob. Then the black notebooks and short pencils came out. It was going to be a *long* night, so Mya rested her head against the fence and closed her eyes.

•••

Mya woke with a start. Someone was shaking her shoulder and there was something soft under her head. In a huge effort, she sat upright. Bugger, she must've fallen asleep on Luca's shoulder. Hopefully she hadn't drooled. A quick inspection revealed a patch of blood, not drool. She reached to touch the back of her head and felt a lump. Her hand came away slick with a dark-crimson mess.

Luca's concerned face was only a few centimetres away. "You okay? Officer Herd needs to ask you about what happened."

Officer Herd stood on the footpath, sucking the end of an HB pencil and surveying Mya with skepticism. Luca jumped lithely to his feet and offered Mya a hand.

"Piss off," she told him, struggling to lever herself on the picket fence. Every bruise and strained muscle in her body cried out for her to lie down. From the corner of her eye she saw Luca grin at her pathetic efforts. Eventually, he supported her under one arm until she was on her feet.

"Is Willy dead?" she asked.

"No, ma'am. Was that your intention?"

Mya glared at Officer Herd and curled her top lip at the plain-faced woman in her masculine uniform.

Luca angled his shoulder between them. "I've already told the officer how I managed to get in a lucky shot and Mr. Mason fell and hit his head." He leaned so close to Mya that his warm breath trickled down her neck. Almost like he was trying to communicate something to her, but her brain was too scrambled to figure out what.

"My *intention* was to walk home from work and go to bed," she told the officer. "These pricks were waiting for me."

The officer rapidly jotted information. "And why do you think that was?"

"Not a clue. They've been nothing but trouble since they moved in."

"Yes, that seems to be the general consensus. The neighbours corroborated your story. One of the ambulance officers should look at the wound on your head."

Mya touched it again and flinched. "Nah, it's nothing an ice pack won't fix."

"You should really get it looked at," Officer Herd insisted, a stern frown in place.

That crap didn't work with Mya. She went to shake her head, but stopped after a single twitch, because it hurt like hell.

"I'd feel more comfortable if you did," the officer added. "The ambulance is here anyway."

"No." She gave the cop a sharp look.

"Well, don't go to sleep for a while. You might have a concussion. Is there someone who can stay with you tonight?"

"I can," Luca volunteered with a twinkle in his eye.

"Over my dead body," she mumbled.

Officer Herd looked from one to the other. It had been a long night for her, too, and Mya guessed the woman was thinking about all the paperwork she had to do back at the station.

"Well, I need to follow the ambulance and get a statement when Mr. Mason regains consciousness." She headed back to the police Commodore.

The crowd started to disperse, and Mya figured she'd better get inside and sit down before she fell down. This had been a hell of a night. Way too much excitement for most of the Railway Terrace residents for sure, and tomorrow ... she had a bad feeling the Mason family wouldn't let sleeping dogs lie.

Chapter 12

All of the neighbours had gone inside—and secured their dead-bolts, no doubt—as Luca and Mya watched the cop car disappear around the bend in Railway Terrace. There were two pools of dark blood visible under the streetlight, one on the road from Willy Mason and one on the footpath from Paula's boyfriend. There was also a smear on the picket fence from Mya's head.

"Yeah, well … I'll be fine now." She flicked a halfhearted smile at Luca and sidestepped into her front yard.

"Oh, no, you don't." He grabbed her elbow but retreated quickly from her ferocious expression.

She didn't like being manhandled. Ever.

"I promised Officer Herd I'd keep an eye on you tonight. You're bound to have a concussion, so you need someone to wake you up every half hour."

She rolled her eyes. The shoulder of his white T-shirt was dark with her blood and she felt bad for ruining it, and for dragging him into this mess, but that didn't mean she owed him anything. No man had any hold over her; she made sure of that.

"I promise not to go to sleep for a few hours," she told him. "I just want to have a shower and relax in my own home. Alone."

"Not going to happen." Unruly blond waves flopped back and forth as he shook his head. His gaze was as solid as steel in the dim light.

"Look, you pushy prick—"

"If you don't want to invite me in, you can always spend the night at my house. On the couch, of course."

"Yeah, right."

With his face partly shadowed, the scar at the corner of his lip made him look dangerous, but it was offset by the amusement in his eyes. There was something very tempting about the whole package. If she weren't so exhausted and in so much pain, she wouldn't mind getting nasty with Luca, but it wasn't going to happen in *her* house.

Damn him, she wished he hadn't come to her aid tonight. Having a man think he was her friend was dangerous. He might even think he knew her well enough to knock on her door and invite himself in for a cup of tea. The next thing she knew he'd be keeping T-shirts in her top drawer and hitting her when he lost his temper. *Not* going to happen.

"We can sit on the porch all night, if you'd prefer," he added, and this time he couldn't hide the smirk.

"Bloody hell." She fished keys out of her back pocket and the twisting movement hurt her ribs. "You can come into the lounge, but if you set foot in any other room, I'll mess your pretty nose up like I did to Paula's boyfriend. This *isn't* an invitation."

Luca raised his eyebrows, palms frontward in the universal sign of submission. She didn't trust him for a minute. Men were cunning.

He held the screen door open. "You think I have a pretty nose?"

She rolled her eyes and unlocked the heritage-green front door. He followed her in and stood in the hallway as she turned the light on, put a booted foot on the hall chair, and unlaced it. When she sneaked a sideways glance, he was staring at the bowl of knives on the hall table. Crap, she'd forgotten about that. Well, maybe he'd be that much more wary, enough to keep his hands to himself.

She tossed damp socks on top of the boots and flicked the lounge light on, waving him toward a worn red-leather couch. He slumped into it, his gaze roaming around the room. It alighted on a photo of her mum, so Mya tipped it face down.

"You want a drink?"

"Sure. What do you have?"

"Tap water." She padded into the green linoleum kitchen, flicked another light switch, and pressed a couple of painkillers from a silver packet on the bench. She couldn't help a soft moan as she reached up to the top cupboard for glasses—recycled jam jars.

"You all right?" he called.

"Yep," she lied.

Every inch of her body ached, her head felt like a sledgehammer was trying to batter its way through her skull, and she was dog tired. The green microwave light read 3:04 a.m.

. . .

Luca settled into Mya's leather couch, checking out the lounge room with more interest than he ought to. Every item potentially had a story to tell. Information to reveal about the woman who lived there. He hadn't known how to play it out on the street when they were facing off the Masons. Probably should've pulled his badge, but his niggling suspicions about Mya stopped him. With the level of disdain and mistrust she already had for him, she'd probably completely shut him down if she knew he was a cop. No, it was better to go undercover on this one, until he had a better feel for the situation.

The reason the whole Mason family wanted to beat the crap out of her was something they needed to discuss further. Willy claimed Mya had assaulted his daughter. Not unthinkable, although it didn't feel right. Mya didn't seem like the type to attack a teenager, unless provoked.

Then again, he didn't know enough about her to come to that conclusion with any real certainty. And the bowl of pocket knives in the hallway wasn't helping her case. What the hell did a woman—anyone—have that many weapons on hand for? He suddenly felt uneasy. Mya might be a lot more dangerous than he'd given her credit for.

Mya walked from the kitchen with a full jar of water in each hand and an ice pack nestled in the crook of her elbow. There were dark circles under her eyes and drips of blood on her T-shirt.

He pointed to a photo of her sparring. "I knew you must be trained. Who's your boxing partner?"

"Just a friend."

He raised an eyebrow. So, she had a friend. A male friend.

She dropped into the recliner chair opposite him and tucked the ice pack behind her head. Her eyes scrunched and the muscle along her jaw flexed. Yeah, she was in a lot more pain than she was letting on.

"So, why did you stick your neck out tonight?" she asked, eyes still closed.

"I've been watching the Masons since I moved in, and I know they've been messing with the neighbours. When I saw them sneak into your yard around eleven, I knew it couldn't be good. You should press charges against Willy."

"Not going to happen."

Just the sort of behaviour he'd expect from someone with something to hide.

She winked one eye open. "Where'd the cricket bat come from?"

"The old bloke next door whacked Willy with it before I could stop him. Broke it, too."

"Mr. Reiner?" She sat forward in surprise but quickly rocked back on the ice pack again. "He's full of surprises."

"You can go to sleep if you want," Luca said. "I'll wake you up in half an hour. I promise I'm not going to mess with your stuff."

She scowled without moving her head. "Like hell." There were flakes of dried blood on her arm and she scratched a few off.

He stifled a smirk at her bravado. There was blood all over her and she looked utterly worn out. It would be a miracle if she didn't keel over any second now. In one long gulp, she drained the last of her glass of water and closed her eyes. Within a couple of minutes her breathing deepened and her head tilted to one side.

He liked the way her face relaxed as she slept. Even covered in grime, she was beautiful. Only a few years younger than him, but world weary. At rest she looked like any other twenty-seven-year-old. He checked the time and crept across the room to turn the light off. Then he settled back on the couch.

With his feet on the coffee table and a cushion pushed behind his head, he was ready to keep watch.

•••

Mya had the sensation of falling and reached to grab onto something. Her hands hit the arms of the chair and she opened her eyes. The room was dark, but a shadow stooped over her. It had hold of her shoulder. She snatched a panicked breath, jabbed an elbow under the person's chin, and dove out of the recliner. Before the shadow had time to react, she slid a bare foot along the floor and contacted its ankle.

"Ow, shit! It's me. It's Luca. Will you stop hitting me?"

"Luca?" In the dark room, on the cold floorboards, Mya sat and listened. Her eyes strained to see him.

"I was just waking you up. Remember, you might have a concussion? Any of this getting through? Geez." He lifted his leg to rub his ankle and flopped back onto the couch.

The wall clock ticked, but she couldn't see the time. She vaguely remembered Luca waking her quite a few times, making her open her eyes so he could see her pupils dilate or something, but she'd just wanted to sleep. Now, there was a glimmer of light outside, so it must be nearly dawn. Wow, Luca had kept his promise.

It was a struggle to get to her feet, so she held the edge of the bookshelf until her head stopped spinning. "You can leave now. You've watched me long enough. I'm going to take a shower."

"You look like you're going to keel over, actually. I think I should hang around to make sure you're feeling okay. I'll sit right here."

His face was in shadow, but she was pretty sure there was a flash of teeth. The bastard was grinning, but she didn't have the energy to argue with him. In fact, if she didn't get to the bathroom soon she might just add puke to his bloody T-shirt. Without another word, she staggered down the hall.

Both hands grasped the sink and she studied herself in the mirror. Wow, not a good look. There was blood and dirt on her face, hair sticking up at the back like one of those freaky catwalk styles, and eyes with dark circles under them. She ran cold water and let go of the sink to splash her face. As she lowered her head, the room started to spin.

•••

"Mya! Mya, can you hear me?"

Something cool and rough moved down the side of her face and she pressed against it. Her eyelids felt like they were glued together, and it took the remainder of her depleted energy to force them open.

She was on the bathroom floor with her head in Luca's lap. "I'm okay," she whispered.

"You're not bloody okay. You fainted and added another lump to your skull. You should go to the hospital."

"No." Her voice was barely audible.

He slid his arms under her and grunted as he lifted her off the cold green tiles. Her head bobbed and lolled as he carried her down the hall, pushing open the spare bedroom door and groaning at the pile of boxes on the bed. He continued down the hall and found her bedroom, where he laid her gently on the bed and disappeared.

She knew she should care that she was submitting to him; that a man was even in her house, but she didn't have the energy to form a coherent sentence, let alone protest. This wasn't what she wanted, but at least she didn't feel like she was in danger.

Kitchen cupboards banged and water ran through the pipes in the walls. Luca returned, carrying a glass of water and a plastic bowl. He lifted her shoulders and held the glass to her lips. She tried to snatch the drink away from him and succeeded only in spilling it down her chest.

He sighed and reached into the bowl beside the bed. A dripping blue flannel emerged and he squeezed it, then proceeded to wipe her face, neck, and arms. The water was warm and it felt good to finally get some of the grime off her skin. His rhythmic strokes were soothing.

"You know, I'm only helping," he said, "not trying to get into your pants or rip you off, or whatever the hell you think I'm trying to do. You must hang out with a lot of arseholes if someone can't even help without getting beat up."

If she'd felt 100 percent, she'd be inclined to back chat, but right now she was happy just to listen to his deep, velvety voice.

The sun glared through the bedroom window now, highlighting the blond stubble on his face. She felt uncharacteristically safe as she closed her eyes.

Chapter 13

When Mya woke, she was lying on top of the quilt with the other half folded over her. Outside she could hear a distant lawn mower, car wheels bumping over the railway track, and corellas screeching in the trees. There was no sign that a man had been in her bedroom.

"Luca?"

The overwhelming emotion inside her this morning was confusion. Sure, she was angry at the Masons for being pussies and trying to take her down in a group, but mostly she was baffled by what had happened with Luca. No one had ever come to her defense before, and it felt both unwelcome and strangely pleasant. The memories of last night were fuzzy—had she imagined him in her house?

Tentatively, she stretched her arms above and legs below to check the damage. Everything felt stiff and sore, kind of like she'd had a vigorous workout at the gym, but there wasn't any sharp pain. Nothing broken, then; that was a good sign. Then the dull throb in her head made itself known. Gently she slid out of bed and tiptoed to the front door. The two bolts were unlocked, which was proof that she hadn't been in the house alone last night. She slid them across and peered into the lounge room.

"Luca?" No response.

In the kitchen a blue plastic bowl rested upside down on the sink drain board. Her cheeks warmed at the memory of him wiping her neck and arms with a flannel. Luca was the first man to ever set foot in her house, so she blamed it on the concussion. She had been in a weakened state. She had also felt safe while he cared for her, which was a completely unfounded and unwanted sentiment.

He was a confident guy, well aware of how attractive he was, almost cocky. Yet he didn't take advantage of the situation. Odd.

After checking every room in the house to make sure she was alone, Mya took a long, hot shower. The lump on the back of her head was tender as she washed her hair. With her back to the mirror, she saw grazes where her shoulder blades had hit the road. All in all, she hadn't come out of the fight too badly, but what about Willy? The bastard deserved to have something broken, but hopefully his head injury wasn't too serious, like brain damage. She shuddered. A brain injury definitely wasn't the kind of thing she wanted on her conscience.

It was nine o'clock; not too early to visit someone, so she swallowed another couple of pain killers, moisturized her face, and blow-dried her hair. It was easier to leave her hair loose, because the lump hurt too much for a hair tie. At least now she felt more civilized.

Wearing navy tracksuit pants, a white singlet, and flip flops, she stepped onto the front porch and scanned the street.

The Masons' house was quiet.

She wandered along the footpath to number twenty-five, steeling herself to say thank you. It wasn't something she did often. But no matter how much she resented his interference, she had to admit that without Luca's help last night, she would've been a bug splat on Willy Mason's windscreen, figuratively speaking.

Luca's front yard was a lot neater than hers, with a recently painted fence and neatly mowed lawn. White and yellow Mexican daisies lined the path and sparrows flitted in and out of a lemon tree in the corner. She made a note to give him some recipes, because it was sacrilegious the way the fruit was left on the ground to rot.

Curtains were drawn in the front windows, but it didn't stop her using the metal door knocker, loudly.

Footsteps thudded down stairs, so he wasn't asleep. When he opened the door, she totally forgot what she'd come to say. She was mesmerised by the way he rubbed a navy towel against wet hair, with a bicep bulging at each movement. A droplet slid to his bare chest and caught in the brown coils. Her gaze trailed down the line of hair to his navel, where too-loose grey tracksuit pants hung low on his hips. So low she could see the dent where his hips and stomach joined.

Luca cleared his throat and her gaze snapped back to his face.

He was grinning. "Looks like you've pulled up all right." He waved a hand in her direction as evidence.

Her face refused to do the polite thing, like smile, so she continued to ogle. Heat travelled up from her toes, like warm molasses moving slowly through her veins. It raised her body temperature several degrees.

Damn, she wanted his body right now, but that would turn complicated into unmanageable. She needed a protective space around her, which didn't include putting her faith in a man. That sort of thing never led to any good.

He looked so powerful and in control now, but last night she'd seen the worry in his eyes as he'd picked her up from the bathroom floor and gently washed grime from her skin.

A line formed across his forehead.

I'm being too obvious. Take a chill pill, girl. It wasn't like she hadn't been attracted to a man before, but this was so much stronger. Nothing she couldn't control, though.

The smell of his warm, damp flesh filled her nostrils and the pit of her stomach clenched and tingled. Willpower was overrated anyway. A girl needed a little fun once in a while.

He lowered the hand with the towel and opened his mouth, but whatever he wanted to say caught in his throat as she crossed the threshold. Her face must've been ferocious, because he stepped back.

She grabbed his hips firmly and pulled herself to him, planting her lips on his still-open mouth. He tensed and she half expected him to push her away, but as she sampled the smooth warmth of his lips, he slowly responded.

The towel dropped quietly to the floor and his strong arms wrapped around her. Luca's leg twitched and the front door clicked shut. He walked her backward and pinned her against it with his hard body. He wrapped her in his heat and strength.

An uncontrollable desire to get closer to him made her skin blaze—hypersensitive and yearning for his touch. She dragged her fingers down the warm flesh of his back and kneaded his solid shoulders. Their tongues twisted together. She slipped both hands down the back of his pants and grabbed his tight arse.

Quick, heavy breaths tickled her neck as his lips danced their way down the side. A large hand brushed her waist and squeezed her left breast gently, sending a thrill from her nipple to her groin. There was no mistaking the erection pressed against her hip. Just two thin layers of fabric separated them.

What the hell am I doing?

Her mouth stopped moving.

He lived two doors from her and would pass her on the street and in the supermarket. She would have to look him in the eye when this was over and …

She gulped the panic.

Luca looked quizzical. His powder-blue eyes were more alight than she'd ever seen them, as they tried to steal some kind of affirmation from hers. A fleeting pucker between his brows was the only hint of doubt.

Rule number one was to never screw around in her own neighbourhood. How could she maintain control if he knew where she lived? Her hand pressed against his chest.

His expression was one of someone torn between a sweet and a healthy snack. Maybe he was having the same doubts. Whatever his reservations, he must have overcome them, because he scooped her legs out from under her in a fluid movement and carried her upstairs.

A tiny voice in Mya's head screamed that it was a mistake. No matter how cute he was, it couldn't end well. Then she nuzzled the smooth curve of his shoulder and inhaled a lungful of cinnamon-scented skin. It had been too long since she'd indulged in human contact, and her body responded with an aching dampness that relegated the tiny voice to background noise.

As he carried her into his dimly lit bedroom, she discreetly gave it the once over, looking for clues about the kind of man he was. No clothes lying on the floor or photos on the cupboards. Surprisingly neat, considering he'd only been in the house for three days. The bed was covered with masculine navy and white linen, and he lowered her feet to the floor beside it.

His eyes didn't leave hers as he slid her track pants down, followed by lacy lilac knickers. She stepped out of them and then pulled the cord on his pants and let them fall. Enough light penetrated the edges of the curtains for her to appreciate the contours of his body. Muscled arms, flat stomach, and sexy as hell.

There was only the sound of shallow breathing and her pulse racing in her ears. Their gazes roamed over their naked bodies, and the radiant heat between them built the tension until the desire to touch was overwhelming. A need.

His expression was filled with lust as he slid his hands down her hips and then pulled her singlet up over her head. When his long arms wrapped around her and pressed her erect nipples against his balmy chest, they tingled deliciously.

The back of her legs bumped against the bed. She toppled backward and wiggled into the centre of the mattress. Luca positioned himself over her, propped on one elbow, his hot, silky erection against her thigh. One hand sashayed from her ribs to her hips and back again, and she closed her eyes to inhale the shampoo smell of his still-damp hair. She shivered as his palm skimmed her nipple and continued down to her stomach.

Luca's lips rested lightly on hers, gazes locked. He cupped her pubic bone and slipped a finger inside. A soft huff accompanied the tilt of her hips against his rhythmic motion. Her fingers eagerly explored the supple dips and bows of his body, committing them to memory, the sensation heightening her arousal.

She slipped a hand between them and delighted as he groaned into her mouth.

He reached into a bedside drawer, withdrew a gold packet, and tore it between his teeth. Mya shuddered with expectation as he unrolled the condom. His face was intense as he moved over her again, held his weight, and nibbled the side of her neck.

Slowly he lowered his hips and she sighed with contentment as he entered her.

Gradually the exchange of gentle moans quickened and became louder until both she and Luca were panting. Her face felt scalded by the flush of desire. Their skin adhered slightly as a sheen of sweat covered them. The ache inside her was answered with every thrust, heightened until she felt her self-control dissolve.

She squirmed in a futile effort to get closer. Deeper. Every one of Luca's muscles tensed and she rested both feet on his butt to bond him to her as he thrust one last time. He collapsed, still twitching inside her.

"Wow," he whispered.

He rolled onto his side and reached for a box of tissues. After a long, satisfied sigh, he closed his eyes. His face looked angelic in the glow from around the curtains. Mya had the urge to stroke a finger across his eyelids and nose and lips, to touch the faint line of the scar on his mouth. Every inch of her skin tingled with satisfaction.

As though he felt her watching, he opened his eyes and smiled. There was a glint of playfulness now.

"And we couldn't have done that at your place?"

She snorted and fell back against a large pillow. The lump on her head made her cringe. "I just came to say thanks for last night."

"You're welcome." He chuckled, rolled onto his side, and traced a finger across her breasts and stomach, his face relaxed. "Did you …?"

"What?"

"You know, come."

"No, I never do."

His eyes darted up. "Never?"

She shook her head. He laid back, arms tucked behind his head, a thoughtful twist to his mouth.

Well, that was her exit cue. She swung her legs to the floor and dashed to the en-suite, where she took a seat on the lid of his pristine white toilet. It felt way too intimate to be in there, which was silly after what they'd just done.

Would he eventually come in if she refused to come out? Now that her hormones weren't the only thing in her brain, cynicism crawled back under her skin. It was great sex—awesome in fact— but was it worth the trouble it might bring her?

Luca's cinnamon body wash wafted from the frameless glass shower cubicle. She splashed cold water onto her face and straightened the navy-blue towels. As she stared at herself in the mirrored vanity cabinet, a burning curiosity to peek inside caught her off guard, and she stepped back from the force of it. It wasn't her thing to open closed doors. It could lead to knowing someone, and that wasn't a road she wanted to travel.

After a fortifying deep breath, she opened the en-suite door, half expecting Luca to have fallen asleep, but he already had pants and shoes on. She felt his eyes scald her back as she set a new world record for pulling on undies, tracksuit, and tank top.

"Yeah, I'll catch you later." She lobbed the brief goodbye with a sideways glance.

The tap of sandshoes following her down the wooden stairs made her feel like she was being chased, which prompted an unreasonable urge to run. Despite her skin still tingling with pleasure, she couldn't wait to get out of there, and she noticed he didn't try to stop her.

Chapter 14

Mya tipped pungent soil from a plastic bag into a trench and shook her fingers back and forth to settle it. Slightly warm, it clung to her skin as she pressed lumpy snow pea seeds in at twenty-centimetre intervals. Last month's crop had already tangled around the chicken wire brace, with radish and feathery carrot tops sprouting in front of them.

"You there, Mya?"

She flinched and then berated herself for being so jumpy. "Yep, just planting snow peas."

Mrs. Elderberry stuck her head over the wood-slat fence that divided their properties and grinned. A halo of white hair drew attention to thick black mascara on her lashes and wine-coloured lipstick that bled into the crevices around her mouth. She hung a plastic bucket over the fence.

"Here's some ash from the fire for your tomatoes."

"You're giving me ash?" Mya raised an eyebrow.

"Put a ring of it around the tomatoes and it'll keep the snails away and plump the fruit. You mark my words."

Mya took the bucket and followed the instructions. "There are a couple ready if you want." They separated from the plant easily and she cradled them gently in her palm.

"Thanks," said Mrs. Elderberry. "There's nothing better than tomatoes on toast, with a sprinkle of pepper."

"Here, have a sprig of basil. Put it on top and drizzle it with olive oil."

"You know, if you didn't grow so many veggies, you wouldn't have to give them away. Anyone'd think you grow them just for us old folks." Mrs. Elderberry giggled girlishly.

"I like to have a continuous supply," Mya reasoned.

"But you eat at the hotel four nights a week."

"And that's why there's plenty for you."

An orange butterfly fluttered around a tomato plant and settled on a yellow flower. Mya twisted to move the bag of potting mix and a pinch of pain sliced through her ribs. She tried to hide the wince.

"Are you hurt, dear?"

"I'm fine."

"That was a terrible business last night." Mrs. Elderberry tutted. "Those Masons have been nothing but trouble since they moved in. I was the one who called the police, you know."

"Thanks, but Luca and I were doing okay by ourselves."

"That's not what it looked like to me," the old lady mumbled.

Mya rubbed her aching side, and it reminded her of the strenuous romp with Luca that morning. His firm body entangled with hers; warm, silky flesh slipping against her skin. She touched her nose to her forearm and inhaled male sweat and soap. It started a tingling sensation between her thighs.

It would've been nice to linger in his rumpled bed, but she shouldn't have gotten into it in the first place. The last thing she needed was him thinking she was his girlfriend, especially after his stalker-like behaviour on Monday night at the pub. What the hell was she thinking? Well, she knew exactly what she was thinking *with*, and it wasn't her brain.

The guy had only moved in four days ago, but a tiny piece of him had lodged itself inside her brain and she wasn't sure why. There was no denying he had the muscled, tough-guy package, but she got the feeling there was more to Luca than a larrikin who beat up neighbours in the middle of the night. Either way, a misplaced crush could be ignored.

"Hmmph. You look like you're pondering the universe."

She looked up at the smiling Mrs. Elderberry. "Yeah." If the old duck knew what she'd really been thinking, it would curl the hem of her petticoat.

"Well, dear, I wouldn't walk around at night by yourself anymore. Not with those Masons down the road."

"I'll be careful. Thanks."

"Do you think he'll go to jail?"

Mya shrugged and stabbed the trowel into the soil. "I have to get going."

She waved and headed inside.

With one finger, Mya gently felt the back of her skull. A helmet wouldn't go over that lump, so she couldn't visit her mum today, but there was one thing she wanted to do.

After last night she didn't fancy getting too close to Willy Mason again, but if he'd stolen her mum's jewelry, he might have stolen stuff from other residents at Rich Haven too. She swallowed a couple of paracetamol tablets before putting her plan into action. If she applied a little pressure, maybe he'd pop like the zit he was.

With a flick of her finger, she Googled Adelaide city hospitals. Willy Mason could have been taken to any of three in the area, but the Queen Elizabeth was the closest, so she dialed it first.

"Mr William Mason, please."

The operator put her through to a ward, but no one picked up, so the call tripped to elevator music. Mya sighed as she rested a foot against the wall. The bowl of confiscated weapons on the hall table had taken close to a decade to amass. It looked impressive, although she'd never used one. Violence wasn't something she particularly liked. It was just a part of life.

After a minute the phone dialed again and this time a nurse picked up and transferred the call to Willy Mason's room.

"Willy? Hi, it's your neighbour, Mya". She held the phone away from her ear as the predictable stream of profanities poured through the speaker. "Yeah, I'm sure I'm gonna be dead, but only if the cops let you—" Pause. "Shut up, Willy, and listen real hard. I know what you've been up to with the jewelry, and you're *not* going to get away with it. Oh, *now* you've got nothing to say."

She hung up while she had the upper hand. Let him shit himself for a bit.

• • •

Luca waited for the traffic lights to change. He had missed the peak hour, thanks to his unexpected visitor this morning. The thought of her flawless skin, pale against his dark-blue quilt, her caramel hair fanned around her oval face, her body arched against his …

The front of his jeans started to feel tight and he shifted in the car seat, glancing at the driver in the next lane.

The lights turned green and traffic started to move. He followed the road up Richmond Hill and turned through the gates of Rich Haven Aged Care Facility.

His head was swimming with contradictory impressions of Mya: from a blood-spattered shirt in the middle of the day and behaviour bordering on reclusive to a talented chef and sex siren. She always seemed so sure of herself and carefully guarded, but last night when he was caring for her, he noticed a moon-shaped nightlight beside her bed.

Then there was this morning—it was as though she was starved for human contact.

He breathed deeply and enjoyed the faint lavender scent that lingered on his skin. Mya was the first woman in Luca's bed since he shared it with his wife. There had been other women, just not in *his* bed. It hadn't felt right before. So what had changed?

She caught me off guard, that's all.

No, that wasn't the whole truth. He'd been attracted to her since she drove that hulking motorcycle past his moving van, and he'd enjoyed every minute of being with her. Maybe it was the announcement of Gabe's engagement. Seeing his brother so happy reminded Luca about how happy *he* used to be. He couldn't know his time with Olivia would be so brief.

After maneuvering his faded red Corolla between a gold Mercedes Benz and a silver BMW, he pulled on his suit jacket and grabbed the buff folder of information Kate had collected.

Rich Haven certainly lived up to its name: manicured gardens, standard roses, gazebos, paved footpaths, a lake, even a brass plaque set into the stone to validate the year of construction.

It was a big commitment Mya had made by keeping her mother there.

Standing in the doorway for a moment, he let his eyes adjust to the dim interior and took in every detail—there was just no taking the detective out of a man. The entrance hall had a twelve-metre ceiling with wide, wall-papered cornices and dark wood panelling around the room. A two-metre mirror, with an ornate gold frame as thick as a man's torso, reflected Luca back to himself. A middle-aged couple sat in high-backed chairs, speaking in hushed tones. A young boy beside them swung his legs vigorously and bounced on the seat of his chair.

A woman, who appeared to be in her late fifties, was behind the reception desk, placing papers into a filing cabinet. Her hair had so many streaks—honey, copper, and white—that it was difficult to tell what the original colour was. He stepped up to the counter and cleared his throat.

The woman immediately abandoned her work. Dentist-white teeth glistened between coral lips.

"Good afternoon. I'm Beverly Aldridge. May I help you?"

"I don't have an appointment but would like to speak to the director, if I can." He extracted his badge.

"Oh." She laid a hand across her heart, as though she'd had a fright. "Is this an official visit? I wasn't expecting you."

"I'm here on police business, but I'd appreciate it if you could keep it quiet."

Beverly picked up a cream-coloured phone and punched three numbers. She flashed another smile while she waited for an answer. "Sorry to disturb you, Mr. Pratt, but there is a Detective Patterson here for an unscheduled visit." Beverly listened and nodded. "Yes, sir." She came through a side door to the reception area. She waved an arm in the direction of another panelled door.

Beverly knocked and stood aside for Luca, and then gave him another toothy smile as she retreated.

Luca suppressed a snort as Humpty-Dumpty approached. Mr. Pratt was round in the extreme and wore a striped shirt and suspenders to hold up his trousers. Precious little hair was combed across his shiny pate; all he needed to complete the image was a red and yellow surf lifesaving cap.

"Good to meet you, detective. Is there anything I can get for you? Tea? Coffee?"

Mr. Pratt offered a clammy hand and Luca shook it briefly.

"No, thank you. I appreciate you seeing me, so I won't take too much of your time. May I?" Luca rested a hand on the back of a tub chair and waited for Mr. Pratt's nod before sitting down.

The director waddled back to his side of the desk and sunk into a voluminous leather executive chair, dabbing a white handkerchief on his brow.

"I trust you understand my need for confidentiality?" Luca widened his eyes in question.

"Oh, certainly, detective. We pride ourselves on discretion at Rich Haven."

Luca wasn't sure discretion and confidentiality were interchangeable, but pressed on. "As part of an ongoing investigation, I need the rosters for two of your staff and photographic ID if you have it."

Mr. Pratt sipped water. "And who would they be?"

"Melanie Lane and Kevin Barnes."

"What are they involved in? Does it have something to do with that missing necklace?"

Luca took a quick breath. "Um … at this stage nothing is substantiated." Hell, it looked like the scam was already under way.

Mr. Pratt wiped perspiration from his forehead with quick, jerky movements as he punched numbers into the phone. He directed someone to bring him the information.

Luca decided to play it cool and go where the conversation took him. "Have there been many jewelry thefts during the past couple of months?"

"Certainly not, detective. Rich Haven is a secure facility, and staff undergoes rigorous background checks. If they were involved in anything untoward, they would be dismissed immediately."

There was a knock on the door and Beverly Aldridge entered, carrying a stack of papers that she handed to Luca. He tucked the proffered documents into his folder and pulled his singing mobile out. Kate's name was displayed on the screen. He pressed the end button and slipped it back into his pocket. "Sorry, but I need to return that call, director. I would appreciate it if you could call me if you think of anything unusual about these staff. Anything at all."

The man bent forward until his belly squashed against the desk. He could only just reach Luca's hand to take a business card.

Luca made his escape and hurried outside, pausing to run a finger along a scratch from the boot of his car to the front panel. He wouldn't leave it in the bloody Croydon Hotel car park again. He threw his suit jacket and the folder onto the passenger seat and fished the hands-free earpiece out of the glove box. With it tucked over one ear, he dialed Kate.

She picked up on the third ring.

"Hi. I couldn't take your call, because I was in a meeting with the director at Rich Haven."

"You were? I was phoning you about Rich Haven. There's been a development."

"Don't tell me, someone reported jewelry missing."

Kate was silent for a moment. "I hate it when you do that. Anyway, I was minding my own business in the lunch room today when I overheard a couple of the guys talking about a jewelry theft. So I listened in and they mentioned Rich Haven. I quizzed Old about it and he told me a woman came in last Sunday to report her mother's jewelry stolen. Only it wasn't just stolen; the woman said it was replaced with exact replicas. He thought she was bullshitting to claim the insurance money."

"Replicas? You have to get a hold of that report."

"Did it. And the woman even handed over the supposed imitations."

"Great. Do you have her contact details?"

"Yes, and you won't believe it, but her current address is twenty-one Railway Terrace. Isn't that your street?"

Luca felt his lip curl as he mentally pictured the house two doors from his. Mya's house. She kept popping up on his radar, and now he'd complicated it by sleeping with her.

Damn it.

"Luca?"

"Yeah, I'm here. I want you to fax a description of the jewelry to every pawnshop this side of the city. Today."

"Sure."

He heard the uncertainty in Kate's voice. "Good work, constable. Is the inspector in his office? I need to speak to him."

"Let me look. Yes, he is. Shall I tell him you're coming in?"

"No, I'll be there in ten. Oh, and I might have my mobile turned off for a while tonight."

"Off? What are you planning?"

"Don't worry about it, Kate. Just find that jewelry."

"Yes, sir. Oh, and I contacted Happy Vale Nursing Home. Someone *did* report their mother's jewelry was a fake. The director called the police as part of procedure, but they wouldn't even attend. Couldn't tell me anything more. Do you want me to track down the family?" Kate sounded eager.

"Don't bother at this stage. Talk to you later."

What the hell was Mya playing at? She reported her mother's jewelry stolen but failed to mention that to him. If her shenanigans this morning had been a ploy to manipulate him, she was messing with the wrong man. When he got home tonight he was going to ask her straight out what was going on.

Face to face he had the upper hand, because he'd be able to read her body language and facial cues. If she lied to him, he'd have a fair idea.

But right now there was an uncomfortable conversation to be had with his boss.

Chapter 15

Luca stopped in the doorway and peered across neat stacks of manila folders to Moss's short, silver hair. "Have you got a minute, sir?"

The inspector scrutinised him through silver-framed reading glasses. "Of course. Make yourself at home."

Luca sat in a vinyl chair opposite Moss and swallowed his hesitation. "Sir, I wanted to let you know I've had some new information relating to Happy Vale Nursing Home."

Moss narrowed his eyes and the black leather of his executive chair squeaked as he crossed his arms. The lines on his face deepened to look like the cracked clay of a dry lakebed.

"I thought you were on holiday," he said.

"I am, sir, other than staying in touch with Constable Derman about the jewelry case. Some new information came to light, and I thought it was worth pursuing." He used one fingernail to hook a broken shard off another, deliberately avoiding his boss's gaze.

"What kind of information?"

He took a fortifying breath—best to say it quickly. "Two staff from Happy Vale moved to another nursing home, and now there has been a jewelry theft and an increase in women without families dying there."

Moss kept his lips firmly shut and stared. He was a pro at staring people down. That was how the old man got information out of you. Luca resisted the urge to fill the uncomfortably long pause.

At last Moss said, "I can't see anything wrong with following a lead, but I can't justify additional resources and"—he held up a sun-spotted hand—"I want you to keep me abreast of your every move. Don't go stepping on anyone's toes and *don't* take unnecessary risks. Do I make myself clear?"

"Crystal, sir."

This whole conversation smacked of the one the inspector had with Luca two years ago, after an unpleasant incident that resulted in Luca's partner being shot. He'd been accused of taking *unnecessary risks*, but if there was a choice between protecting someone and following protocol, he'd be a protector every time. It's the whole reason he took an oath and did the training. Some people needed someone else to stand up for them. Even the murdered needed a voice.

"Sir, can I also request a Banker's Record? I want to look into the financial records of someone involved in the case. I'm not sure if she's a suspect or victim yet."

"Sounds interesting. You can have the form, but you'll need to have it approved by a magistrate."

"Will do." Luca stood.

Right, that was the easy part of his plan. Now for a potentially boring afternoon in his car. His primary objective now was to find out who Melanie Lane and Kevin Banks were.

• • •

Luca unwrapped greaseproof paper from around a chicken salad roll and bit into it. Tangy mayonnaise and Dijon mustard combined to form a creamy dressing. It was four in the afternoon and his stomach had been growling for a while. He washed it down with a swig from a carton of chocolate milk. Not a gourmet meal, but very satisfying. He had been sitting in his car across the street from the entrance to Rich Haven since his meeting with Moss.

According to the work schedules Beverly had provided, Melanie Lane should be finishing work about now. He planned on following her home. Kevin Barnes would finish at four thirty and Luca couldn't be in two places at once, so he'd have to come back tomorrow. He didn't know what cars they drove, but he had both photo IDs on the seat beside him. One way or another he was going to find out where they lived and what they were up to.

The thefts he'd originally followed at Happy Vale Nursing Home had ceased when he started asking questions. But had they really stopped, or did the thieves just get smarter and replace the jewelry with replicas?

He screwed the sandwich paper into a ball, tossed it on the passenger floor, and dusted sesame seeds from his lap. With teeth bared at the rear view mirror, he checked for seeds. The white scar he got playing backyard cricket with Quinton and Gabe radiated from the corner of his lip like a faint vein.

At ten past four, a ginger-haired woman wearing the Rich Haven uniform approached the roadway on foot. She carried a large black handbag. He glanced at the photo of Melanie Lane—definitely one and the same.

Melanie strolled along the Rich Haven driveway, through the pedestrian gate, and sat on the bench at the bus stop, 100 metres away. She bent to rub the side of her ankle. Why did that seem familiar? He ran a finger down the margin of Kate's notes as he scanned the lines. There it was—Melanie was a registered nurse who'd had an accident at work fifteen years ago. It left her with permanent damage to the lower right leg and a limp.

Luca knocked back the rest of the chocolate milk and compacted the carton as he Googled the bus timetable on his mobile. The next one was due at four twenty. Right on time, a bus squealed to a halt across the road and sunk closer to the ground with a hiss of expelled gas.

Luca put the folder on the passenger seat and started his car. As the bus pulled away from the curb, he put the Corolla into first gear and rested his fingers on the handbrake. The bus groaned from first to second gear and … Melanie was still seated at the bus stop. He had no idea what was going on, but turned the car off, hoping the noise of the bus had masked the engine noise.

If Melanie had made him, she might be waiting for his next move. He sunk lower and watched her in the side mirror. She pulled a compact from her handbag and applied lipstick, mushing her lips together to set the colour.

Fifteen minutes passed and his lower back ached from the slumped position he held. He could abandon the stakeout, but the woman had to leave some time.

At 4 thirty-seven a white Holden Commodore turned out of Rich Haven and pulled alongside the bus stop. Luca sat taller and looked over his shoulder. Melanie smiled and, without hesitation, got into the passenger seat. It was clear she knew the driver and was probably waiting for him, rather than accepting a random lift. Interesting.

Luca jotted down the registration number and waited until the Commodore pulled away from the curb before restarting the Corolla and pulling a U-turn.

• • •

"Thanks, Miss Ballinger." Mya held the plate of blueberry muffins higher to show her gratitude.

"Oh, call me Doreen, dear. And you're most welcome. Perhaps those Masons will think twice about terrorizing the neighbourhood now that you and Mr. Patterson have showed them who's boss." Doreen dabbed gently at her stiff, white hair as she backed out of Mya's broken gate.

"Well, I'm not sure it'll be *that* easy," Mya told her.

Great, now half the neighbourhood expected her to perform some vigilante service. There had been two jars of cloth-covered homemade jam on her doorstep in the morning, and now the muffins.

"Hi, Mya."

Mr. Reiner from next door dodged a geranium bush that overhung the footpath. The scrawny old bloke had a fistful of tools and a goofy grin.

She smiled. "Hey, my lawn isn't long enough to hide snakes yet." She tried to sound indignant.

"It can go another week," he replied jovially, "but that gate is going to trip one of your fans." His bony shoulders jiggled as he sniggered.

"Yeah, just what I need, a bunch of old folks thinking I'm going to save the neighbourhood." She met him at the gate and extracted a handful of paper from the letterbox.

"Don't worry. I don't expect such heroic deeds every week." Bert grinned and knelt to work on the broken gate hinge. "Besides, I reckon it was that strapping young man from the other side of my place who did most of the work."

"Way to flatter me, Bert. And don't think I didn't hear about the cricket bat. You shouldn't be getting yourself involved in scuffles like that, you know."

Bert lined the end of a screwdriver up with a loose screw and started turning it clockwise. Mya flicked through junk mail. There was a sale at the local car yard, it was time to treat herself to a facial at Belinda's Beauty Barn, and if she bought fish and chips for six dollars, she'd get a free soft drink.

"There. Good as new." Bert stood and, with hands on his lower back, stretched backward. "Damn these old bones," he mumbled. "Your fence is going to need a paint before long, too."

She nodded agreement and scraped at a sliver of peeling paint.

"I saw Mr. Patterson leaving your place this morning." Bert smiled hugely. "That was nice of him to take care of you *all* night."

She swatted him with a take-away brochure, hoping her cheeks weren't as flushed as they felt. "Don't be such a gossip. Hey, you want a blueberry muffin?" She shoved the plate at him and peeled back the ClingWrap.

Bert left, stuffing his mouth. There was one drawback to living in a street of old people. They were snoops.

With the plate of muffins balanced in the crook of her arm and junk mail between her lips, she opened the front door and an envelope at the same time. Halfway to the kitchen, the plate nearly came a cropper, so she put it on the dining table. She spit the junk mail on top and shook out the thrice-folded paper. It was jagged down the left margin, and her heart skipped a beat. The same backward slanting writing confronted her. Not another one!

Did you miss me, Mya? Living it up in that nice house, with that big motorbike you ride. I'll bet it cost a small fortune.

Can you feel me breathing down your neck yet? It won't be long before it's time to pay up.

Mya's hand went limp and the paper glided to the floor. She couldn't suck air into her lungs, so she gasped short, unsatisfying breaths.

Suddenly she didn't feel safe in the house. She ran to the front door and checked the bolts, then sprinted from room to room checking window locks. She turned the stereo on loud and checked the front door again.

When she'd finished, she stood in the hallway panting and concentrated on clenching and unclenching her teeth and breathing in and out. Her heart still beat faster than before. Shit, she was dealing with a psycho. What had she ever done to this woman?

Was Mya in real danger—or her mum? The thought of Rosalie sitting, quiet and non-responsive in her floral armchair, squeezed her lungs tighter still. Who the hell knew what this crazy woman was capable of, or if she was a puppet for someone else.

"I'll change our names and move again."

Overreact much? Take a chill pill! Besides, changing names takes ages, and getting Mum into another nursing home would take eons.

No, she'd wait and see how things panned out. She could take care of herself.

She glanced at a photo on the bookshelf of her mum in a floral summer dress, eating ice cream by the beach. It couldn't hurt to make enquiries about moving her to another nursing home and changing their identities. After all, they only had each other.

Chapter 16

Luca wasn't sure how long he planned to sit in his Corolla watching, what may or may not be Melanie's house. He swigged water from a two-litre bottle that he kept on the passenger floor for emergencies. Spending a whole afternoon and evening in his car definitely constituted an emergency. After fossicking in the glove-box, he located a stick of chewing gum wrapped in green paper and wished he'd bought a second chicken roll and chocolate milk at the deli.

He saw the couple go inside sixty-three Listing Street three hours ago. Now he was bored, and worse, he had time to think. Sitting alone here was much the same as sitting alone at home. Having Mya in his bed made him tired of flying solo. Maybe he was really bad at reading women—out of practice—but she'd made it abundantly clear she wasn't interested. Then she'd knocked on his front door and … Wow.

Maybe the way she acted and felt weren't as transparent as he first thought.

She was so different from his late wife. Olivia had been graceful, softly spoken, nurturing. His best friend. Mya was guarded and independent, but it was the passion he liked about her. It was the autonomy that bothered him. Was she acting outside of the law? Willy Mason obviously had a beef with her—could it have something to do with the jewelry?

To pass the time, he radioed dispatch to request a registration trace on the car that had picked Melanie up. Surprisingly, it was registered to a Kevin Walker, not Barnes, at the same address. Surely it couldn't be that easy. Changing a surname wasn't much of a cover.

By eight o'clock the sun set and only dusky shadows were left as streetlights flickered on. He alternated between rotating his cramped ankles and stretching his arms over his head.

Then the front porch light went on. Melanie and Kevin jostled one another out the front door and clinched passionately. They trotted down the porch steps hand in hand and took off in the white Commodore again.

Luca's hand shot to the ignition key, but he didn't turn it. He watched the red taillights disappear around the corner and sat for another five minutes, clock-watching and thinking. Entering the property without just cause was illegal, but strictly speaking, he wasn't on duty, and it couldn't hurt to look around. He needed some concrete evidence to tell him who Kevin and Melanie really were.

The street was dark. He stepped out of the car and searched the boot for his crime scene kit. From it he extracted a pair of latex gloves and shoved them in his back pocket. He swapped his police-issue blue shirt for a less conspicuous black one and crossed the street at the darkest point, between the soft pools of illumination cast by the streetlights.

Searching the footpath and front yards, he strolled toward number sixty-three and stepped over the low iron fence. In the blackness cast by a tall ash tree, he pressed his back against the warm house bricks and listened.

Excessive risk taking, that's what Moss would say. Luca pulled on the latex gloves and circumvented the porch light on his way to the side of the house.

The gate squeaked and he paused. Nothing and no one came running. There was no turning back now. Melanie and Kevin could be back any minute, so he made a quick visual sweep and moved forward.

Extracting a penlight torch from his trouser pocket, he held it low so the neighbours wouldn't notice the glow bobbing. He hoped to hell there wasn't a dog in the yard. All of his senses were alert, and he could smell the dampness on the lawn. He pointed the torch at the path and crept forward. There was only a footpath distance between the house and fence and he had to step over stacks of empty plastic plant pots, half a bag of cement dust, and planks of wood stacked against the house—termite heaven.

The backyard was softly illuminated from a far window. With his cheek pressed to the glass, he saw a dining table. The decor was right out of the '70s, with orange pendant lights and sliding doors with bubbled-orange glass insets.

Car lights bounced into the driveway and through the front window.

Luca threw himself on the ground and scrambled to switch off the torch. Flat against the ground, he lay still.

The car engine revved. The lights changed direction, and then he heard it reverse. He commando-crawled to the corner of the house, jumped to his feet, and watched the car disappear down the road. Just someone turning around.

His heart tried to punch a hole in his chest and moisture prickled his upper lip. He needed to hurry this up. After a deep breath he peered through the dining room window. A mosaic lamp cast a distorted rainbow across shag carpet. To the right was a speckled laminate breakfast bar with dark wood-look cupboards and lime-green tiles over the sink. On the bench was a pile of opened mail. What he wouldn't give to get his hands on it.

He spotted a hefty cement pot with an insipid palm in it. With a foot on each side of the rim, he held onto the window ledge and pulled himself up, tightening his fingers on the ledge as the pot rocked slightly.

The mail was clearer from this position. Bills, but he couldn't read them. With one hand he pulled his phone from his pocket and angled it in the direction of the kitchen bench, zoomed in, and clicked.

The flash was super bright in the dark yard. He jumped to the ground and crouched under the window. Besides the thunder of his pulse, he didn't hear any disturbance. He flicked the torch over his watch. Fifteen minutes on the property. Time to get out.

On the way out he shone the torch into the bathroom window. Although he was the first to admit he was no expert on women, it seemed that there were very few signs of a female living in the house. No woman's touch, no underwear hanging on the shower rail, no makeup on the sink. Melanie Lane might have her own place.

As he passed the back door his shoulder brushed the silver handle on the screen door and it knocked against the frame. Surely not. He tried it. Unlocked. Seconds ticked by as he stood in the dark, trying to shake conflicting thoughts into a logical order. Nothing he found tonight would be admissible in court, and worse, he could lose his badge or end up in jail.

But he needed to know who these people were.

If they'd set up the same scam at Rich Haven, then the jewelry theft was just a front. Elderly women could die, and no one else was in a position to prevent it. With his gaze fixed on the old-fashioned lever handle, he ran a tongue around his dry mouth.

After another minute of indecision, he stepped back and closed the screen door.

• • •

Mya watched a short man with thick caterpillar sideburns, measure chips into a metal basket and plunge it into hot oil. The surface of the deep fryer turned into an ale-coloured foam, and she regretted her decision to get take-away for dinner. Boiled chips, gross. She leaned against the soft-drink fridge and felt a bead of sweat trickle down her cleavage.

Within five minutes she was headed home, swapping the butcher's paper parcel from arm to arm to avoid scalding. She alternated it with a cool can of lemonade.

A familiar cricket-like chirping brought a smile to her lips. Her gaze followed a two-tone Volkswagen Kombi as it rattled past. It had a white roof and a pink lower half. Not the same as the one she coveted as a child, but it still reminded her of a happier time, when she was part of a real family. Jack hadn't always been an abusive drunk.

On the day of her fourth birthday party, Mya sat on the lounge room floor in a circle with five kindergarten friends, playing pass-the-parcel. Jack Roach tousled her hair and knelt beside her.

"Happy birthday, Mya. I got you a little something."

The game was momentarily forgotten at the sight of a square box wrapped in iridescent-blue paper. She picked at the sticky tape, carefully peeling and folding it. It was going into her collection of precious things. Inside the plain brown box, she lifted a yellow VW Beetle. The cutest car she'd ever seen, complete with a daisy painted on the bonnet, just like the one she'd fallen in love with on their beach holiday. He'd remembered.

"I'm going to drive one like this when I'm a grown up," she told him.

"No doubt." Jack smiled.

Mya blinked the childhood memory away. Jack might have started out kind, but after his mother died …

Her shiver contradicted the humidity. Cockroach spent far too much time in her nightmares to deserve space in her consciousness, so she trudged on.

A full moon hung just above one horizon as the sun melted into the other. People were out enjoying the summer evening: couples holding hands, teenagers smoking and laughing. Mya stepped around a purple-flowering westringia, her gaze on the now grease-soaked parcel in her arms.

The quick footfalls didn't catch her attention until the last moment. She braced as a pale figure collided with her. Air grunted from her lungs and the momentum knocked her back several steps. The soft drink can thudded to the ground, but she saved the fish and chips.

Wide panda-eyes glared at her. Two eyeliner trails trickled down pale cheeks and there was a small gash at the top of the girl's left cheekbone. Blood was smudged into her hair as though she'd wiped it with the back of her hand.

The girl's hand flew up and Mya wrapped her fingers around the exposed wrist to prevent an attack, if it was intended. It was Blondie—Paula Mason's live-in friend with the multi-coloured hair.

The girl's eyes expanded. She struggled, no doubt remembering the beating Mya gave Paula in the park. Blondie's eyes filled with tears and she whimpered.

Mya let go of her wrist and took a step back. "Are you okay?"

"Leave me alone!" Blondie glanced over her shoulder.

"I'm not going to hurt you." Mya took another step back.

"I don't need your help. What the hell do you care anyway?" Bangles jangled on the girl's forearm as she shifted from foot to foot, looking for an escape.

"I'm sure I'm the last person you want help from, but in my experience when a woman has a mark like that on her face, it's from a bloke."

Blondie frowned, stilled. She glanced over her shoulder again and then pushed past and ran along the bike track. Same old, same old—what people needed and wanted weren't always the same.

Mya half expected to see a bloke in pursuit on Railway Terrace, but the street was empty. The only sounds were crickets clicking like the party favours at her fourth birthday party, and the hiss of a sprinkler. There were lights on in most of the houses, but not Luca's.

The paper around her dinner was now slick. That was the last time she got sucked in by junk mail specials. Car headlights bounced on the road and she hurried to the footpath, watching it slow. She didn't have a clue what kind of car Rhonda drove, or what the nutter was planning, but a drive-by shooting might be in the newspaper tomorrow.

She opened her now-functioning gate and turned to face the car, tensed to throw herself on the ground behind the fence. The car crawled to a halt and the driver's window rolled down.

She held her breath. Step back. Step back.

"Hi, Mya."

Luca's smiling face came into view and she swallowed her panic down like a mouthful of Brussels sprouts. A flutter started in her stomach and gave her heart palpitations as it caught in her chest. Blondie's problems could wait.

"Hi, Luca."

"What you up to?" He hung a long arm out the window and drummed his fingers on the side of the door.

Yep, still nosy. Sexy, but too inquisitive for his own good. "I'm about to eat some grease for dinner."

She shrugged the parcel forward to show him the semi-translucent paper. He had better not take it as an invitation. He'd seen the inside of her house for the first and last time.

"Anything sounds good to me. I'm starving. How are you feeling after last night?"

She narrowed her eyes when his gaze travelled briefly down the length of her body. Was he sniffing around for more of what he had this morning?

"Head still hurts," she said bluntly.

"Maybe you should see a doctor."

Yeah, or he could give her a sponge bath again. Whoa, that was a stupid idea out of fantasy land. The last thing she wanted was him in her house again. One-night stands, that was all she needed. Luca was going to be disappointed if he had something more in mind.

"I'll be right," she told him. "Was there something you wanted?"

"Oh yeah, I'm glad I caught you. Willy Mason was released from hospital this afternoon, so I wanted to tell you to watch your back." His head disappeared into the car and she heard a ripping sound. A few seconds later he leaned out the window, arm extended. "Here's my mobile number, just in case."

A gentle breeze caught his soapy scent and wafted it across Mya's face. An unwelcome vision of tangled limbs and his big bed surfaced.

"I'll be fine."

"I'd really feel better if you'd take it. I'm not expecting you to call or anything, but if you get into a sticky situation you can. If you need anything."

She hesitated, returning Luca's cool stare. Finally she stepped back through the gate and took the slip of paper. "See ya 'round."

"Um, Mya …"

"Yes?" she snapped. Hell, she'd lost her lemonade and now her dinner was lukewarm. What now?

"Never mind. I'll see you later."

Mya pursed her lips and glared at the faded taillights as his car coasted home.

Chapter 17

It was just before nine a.m., so the Triumph was the only vehicle in the Rich Haven visitors' car park. Mya's hair was damp with sweat when she pulled her motorbike helmet off and placed it on the ground. The air was already oppressive, but the weatherman had predicted rain by the weekend. She tilted her face to the cloudless sky and doubted it.

She took the slate steps two at a time and tried the front door. Still locked, so she pressed a code onto the keypad and waited to hear the doors click unlocked. Hansi, a stiff-backed Sri Lankan security guard, shuffled across the reception foyer and, after recognition lit his eyes, lifted a cluster of keys dog-clipped to the belt loop on his pants.

"Good morning, Miss Jensen. You're early today."

"Hi, Hansi. Yeah, I just wanted to see Mum before work."

He raised his left arm to check the time on a silver dive-watch. "It's nearly nine anyway, so I'll leave the door open. Don't forget to sign in, please."

Mya signed the visitor's book on the reception desk and headed down the left hallway to door number thirty-two. She let herself in. Her mum was still asleep, and Mya let out the breath she didn't realize she'd been holding. The letters from Rhonda, or whoever this nut was, had spooked her, but she felt better seeing her mum safe.

There was a desk in the corner, so she dragged its chair closer to the bed and sat. It was calming to watch her mum sleep. She looked like a regular forty-nine-year-old lying in bed, hair the colour of Werther's caramels tangled around her face. With her fingertips, Mya gently stroked it back onto the pillow. Her mum's lips were full and pink, but the dark circles under her eyes made her look tired all the time. Not tired from lack of sleep—more world-weary. The blankets moved up and down slightly with the rhythm of her breathing. She looked peaceful.

Someone had delivered her breakfast on a tray but must have decided not to wake her, so it was untouched. The wall clock ticked away half an hour and then it was time to kiss Rosalie's forehead and go to work.

•••

Luca nodded to a middle-aged woman being towed along the bike track by a white and tan Jack Russell.

He had seen Mya leave early this morning on her motorbike, and wanted to know where she had gone. It had been too early for a shift at the Croydon Hotel, but he'd still walked to the pub to check that she wasn't there, although it made him feel a little creepy to admit.

He couldn't marry the way he felt around her with his suspicions. Every time he looked out his house windows or stepped into the front yard, he hoped to catch a glimpse of her. It was ridiculous to be acting like a horny teenager, but he hadn't felt this attracted to a woman in a very long time. He wanted to unravel the mystery that was Mya Jensen.

He ignored the bitter taste in his mouth that warned he was better off not knowing.

Mr. Reiner was pruning his immaculate front garden next to Luca's house. They both waved. Friendly neighbours, except for the Masons. Once inside, Luca turned the kettle on and waited for his laptop to boot up. According to the thermometer on the kitchen window, the outside temperature was already thirty-five degrees Celsius. He made a mental note to turn the garden drippers on later.

With his mobile phone plugged into the laptop, he hit enter and waited for the photos to import. There were a few mail items in his inbox, but one in particular caught his attention. He had pulled a favour from a buddy in the Fraud Squad to fast track a copy of Mya's financial records. "Call me," it said.

"Hi, Nielsen, it's Patterson. What've you got for me?"

"Hang on, let me open the file. Yes, Mya Jensen. Can't say I found anything that stood out, other than the fact the report was sparse. Doesn't have a credit card, no repayments, bank balance is $2,163.54."

Not what Luca would expect from someone on the take, or someone keeping her mother in Rich Haven, where the fees must be astronomical. Certainly higher than a single girl working at a pub should be able to afford.

"No repayments?"

"Nope. Owns a property at twenty-one Railway Terrace outright and a vehicle."

Considering she wasn't yet thirty years old, that was a stretch when added with the Rich Haven fees.

"Any indication of how she came to pay off these assets?" he asked Nielsen.

"Let me see. It looks like there was a huge injection of cash in 2001. The money came from a trust account in the name of Jean Roach."

Luca flicked through his notebook to find the page of information about Mya. Her mother received a traumatic brain injury in 1999. "Why would money in Jean's name be transferred to Mya? Especially in a lump sum."

"Let me see what it says here. Oh, it seems Mya Jensen was granted guardianship of a Rosalic Jensen. Hmm, there must've been a name change somewhere along the line."

"Yeah, I know about that."

Neil grunted his assent. "Most of the money went straight out to Rich Haven Aged Care facility."

Luca was amazed that a teenager from an underprivileged home could make such smart financial decisions. Instead of blowing the dough, or buying herself a flash house in a nice suburb, Mya had made sure her mother was taken care of first.

"You still there?" Nielsen asked.

"Yeah, sorry. You said *most* of the money went to Rich Haven. What about the remainder?"

"Looks like she paid for the property at Railway Terrace outright and then nearly $20,000 went to a private account, which might indicate a vehicle."

"One more thing, Nielsen. What's her current status?"

"Looks like she has a steady but modest income. Half of her wages are direct debited by Rich Haven each month."

So, Mya still took care of her mother first.

"You've been a big help. Thanks for pulling the file."

"No worries. You can take me for a beer one Friday."

"Sure thing."

The enigma of Mya was slowly unravelling, although every step seemed to raise more questions. Right now he needed to focus on his investigation, but that didn't put Mya out of his mind. It only made him more determined to figure out how she fit into this whole mess.

Luca clicked the camera icon on his laptop and opened the photo of the mail on Kevin Barnes's kitchen bench. It was a bit dark, because the phone flash didn't quite reach the distance, but with the zoom he could make out some of the details.

There was a vehicle registration renewal, but he couldn't see the name or registration number, some junk mail, and an electricity bill in the name of Kevin Walker. So, Kevin was paying the bills. It must be his house.

There was no mail with Melanie Lane's name on it, and he wasn't authorised to put a tail on her yet—so he'd have to dig around some more. It meant more time sitting in his car until he figured out if she had her own place.

His mobile sang on the table beside him.

"Hi, Luca. Feel like visiting Pete's Pawn Shop?"

These were Kate's first words, no hello.

"Should I?"

"Pete himself called me this morning and said a woman was in his store two days ago looking for the necklace in the fax I sent."

"A woman. What's Pete's address?"

"It's on Blewitt Boulevard, 147 to be exact. I'm heading over there now," Kate said.

"I'll be there in ten minutes. Don't go in without me."

"Will do."

He rushed to change into his police uniform, strapped the utility belt and holster on, and shoved the muzzle of his standard-issue .40 Smith & Wesson compact pistol into its slot.

• • •

Luca angled his car into the parking space beside Kate's police Commodore and they met on the footpath in front of Pete's Pawn Shop.

"Let's do this," he said.

"What did you get up to last night?" Kate chewed her bottom lip.

"Later."

A bell jingled above the door as they pushed their way through and an overweight man looked up from the newspaper he was reading. He had two black eyes. He scanned their uniforms and ran a hand over what little fly-away white hair remained.

Luca scrutinised the disarray of the shop interior. The right side had antiques: dusty, glass-fronted cabinets full of silver spoons and mismatched crockery, paisley-covered chairs with threadbare arms, gilt-framed oil paintings, and a copper diving helmet. The left side had modern junk: boxes of CDs, a rainbow of vases and beer steins, box-style computer monitors, and bookshelves spewing paperbacks.

Kate marched straight up to the counter. "Good morning. I'm Constable Derman—we spoke on the phone earlier—and this is Detective Patterson."

Pete extended a flabby arm and shook her hand while his eyes travelled up and down her body. It made Luca want to position himself between the two.

Kate smiled. "I'd like to ask you a few questions about the jewelry you recognized." She placed the original fax on the counter, facing Pete. "You said you had this necklace. Would you mind showing it to us?"

"I wouldn't mind a bit, luv, but I ain't got it no more."

"Why?" Her voice went up an octave.

"The girl who was looking for it on Tuesday took it."

Luca stepped up to the counter and Pete tilted back on his stool, crossing his arms in front of him.

"She bought it?"

"Nah, the bitch stole it. And a ring."

"What did she look like?" Luca rested his hands on the counter as Kate wandered around the shop.

"Average height, good looking, brown hair, tight jeans, leather jacket, and she was carrying a motorbike helmet."

"What colour was the helmet?"

Pete tilted his head to drain a can of lemonade into his mouth, and then scrunched and tossed it under the desk. "Red."

Luca pictured Mya in her leather jacket and red helmet and his stomach knotted. "Did you see what bike she was riding?"

"Big red and black thing. Maybe a Triumph." Pete looked pleased with himself.

Luca clenched his teeth. He didn't like the way this was panning out at all. This case (or cases, he wasn't sure yet) was turning into quite the conundrum.

He fixed Pete with a steady glare. "And what exactly did she do when she came into the shop?"

"She was acting real friendly and leaning over the counter and stuff, so we got chatting and that's when she hit me."

Luca looked up from the file. Mya was being overly friendly to Pete? There was something wrong with that picture and not just because it stirred a fire in his belly. He hadn't seen Mya be friendly to anyone. Pete started flicking through the newspaper again and Luca slammed his hand onto it.

"We haven't finished yet. What happened to your eyes?"

"That bitch did this." Pete got to his feet and moved away from Luca's scrutiny.

"Let me get this straight," Luca said. "A girl came into your shop on Tuesday, beat you up, and took that necklace."

"And a ring," Pete mumbled. "She must have been an ex-cop or a black belt or something, because I didn't get a punch in."

Luca chewed on his bottom lip to suppress a smile. He'd seen Mya in action and knew how lethal she could be. It didn't surprise him at all that Pete had two black eyes.

"Do you want to press charges?"

"Nope." Pete smirked.

Luca figured as much.

Kate wandered over to the locked cabinets. "How did she get the necklace out of here?"

Pete dropped his gaze to the floor and shrugged. "She asked to see it, so I unlocked the cabinet."

"Did she tell you why she wanted to see it?"

He straightened. "Not until after she had it. Said it was stolen, but the police were too lazy to do anything about it." He glared at Kate.

Luca stepped around the counter and stood uncomfortably close to Pete, getting a whiff of sweat-soaked fabric. He straightened his spine so all six feet three of him was towering over the other man. "Where'd you get the jewelry?"

Pete swallowed and swiped at the sheen of sweat on his forehead. "If I'd known this shit was gonna get me in so much trouble, I wouldn't've taken it." His back was against the wall now, literally.

"Tell me who sold it to you, or Constable Derman here is going to slap a set of police-issue bangles on you and take you down to the station for a chat."

"Okay, you don't have to get heavy. I'm just tryin' to make a livin' here."

"Perhaps you should be more careful about who you buy jewelry from then," Luca said.

"It was Willy Mason sold it to me. He brings me stuff all the time. I've never had any trouble before—"

Luca put his hands up and stopped Pete's blather short. "Did you tell the woman who gave you those black eyes that?"

"Of course I did. She was hittin' me." Pete sagged onto the stool again.

"I'm going to talk to Willy Mason, and if he doesn't corroborate your story, I'll be back."

•••

Outside Pete's Pawn Shop, Luca paced back and forth, while Kate stood silent.

Maybe Willy Mason came to Mya's house the other night to silence her, because she found out about the scam, or she was already involved in it.

"Let's get a drink and think this through," he told Kate.

They headed across the road to a cafe with round, plastic tables under a bullnose veranda and settled in a quiet corner inside. Luca spread paperwork across the table. A waitress delivered two cappuccinos, a custard tart for Luca, and a chocolate doughnut for Kate.

"What's going on?" Kate tore the top off a tube of sugar and stirred it into her cappuccino.

"I don't know, but it's tied to the Happy Vale scam."

"You mean Rich Haven?" Kate frowned as Luca shook his head.

"I mean the same group that I suspected at Happy Vale Nursing Home has set up at Rich Haven and they're stealing jewelry from little old ladies. But I don't think that's all."

"You're not thinking along the same lines as nine months ago, are you? It's highly unlikely they're knocking off little old ladies without leaving a shred of evidence, Luca. Besides, Moss told you to leave that alone."

"No evidence that we've *found*, but there's a whole lot of something going on with this group. I just don't know how it all fits together yet. Anyone can kill, Kate."

"Everyone is capable of it, but most of us have a mechanism that stops us from going that far. You're talking about a serial killer."

"I don't know what I'm talking about," he mumbled. "I'd like you to come with me when I talk to Willy, because I don't think it's a good idea for me to see him by myself after what happened on Tuesday night."

"Do I want to know what happened Tuesday night?" She scowled.

"Willy Mason also lives on Railway Terrace."

"Nice neighbourhood."

"Anyway, Willy was trying to beat up another neighbour, so I stepped in." He shrugged and concentrated on pulling the crust off his custard tart.

"You stepped in with your badge and broke it up?" Kate's hands were on her hips, projecting an exasperated tone, even though she was sitting down.

"No, I mean I beat the shit out of him."

"Bloody hell, Luca."

"Well, I didn't know he was involved in my case then. Besides, he didn't give me much choice. He wasn't interested in talking. Anyway, I didn't want to pull my badge and give myself away. There's something suspicious about this lot."

"I'll say. And I take it there's a good reason you aren't hauling Pete down to the station to see if he can identify the woman who robbed him?"

"I know who it is."

Kate shook her head and wiped milk foam from her top lip. "The woman who reported it stolen?"

"I reckon so."

"Another one of your neighbours?"

"Mmm. I don't know if she's linked to this group, but her name keeps cropping up. Something about Pete's account of how she took the stuff doesn't feel right. I've met Mya Jensen a couple of times and friendly isn't how I'd describe her." He felt his ears warm—well, except for their morning tryst.

"Maybe she thought it was the best way to get the necklace." Kate bit a chunk of doughnut.

Luca's automatic response was to protect Mya's reputation, but he didn't really know her. Maybe that *was* her motivation.

So what was her motivation to jump his bones yesterday morning?

He cradled his cappuccino. "I'll talk to Mya tonight."

Kate's eyes widened.

"She works late," he explained. "And you and I will go see Willy Mason tomorrow morning."

Kate was silent as the waitress cleared their empty cups and plates and ran a wet cloth in a perfunctory sweep across the table.

"Are you going to tell me what you were doing last night?"

He looked up from browsing his notes. "I'm not sure if I should."

"You should know by now that I'm 'on board'." She made inverted commas in the air with her fingers.

"It's not your commitment I'm worried about, Kate. I don't want to get you involved in something that could go against you."

She nodded, but he wasn't sure if it was in agreement or acceptance of his decision. He intended to do another stakeout that night, so he might have something more concrete by tomorrow.

"By the way, I've got a name for you to run down: Kevin Walker."

Kate jotted it down and then collected her handbag and left without another word.

Great, now she's pissed at me.

Chapter 18

The dinner crowd came and went early at the Croydon Hotel, so Mya shut the kitchen at eight. She stepped through the back door and the fog of insects clamouring for the light, and assessed her motorbike. She wasn't fond of bringing it to work, but there hadn't been time to drop it home after visiting her mum that morning. It had been such a relief to see her, but during the day the feeling of dread had slowly crept back into her bones.

The bike was in one piece. A quick glance around the car park confirmed that she was alone, so she bent and removed the disc lock from the front wheel. The engine warmed up while she donned gloves and helmet—hardly worth the effort when she'd be home in two minutes. The Speed Triple spluttered through the pot-holed car park. It wasn't made for puttering; it was made for flying.

Movement caught her eye and yeasty beer wafted from the front door of the pub as one of the regulars tumbled out.

"See ya, Mya." A wrinkly specimen with straggly silver hair waved in her direction.

She nodded and accelerated onto the road. There wasn't much traffic, but she expected every idiot on the road to try and run her down. It was part and parcel of riding a motorbike. So she made a mental note of the guy sitting in his idling car and the girlie riding a lime-green scooter in a summer dress and sandals—idiot. Obviously she didn't know how the hospital used a scrubbing brush to remove gravel from skin.

Despite the railway signals being silent, Mya looked up and down the track as she bumped across, and then indicated to turn into Railway Terrace. A black four-by-four rocketed across the intersection and her buttocks contracted. It was coming right for her with no headlights. Mya caned the bike, swerved left, and jumped the curb as the vehicle veered closer.

She grabbed a handful of brake and felt the bike lean. A couple of hundred kilos was more than she could hold, so she put a foot down and let it topple.

Her heart rate spiked. The four-by-four skimmed the gutter and she held her breath, knowing there was no way to move fast enough to avoid it if it mounted the curb. By the glow of the console light there was a frizz of red hair, but the face was shadowed. Then, pedal to the metal, it tore down the road.

Her first instinct was to follow, so she grabbed the handlebars and yanked.

"Shit!" She rested the heavy Triumph back on the footpath. "Shit. Bugger. Shit!"

She kicked the nearest fence post and her toe started to throb. Then she rolled her shoulders a few times, took a deep breath, and seethed silently.

"You okay, Mya? What the hell happened?"

She knew the voice instantly. Luca was parked with the passenger window of his car open and head ducked down so he could see her. He turned the car off and got out.

"Want some help to get that thing up?"

"Nah, I'm just shooting the breeze here while my bike takes a nap." She knew the sarcasm was a bit much, seeing as he was offering help, but there was something about the man that put her on edge. Of course, she'd be there all night if he didn't help. "Sure."

She grabbed the handlebars with shaking hands and waited for him to take hold of the frame under the seat. His soapy scent had faded during the day and was now tinged with sweat. It only made him more appealing.

"One, two, three," he counted.

They heaved together and once the bike was vertical, she kicked the side stand down and inspected the damage.

"So, what happened?" Luca asked.

He moved to stand beside her and his arm brushed hers. A tingle shivered up to her scalp. His hawk eyes scanned the street, sized up the bike and Mya. There was something odd about the way he took in his surroundings and the kinds of questions he asked, but she couldn't pinpoint what exactly.

"Some bitch tried to run me off the road," she told him.

"Yeah, there are some rotten drivers out there. Is the bike all right?"

She didn't bother trying to explain. It wasn't just a bad driver who did this. It was deliberate. "It's hard to see in the dark, but it looks okay. A scratch or two on the tank."

"Um, Mya, perhaps we should talk about what happened yesterday."

"What for?"

"I don't want it to be weird between us. We're neighbours."

"I've already forgotten it," she lied. Even with her legs about to collapse, she remembered the curve of his firm chest and flex of his bicep as he held himself over her.

It might be her imagination or the shadowy streetlight, but she could swear Luca frowned. She didn't want to continue the conversation, so she pushed the bike onto the road and swung a leg over.

"You're welcome." Luca shook his head and headed for his car.

She followed his swagger and watched him slide into the car. It wasn't fair to be a bitch, especially not to someone with such a cute arse, so she amended her attitude. "Hey, thanks for that."

His head appeared through the open window with dull eyes. "I meant to ask you why Willy Mason wanted to mess you up the other night."

Mya turned the ignition key. With a minute twist of the throttle, the engine roared and she pulled onto the road.

When the Speed Triple was safely locked in the shed, she had time to relive the almost accident. It had been dark and yet the four-by-four didn't have lights on. It hadn't been waiting to cross the intersection or she would've seen it, so it must've been parked on the side of the road. She had caught a glimpse of red hair, but there wasn't enough light to see the face.

It had to be Rhonda. Shit! The woman really was trying to kill her.

Tomorrow she would make enquiries about other nursing homes—interstate.

• • •

Luca whizzed a spoon viciously around a cup of chicken soup and blew on the surface. It was a bit late to stake out Kevin's place now, but he was too pissed off to go to bed. What he *should* do was march down to Mya's house and ask her outright why she beat up Pete instead of going to the cops. He should, but he was worried about what would happen if he was alone with her again. The woman gave off pheromones.

If she was ballsy enough to retrieve her mother's jewelry alone, then it wasn't a huge leap to assume she planned on handling Willy Mason on her own, too. That wouldn't end well. Then again, maybe she didn't go to the police because she already knew who had the stuff. He shook his head to try and make sense of it. In one mouthful he skulled the last of the lukewarm soup and banged the mug on the sink drain board.

"Damn!"

He was too wound up to sit at home, so he grabbed his car keys from the wooden bowl on the kitchen counter and headed out to the garage.

It only took twenty minutes to reach sixty-three Listing Street in Holden Hill. Luca parked his Corolla a few doors down, on the opposite side of the road, so he could see Kevin's house and not look suspicious. Nine thirty. There were two cars in the driveway and several lights on in the house. He knew the layout well enough to guess they were from the lounge, kitchen, and a bedroom.

Since last night, he'd thrown more emergency supplies into the car: non-perishable snacks, an extra bottle of water, blanket, change of clothes, a multi-tool for good luck, and binoculars. He grabbed the green and blue tartan rug, threw it over his knees, and settled in.

Should've brought a pillow.

Twice in the next hour cars came up the road and he ducked down. Just after ten thirty the kitchen and lounge lights went off. He waited to see silhouettes in the bedroom, but instead the porch light flicked on and the front door opened. First Melanie and then Kevin stepped onto the porch. They embraced and kissed, lingering.

Melanie made her way to a Toyota Land Cruiser, waved over her shoulder, and got in. Once she backed out of the driveway, Kevin closed the front door and the porch light went off.

This might be the chance Luca was waiting for, to find out where Melanie Lane lived and her real identity. He watched her taillights turn right at the end of the road and quickly pulled a U-turn to follow.

At the end of the street he turned right as her taillights disappeared around the next corner. There were lots of twists and turns, but he kept the four-wheel drive in view. Once they were on the Freeway, he backed off and stayed in the left lane. Melanie set a cracking pace—fifteen over the speed limit.

Thirty-five minutes later she took the Hahndorf exit and then veered left. Although the rolling hills were black, Luca had been through there before and knew how beautiful this part of the country was. Unfortunately, the government hadn't seen fit to put streetlights out here, which wasn't good for a tail. He'd be easy to spot at night.

He kept his distance as Melanie passed the cold store where travellers picked up fruit fresh from the farm, and over the railway line. A huge hardware store whizzed by on the left, then a radiator shop, and they were in the Balhannah township proper with its half a dozen shops and pub.

When Melanie turned left onto a minor road, he switched off his headlights. Dangerous, but he couldn't risk being seen. The Corolla crept forward along a minefield of potholes and loose stones. Once his eyes finally adjusted, there was enough moonlight to get up to forty kilometres an hour. Melanie's lights disappeared over a crest. At the peak he braked. Her taillights were gone.

"Damn it!"

He contemplated illuminating the road ahead, then a stand of pines started to glow. She had turned off the main road. With his Wolf Eyes tactical torch shining out the passenger window, he coasted the car slowly forward. When he located a letterbox, he pulled onto the dirt verge and loaded as much gear as he could comfortably carry into his pockets.

Swapping the powerful torch for a discreet penlight, he made his way along the dirt driveway, trying not to twist an ankle in deep ruts. A warm breeze rustled the black vegetation either side, making him weave the torch back and forth as he stared into the night. The glow continued through the foliage and, as he rounded a bend, a lavish ranch house sprawled across a lush lawn. Standard roses lined a paved path to the front door.

One end of the house was lit, so he turned the torch off and circled the lawn to the dark end. One careful step at a time he stalked along the porch, scanning for automatic spotlights and booby-traps. Nothing. At the edge of the light spilling from the house, he pressed a cheek to the glass and moved his face around just enough to look in.

Melanie Lane lounged on a velvet modular suite with a glass of red wine in hand—cabernet sauvignon, according to the bottle on the coffee table. A fluffy white cat was curled at her feet, and the room looked considerably more luxurious and tidy than Kevin's place. She spoke to the cat and rubbed behind its ears.

A light went on above Luca and he ducked and held his breath. A large shadow, cast from the window above, lengthened as it approached. He strained his neck to peer over the brick windowsill and saw a wide, dark-haired man bent over, what he assumed to be, the kitchen sink. The guy had to be seven foot tall and his shoulders three feet across. His face was ruddy, and the hair poking out of his pressed collar reached halfway up his neck.

This had to be the same guy that threatened Linda and Agosto from Rich Haven, to make way for Melanie and Kevin. Now Luca was getting somewhere.

The kitchen light went out and Luca maneuvered along the wall until he could see Melanie again. The wide man batted her feet off the end of the lounge and sat down. She kicked off her sandals and put her feet in his lap, rubbing them against his crotch, until he wrapped hairy-knuckled fingers around them and massaged.

Luca had no desire to see the end product of this and so circled around the house trying doors and windows. It was locked up tight. Surprisingly diligent for a rural property. Someone wasn't very trusting.

At an open laundry window he paused.

A deep voice carried to him. "The funds have been moved to the offshore account, but I'm still waiting for the sale of her house to go through. Did you get the info I sent about the next mark?"

Damn skippy! Luca had hit the jackpot.

A female voice responded, presumably Melanie's. "Yes, I'm working out the best plan of attack as we speak. Her husband died of leukemia, so a cancer charity is our best bet. Ev, would you mind shutting the hall door? It's cold in here."

Luca leaned closer to the fly screen. There were heavy steps on the wood floor and a door banged shut. Typical, now he couldn't hear a thing. He continued his sweep of the outside and tried the garage. Locked. He very gently tried Melanie's car door, in case it was alarmed. Locked.

Time to call it quits. Better to have the information he had and live to see another day.

Chapter 19

Luca ambled through the front doors of the police station and spotted Kate parked in a loading zone. He slid into the passenger seat with a grunt.

"How'd it go with Moss?" she said.

He rolled his eyes. "He said I don't have enough to warrant more manpower, but I'm free to follow the leads myself."

"Well, at least it's not a no."

"Might as well be. I can't be everywhere at once." He scowled at the dashboard as she put the automatic into drive and pulled away from the station.

"And by everywhere you mean …"

He sighed loudly. Without back-up, he would need Kate's help, so he might as well 'fess up. "I've been following Kevin Barnes and Melanie Lane." He glanced sideways to see how the revelation had been received.

Kate's gaze didn't deviate from the road ahead. "I gathered that. And …"

"Last night I followed Melanie all the way out to Balhannah, and she appears to be shacked up with none other than the wide man."

"*The* wide man?"

"Wide and hairy. It's gotta be the same guy. I suspect he's the leader of this little group, only I can't figure out how Melanie fits in. Looks like she's been cozying up with both of them."

"Playing them, no doubt. Did you find her real identity?"

"No." Luca slumped further into the car seat. "Which is why I need to go back."

"That's not a good idea."

"I overheard a name, well, part of a name. Ev. Could be short for Everett, Everard, Evan, or something foreign. I've emailed you the address. Could you look into it later?"

"Sure. Luca, did you talk to Mya Jensen last night?"

He glared out the window at cream-bricked Housing Trust homes set on raised foundations. "No, I got busy following Melanie."

"We need to talk to her, sooner rather than later. I asked the Fraud Squad to flag anything that came up on her and something has."

"You're watching her?" He was appalled, but couldn't fault Kate's logic.

"I'm following leads," she said frostily.

"What have you got," he mumbled to the window, watching it fog and clear with each breath. Kate had only done what he should have, if his mind weren't clouded when it came to Mya.

"She put an application into Deed Poll yesterday. An application to change both her own and her mother's names. I think she might be doing a runner."

"Shit."

He could feel Kate's eyes boring into the back of his head and, when he finally stopped pretending to be interested in the scenery and turned to her, she was chewing her bottom lip.

She glanced at him with a pitying look. "*Please* tell me you don't fancy her."

"Just drive, will you?"

"Bloody hell, Luca." She shook her mouse-brown bob and huffed.

They undertook the remainder of the journey in silence. He tried to focus on Willy Mason and how this visit was likely to play out. When they parked out front of eleven Railway Terrace, Kate took the lead, as instructed. Luca wore his full police kit today, including the Akubra hat and capsicum spray tucked into his utility belt. Might come in handy with Willy.

He stood aside while Kate knocked on the door, because he didn't want to be the first thing Willy saw. Heavy footsteps approached the other side and a key turned in the deadbolt. It cracked open and Kate's stare moved up as she sought Willy Mason's face.

"Good morning, sir. I'm Constable Derman and I'm looking for Mr. Mason."

Willy squinted down and then over her shoulder. He ground his teeth and threw the door open. "What's this fucker doing 'ere?"

He shoved past Kate and towered over Luca, who rested a hand on his gun.

"Excuse me, sir." Kate bravely moved in front of Willy. "I need you to step away from Detective Patterson. We're here to ask you a few questions about jewelry you might have pawned at Pete's Pawn Shop on Blewitt Boulevard."

"I don't know what you're talking about."

"I'd like you to take a look at this picture." She waved the fax sheet in front of Willy to get his attention. "Pete said *you* sold these items to him. Items that turned out to be stolen from an elderly lady."

"I don't know anything about stolen jewelry. Don't even know this Pete guy. He's lying."

Luca smirked. "Of course he is."

Willy stepped forward and Kate moved her hand to the butt of her pistol. "You understand that these items will be studied for forensic evidence, and if we find anything that matches you, you're going to be locked up faster than you can sneeze?"

Willy visibly relaxed. "I understand that you ain't got shit on me, or you'd be arresting me right now. Get the hell off my property." He gave Luca one last look. "You'll keep."

Then he went back inside and slammed the door shut.

"That went well," Luca quipped.

"He knows something," Kate added. "Maybe applying a little extra pressure each day will bring him around."

"Sounds like you don't like Mr. Mason." Luca chuckled. "Can you drop me at the station, so I can pick up my car? I'll go through my case files and catch you tomorrow."

She nodded.

• • •

Luca drove past the cafe, laundromat, and Pete's Pawn Shop along Blewitt Boulevard and turned down Josiah Mitton Parade. With his eyes on the road, he reached his left hand to the passenger seat and flicked the lid off a small cardboard box. He wrapped his fingers around a couple of hot chips and stuffed them into his mouth.

It had been good to spend time looking at all the evidence and theories as a whole that morning, although it hadn't triggered any revelations. At least it reaffirmed his belief that the deaths of old ladies without families were somehow linked to the jewelry thefts. The same anomaly he noticed nine months ago at Happy Vale. He could feel that he was closer to finding the key and unlocking the mystery. Something had to go his way sooner or later. Tenacious: that's what his wife had called him.

As he passed Josiah Mitton Reserve, a babe in a tight tank top caught his eye. She threw a fluoro-yellow Frisbee and laughed as a scruffy terrier chased it. A ripped bloke wrapped a protective arm around her waist. A family rode along the footpath on a line of bicycles in reducing sizes, the last one with a plastic basket on the handlebars. A pang of regret clenched his heart that his opportunity for children had passed him by.

There was a troupe of women by the fountain, gaily dressed in pastel leggings, bright tank tops and headbands. In the shade of a knotted gum tree, the aggressive stance of two women made him pay closer attention. One suddenly attacked the other with a lightning-fast kick. The victim barely managed to block it.

Luca's foot came off the accelerator and the car engine faltered. He knocked it into neutral and parked on the roadside. The attacker was fast and there was something familiar about the way she moved. Caramel-coloured hair tied in a ponytail. Mya.

He grabbed the door handle as Mya came at her target again. With one foot on the tarmac and the car door ajar, he watched the victim overbalance and fall onto her bottom. Mya laughed. Hell, she really was nuts, and she was going to beat the shit out of this woman if he didn't stop her.

Then Mya offered a hand and pulled the woman to her feet. What the—?

The woman stepped to the side and waved another female into position. Luca studied the group more closely. They were practicing kickboxing maneuvers. Mya appeared to be moving from one pair to the next, as though giving instruction.

He backed into his car again and pulled the door shut, but couldn't bring himself to leave. After several minutes of watching, he turned the engine off and wound down the window. He wasn't sure why, but he couldn't take his eyes off Mya. She looked different—carefree—and it was mesmerizing. The women in the group seemed to really pay attention to her.

She was fast and strong but graceful at the same time. Her moves were precise and controlled. She wasn't a kickboxing street thug. It was clear she'd been trained.

So it was possible Mya might be the brawn in the scam group. A hired thug? No, that didn't feel right. They—meaning Kevin, Melanie, and Ev—wouldn't need a kickboxer when they had Willy Mason. They certainly weren't keeping that man around for his brains.

So maybe Mya was the brains of the operation. The woman wasn't stupid, considering what she'd achieved after such a brutal childhood. He'd seen the outcome of abusive homes before. Teenagers often didn't have the strength or resources to climb out of the cesspool and into a new life. Mya had.

But how did she fit with Melanie and Kevin?

Luca's temple started to ache as he tried to puzzle it out. He shoved a couple of cool chips into his mouth. The kickboxers smiled and waved to Mya as they dispersed. A lanky woman jogged across the park, over the footpath, and crossed the road in a direct route to Luca. He fumbled with the key in the ignition, conscious of what Mya would say if she caught him spying on her, but the jogger was too fast.

"If you're looking for your wife or girlfriend, you're not welcome here, mate. I suggest you move along before someone calls the cops." The bony brunette's lips were pursed.

He checked out her grey leggings and cropped pink T-shirt and smiled politely. "I *am* the cops, actually." He flashed his badge at the still scowling woman. "I only stopped because I think I know the instructor. Is this some kind of class?"

The woman glanced over her shoulder at Mya, who was talking to a couple of students and then back at the badge. "Nothing you'd be interested in, sweetheart. It's self-defense for women."

"Oh?"

She hesitated and then rested her elbows on the edge of the open window. Luca had to avert his eyes from the front of her top.

"You'll have to excuse my suspicious nature," she said, "but we sometimes get husbands hanging around, looking for their wives. Now and then they cause trouble."

"How so?"

"Most of Mya's students are from the battered women's shelter in Woodville."

"Huh. I'm sure she sets them straight," he said cynically.

"Yeah, she's brilliant. Makes us feel like we have some control."

"Thanks for your help. Enjoy your run." He placed both hands on the steering wheel as an indication that the conversation was over.

"Sure." The brunette straightened and took off at a brisk pace.

Luca arrived at his home without remembering going over the railway track, past the Croydon Hotel, or turning into Railway Terrace. His mind was spinning like a fast-bowled cricket ball. Mya helping battered women. Go figure. She was like a club sandwich; every time he thought he had the flavour figured out, another bite revealed one more unexpected taste.

Chapter 20

It was Friday, so Mya didn't have long before her next shift at the Croydon Hotel. There was a lot of prep to do for a busy night, but she'd make time for a quick workout at her second home: Railway Fitness Centre.

Mike waved as she passed All Car Motors. "Hey, Mya," he called.

"Hey, Mike. Business good?"

"'s okay. You had an accident?"

"What?" She stopped in the middle of the car park.

"The Triumph's got a few scratches." He jerked his head in the direction of the parked motorbike.

"Minor damage. It's a jungle out there, Mike."

He laughed and disappeared into the cave of his garage.

The scratches on the tank reminded Mya that she had to make a few phone calls tomorrow. She needed to put her mum's name—well, the one she'd have as soon as their Deed Poll change went through— on the waiting list at a few nursing homes. If she was prepared and kept their options open, they could move as soon as it became necessary.

An electronic beeper sounded as she pushed the grimy door open, distracting the few hardcore gym junkies who had nothing better to do mid-afternoon. The place smelled of stale sweat, machine oil, and dust. It was familiar and comforting. Her shoulders relaxed as she crossed the threadbare carpet to the boxing ring.

"Hey, MJ." Tommy stepped away from the sagging ropes and high-fived her.

He looked too upmarket for the dingy sweat room with his bright green shorts, muscle top, and gel-spiked hair, but he was fast, and as close to a brother as Mya would get.

"How'd the class go?" he asked her.

"Good. The girls are getting more confident, slowly."

"Chick came in this morning, asking about your classes, so I gave her a flier. You oughta start charging. We could make a killing."

"You know I don't do it for people who can afford to pay."

"Yeah, you're a bloody saint."

"How's Ned?" Mya hated that her mentor was too sick to run the gym now.

"Dad's fine. He's a tough old bastard. The doc says he can come back to work so long as he doesn't put on the gloves."

"Yeah, like that'll happen."

They both grinned.

"Up for a few rounds?" Tommy pointed to the boxing ring.

Mya had been sparring with him for a decade, since his old man found her peering through the window—in those days you could see through the glass—and took her under his wing. Turned her life around, in fact. Taught her that she didn't need to always be on the attack, if she knew how to handle herself. It was Ned's ideals that she taught during her self-defense classes.

"You know there's nothing I like better that hitting something, Tommy. You up for it?"

"Not me."

"Who'd you talk into it?" Most of the regulars wouldn't get into the ring with her anymore, because she never gave up. That wasn't *all* Ned's doing. Life had taught her to keep facing her fears until she beat them down.

Tommy waved a thick arm in the direction of the boxing ring, making a bicep bulge under his sleeve of Maori tattoos. He smiled slyly and called to the couple of young guys already in the ring. "Hey, tough guy. I've got a new sparring partner for you."

Mya hadn't seen one of them before, and from the look on his face, he wasn't impressed about being paired with a girl. She pulled the headgear on and wrapped strips of fabric around her wrists and hands to protect them. Tommy pulled gloves over the top and strapped her shin pads on.

The regulars gathered ringside as Mya climbed between the ropes, because they knew exactly what was going down: new guy initiation. The guy looked to be in his early twenties, with a silver stud in his left ear and a skull tattoo on his shoulder. She knocked gloves with her opponent and headed for her corner, but not before she caught him rolling his eyes at his mate. He'd pay for that.

Tommy stood at the side, one tree-trunk leg hooked through the ropes for support. "Fight," he called.

She danced out of her corner, circling the newbie and giving him time to size her up, as she did him. Lazy footwork. Probably figured he didn't need to expend too much energy to beat a girl.

He led with a right hook and knee strike, which she blocked. She moved away from his favoured hand. With fists up and chin down, she felt him out with a kidney kick. It landed solidly, and the newbie wavered. Her own ribs still hurt like hell from Willy Mason's beating.

She gave her opponent a moment to gather himself. Fighting for the sake of it wasn't her style. He glanced at the spectators and straightened. His retaliation was a front kick and a couple of punches, which she dodged, her feet constantly dancing.

There were whistles and whoops as he landed a blow to the side of her head and the room blurred. His skin glistened and the scent of deodorant kicked in. Time to attack. Forward, forward. He led with his right hand, so she moved right. He looked down for a fraction of a second and she hit high. Once she had him against the ropes, he tried to neutralize her with a grab, but she pushed him away.

With her back to him, as though she was going to walk away, she lashed out with her leg. A foot connected with his gut and she spun to deliver a powerful left hook. The newbie stumbled, lost his balance, and sat on the mat.

Tommy slapped his thigh and sported a thousand-watt smile. "And that's how it's done, boys."

She offered the stunned guy a bent arm and he begrudgingly allowed her to pull him to his feet.

It was nice to know she could still put a guy on his arse. Since someone had tried to run her off the road, personal safety had become a priority. Keeping her combat skills in top shape was her best strategy. The woman may or may not be Rhonda. Either way, there was no telling if she had a male accomplice, and Mya wasn't taking any chances.

Chapter 21

Mya tipped whisked eggs over sizzling mushrooms, home-grown tomatoes, red capsicum, and onion. Chester Bennington from Linkin Park screamed at low volume from the stereo. Ten thirty was too late for most people to eat dinner, but after a decade in the hospitality industry, her hours were out of whack. The sink was full of vegetables picked from the garden only minutes ago. She tossed the colourful salad and finished it with a drizzle of lemon-infused olive oil.

Once the omelette was set, she sprinkled cheese across the surface, folded it in half, and slid the lot onto a plate. It was a balancing act to arrange the plate, bowl, and a jam jar filled with tap water in her hands, and then carry it all to the dining table.

What a relief to sit after a long day on her feet. Comfy Ugg boots were under the table and she slid her aching feet into them. Steam from the omelette wafted to her nose and made her salivate. Her stomach grumbled urgently. Teaching a self-defense class, doing a round of kickboxing, and working could work up a serious appetite.

It would be nice to have dinner conversation, but then she remembered where that got her mum. There was a lot to be said for peace and quiet.

Opening the mail caused knots in her stomach lately, but there was nothing from Rhonda today. She couldn't know for sure that Rhonda was the one who tried to run her off the road last night, but if it was, then Mya needed a plan to find out where the woman lived, but there was nothing to go on. Sitting there, waiting for the bitch to strike went against everything Mya had fought for during the past twelve years.

Pity she didn't have a cop friend who could massage an ID out of the Big Brother database.

After dinner, she turned off the stereo and reclined in her favourite armchair. She flicked on the reading lamp and picked up *The Girl with the Dragon Tattoo* by Stieg Larsson. She was halfway through it and dying to find out what happened next.

• • •

Mya jerked awake, her eyes struggling to focus, heart thundering. The wall clock showed ten past twelve. With a hand on her heart, she realized she had nodded off. She tucked a strip of leather between the pages of her book and levered herself out of the armchair, stifling a yawn. Like always, she flicked the lace curtain aside and looked up and down the street.

Hers was the only light still on, but there was a shadow moving down the road. It leapt from the footpath to the road and back, as though it couldn't decide where it was going.

With her face pressed to the glass, Mya still couldn't recognize the gangly, pale-limbed person, but they were running fast. Another couple of seconds and she saw long hair. A girl, who stopped beneath the streetlight in front of Mya's house.

The blond hair had multi-coloured streaks in it. It was Paula Mason's friend, the one from the park. The same one who'd literally bumped into Mya on the bike track. The girl searched left and right in quick, jerky movements, her hands tensed by her side.

An almighty roar sounded from further down the road and Blondie startled like a deer. She scaled Mya's picket fence and ran up the alyssum-covered path.

Bang! Bang! Bang! The front door vibrated.

What the hell?

Mya didn't want anything to do with the Mason family or their multi-coloured pet. She ignored Blondie, hoping she'd go away.

There was another knock and a whimper. Mya remembered crashing into the girl the other day, and curiosity got the better of her. Without turning the porch light on, she slid the two bolts aside and cracked the door open.

"Stop banging. What do you want?"

Blondie tried to push her way in, but Mya's shoulder was against the door.

"P-please let me in. He's g-gonna k-kill me."

Even in the dim light the girl looked worse for wear. There was more damage than the cut cheek from the other night, and her eyelids had rolled wider than Holland blinds. This girl needed help.

Mya stepped back and Blondie fell inside. Swiftly she turned, pushed the door shut, and slid the bolts into place. Wow, the girl must be in real trouble if she was prepared to be locked in with Mya.

"What's wrong—"

"Shhh!" Blondie's eyes darted back and forth in the narrow hall and rested on the bowl of knives; they couldn't go any wider, but her pale face turned ashen.

Mya assessed the bruise starting to blossom on the girl's cheek. There was an assortment of welts and blood trickled into her eyebrow, presumably from a cut on her head.

"I'm not going to hurt you," she said, staying still and waiting to see what the girl did next.

Blondie stared at Mya, hands clenched, body tense. Without warning she darted into the lounge room, turned off the reading lamp, and crouched by the window. With a shaking hand she lifted the side of the lace curtain enough to peer outside.

Mya followed suit on other side of the window, not sure what or who they were looking for, but expecting a pimply, drugged-out boyfriend. She didn't have to wait long. A dark figure loomed in the middle of the road. Massive hands shone a flashlight first on one side of the road and then the other. He checked front gardens and under bushes as he went. She remembered those huge hands as she prodded the still sore lump on the back of her head. Willy Mason was dangerous.

The flashlight beam hit the front fence. Blondie whimpered and threw herself to the floor, knees pulled to her chest and hands over her ears. Without thinking Mya ducked away from the curtain. Great, now she was acting like a teenager pulling a prank and hiding in the bushes. She wasn't big on hiding and she had business with Willy.

Jumping to her feet, Mya watched the yellow beam of light bounce across her yard and linger on her front door. Her foot slid toward it.

"Don't!" Blondie's bright blue eyes were glassy. "Please," she whispered.

Mya nodded. She stood to one side as Willy rechecked the front yard. Finally he moved on. Once the bobbing glow was out of sight, she sat on the floor and waited until the frightened girl was game enough to look at her.

The streetlight caught a sheen on the girl's eyes and, at first, she looked sheepish. Next she glanced toward the front door, as though she might bolt.

"He's gone for now." Mya tried to put the girl at ease. It wouldn't be safe for her outside with Willy looking. "What's your name?"

"Natalie." The girl's eyes narrowed beneath thick, smudged makeup.

"Mya. So, why's Willy after you?"

Natalie's bottom lip trembled. She wiped her eyes and long spiral earrings twirled beside her throat. A web of beaded bracelets jangled on her wrists as she got to her feet and headed for the hall.

"There's no guarantee he won't be back," Mya told her. "Why don't you hang here for a while?"

Natalie froze. Tailored navy slacks sat nicely on her slim figure, and a white and red babydoll top was complemented by red sandals. The girl might hang out with dubious folk, but she certainly had style.

Mya imagined the teenager's eyes were trained on the bowl of knives again. The girl wasn't likely to trust the woman who beat up her friends, but Mya didn't want Willy Mason getting his hands on her. She pulled herself off the floor and pretended not to notice Natalie flinch.

"I won't hurt you," she repeated. "You want a cuppa?"

Natalie went back to the window and lowered herself to the floorboards. Mya took that for a yes and headed for the kitchen.

"He'll kill me if he finds me," Natalie whispered.

Turning slowly so as not to spook her, Mya whispered, "I won't let him get near you. Why did you knock on *my* door, anyway?"

"I seen what you did to Paula and her boyfriend, and figured you'd protect me."

One of Mya's eyebrows shot up. First the neighbours and now Natalie thought she could protect them. They were overly optimistic.

"You can stay here tonight and we'll figure something out in the morning."

A long breath huffed through the girl's lips and she visibly sagged. "Why are you helping me? Paula and I were … mean to you in the park."

Mya considered carefully before answering. "I don't like men who beat up women, and I don't want to see anything bad happen to you. You oughta come along to one of my self-defense classes one day. They're free."

"Yeah, I might."

Tap, tap, tap. They both jumped.

There was the soft sound of feet shifting on the porch. Natalie huddled against the wall. Mya pressed a finger to her lips and crept to the edge of the curtain. Carefully, she prised it away from the window pane, just enough to see the outline of someone standing there—male, from the shape and black T-shirt. When he turned to scan the street, she saw a blond ponytail tied at the nape of his neck.

"Luca." She said it like an expletive.

Natalie tilted her head in question and Mya shrugged. She sat on the edge of the couch in the dark. They could wait him out.

There was a louder knock. "Mya, it's Luca. Let me in."

There was only one thing he could want at that time of night, and it wasn't going to happen. There were more strings attached to her morning romp with him than to a marionette.

"Mya. I know you're in there with one of the Masons. Can you please let me in?"

A tiny pang in the centre of her chest brooded that he wasn't there to see her. She frowned at Natalie and mouthed, "What does he want?"

The girl shrugged. "How does he know I'm in here? Could be working with Willy."

The indignant look Luca would give that comment made Mya smile.

"Remember, he's the one who put Willy in hospital this week. Let's go to the bathroom and get you cleaned up. He'll piss off soon enough."

"Tell the girl I can help her." Luca's voice was soft. "I'm going to wait here until you open the door." There was a sliding sound, followed by a long sigh.

Mya crept closer to the door and listened to Luca's steady breathing on the other side. Not so long ago it had been beside her ear, trickling down her neck. Its rhythm ignited a smouldering sensation in the pit of her stomach. The tips of her fingers slid down her bare arms with a feather-light touch, just like Luca's balmy skin had slid across hers. A shiver of ecstasy trembled clean down her spine.

"Maybe he *can* help," Natalie suggested. "Let him in, will ya?"

With a huff and head shake, Mya pulled the bolts back and wrenched the door open in a fluid movement. Luca must've been sitting against it, because he fell backward.

Smiling up he said, "Nice to see you, too."

He did some kind of break-dance move where his legs kicked out and he was suddenly on his feet, inches in front of her. She grabbed a handful of his T-shirt and pushed him against the wall, causing the smile to slide right off his clean-shaven face.

"What the hell do you want?" she growled.

Luca's hot breath cascaded across her face and raised the hairs on her arms. A light cinnamon scent came off his skin. His head tilted the tiniest bit toward her, and then he blinked.

He slid from between the wall and her. "I saw the girl run down the road and knock on your door."

The reason he'd been watching the street late at night from a dark house was definitely something they were going to discuss later. Right now she needed to put some space between them, so Mya headed to the kitchen, grabbing dirty dishes from the dining table on the way.

As she filled the kettle, she could hear the front door lock and someone flop onto the couch. Neither Luca nor Natalie spoke.

With three mugs of tea, a sugar canister, and a milk carton on a tray, she sauntered back into the room. Natalie was still crouched on the floor and Luca was watching her. Mya pushed a book and mail aside so there was space for the tray on the coffee table. Then she closed the block-out curtains and flicked the light on. Natalie blinked. The damage to her face looked worse in the bright light.

Mya turned to glower at Luca. "So, why are you sticking your nose in where it's not wanted again?"

He poured milk into a mug of tea, looking as cool as a cucumber. "When I saw Willy Mason come down the street, I figured Natalie could use my help."

Mya stood with hands on hips. "Why do you think you can help her more than me? Because you're a bloke?"

"No." He lowered his eyes and blew a thin stream of air across the surface of his tea. "Because I'm a cop."

Shit!

Chapter 22

Mya's legs felt rubbery as she sank into a chair. Luca was a cop. No wonder he sized people up like he was suspicious. He was. She could usually pick law enforcement. He certainly had the arrogance, but coppers didn't beat up neighbours.

The intensity she previously noticed had turned to concern as he focused on Natalie.

The girl nursed her tea like a security blanket. "You're the cop who came to the door today, aren't you?"

"Yes. Natalie, if Willy has done something to you, I can help."

Mya stewed as she stared at him. He had lied to her. Well, not an outright lie, but a falsehood by omission. He'd had plenty of opportunities to tell her. Of course, there was the covert look and whispered conversation with Officer Herd out front of her house the other night, but it didn't make sense. Why didn't Luca just pull out his badge and put a stop to the fight with Willy? It looked like the bastard deliberately deceived her and had an ulterior motive.

Typical bloke.

"I can't go back there, ever." Natalie was teary again.

"How old are you, Natalie?" he asked.

"Nineteen."

"You're old enough to live wherever you choose, but I can't help if you don't tell me what happened. Where are your family?"

Natalie shook her head. "Dead when I was eight. I lived with Nana Hilda for a while, but when she got Alzheimer's, I got put in foster care."

Luca put his elbows on knees, his undivided attention on Natalie. He kept his voice low and soothing. "I'm sorry to hear that. So, how did you meet the Masons?"

"I met Paula at school and her family was nice to me." She shrugged, her voice barely a whisper as she continued. "I did a jewelry-making course and sold the stuff at markets, but I couldn't get enough cash. When I turned eighteen, Paula said I could live with her. I thought the Masons were my friends."

Luca sipped his tea. "What happened after I came to see Willy today?"

"I was in the front room, and I heard what you said. I knew that job was too good to be true! Willy said it was a sweet deal and he needed someone like me." Natalie's voice choked and she sunk closer to the floor.

"What was the sweet deal?" Luca's hands reached forward.

"He said rich, old ladies worried that someone would mug 'em and steal their jewelry, so they paid him to get exact replicas. That way they could still wear the stuff, but the real McCoy would be locked away. It made sense."

Luca scribbled on his notepad. "Did he bring the jewelry to you?"

"Nah, he brought photos and measurements. I swear I didn't know what he was gonna do with it. Then I heard what the lady cop said about stuff being stolen , and I knew right away what he was doing with *my* jewelry. I said I didn't wanna do it no more and he just … flipped." She buried her face in her hands and sobbed.

Luca looked pleadingly at Mya. "Can she stay here tonight?"

"I've already offered."

With Natalie still snivelling, Mya led her down the hall to the bathroom and ran warm water onto a flannel. "Here, you can clean yourself up, and I'll get you something to wear. The next door on your left when you've finished."

It wasn't possible to find pajamas where there weren't any, so Mya dug a pair of cotton shorts and a tank top out of her drawers and tossed them on the spare bed. By the time she'd put a glass of water on the bedside table and set the digital clock, Natalie stood in the doorway.

Mya gave the girl what she hoped was a reassuring smile. "I'll leave you to it. Help yourself to breakfast in the morning."

"Thanks," Natalie whispered. "I don't know why you're doing this, but he would've got me if you didn't let me in."

"Willy Mason is going to get what's coming to him."

She pulled the door closed and found Luca in the lounge, running his finger along the spines of her book collection. "She's in bed now, so you can leave."

"I've got *déjà vu*. Weren't you trying to kick me out the last time I was in your house?" He grinned.

"You're slow to take a hint, aren't you?" She tried to outstare him.

"You send mixed messages," he retaliated.

He had her there.

"Did I do something to offend you?"

"What gives you that idea?" She laced her voice with as much sarcasm as possible.

"Well, you're hostile, although I'm gathering you're equally charming to everyone."

"No, you haven't offended me. I expect all men to lie and sneak around, so it's no big deal."

He stepped closer. Mya straightened her spine.

"It's a bit arrogant to lump me with *all men*. You don't even know me."

"Arrogance is thinking you can follow me around. It was just one fuck."

"Oh, I'm not following you around like a lovesick puppy, Mya. I'm watching you, because I think you're involved in this mess."

She recoiled. There wasn't time for calming breaths. Her hand whipped up. Luca blocked it. She glared from his face to the hand wrapped around her wrist.

"Get. Your hand. Off me."

"If you try to hit me again, I'll cuff you," he threatened.

As they stood toe to toe, staring one another down, the atmosphere changed from scorching anger to static desire. Shallow breaths collided in the void between them, and a tingle started in Mya's chest and fluttered down to her stomach. She looked into his hungry eyes. The anticipation built. Her fingers twitched at her side as she ached to touch his taut, naked body.

Abruptly, he blinked several times and backed away. He flopped onto the couch and puts his heels on the coffee table.

"Why don't you tell me about your visit to Pete's Pawn Shop on Tuesday?"

"Is this an interrogation?"

"No, just a friendly chat with a concerned neighbour. Look, Mya, I know you're planning on handling Willy Mason on your own, but I can't let you do that."

With a shake of her head, she stalked to her favourite armchair and dropped into it.

"The guy's a nut job, not to mention huge," Luca said.

She remained silent.

"Look, I'm pretty sure he's involved in a bigger scam, and this is the opportunity I've been waiting for. I might be able to solve, well, a lot of crimes."

"I did the right thing and reported Mum's jewelry stolen," Mya said.

"I know."

"But I knew the cops wouldn't bother looking for it. They never protect people when it really counts."

"What?" Luca was on his feet again. "That's what cops do. We protect civilians."

"You make a big show of locking the bad guys up, but you let them right back onto the street."

A peculiar look crossed his face. Guilt or maybe understanding, but he soon distanced himself from it.

"I think we're getting off track here." He sat down again and waved a hand to encourage her to continue.

"I canvassed every secondhand shop in the district. It was pure luck I found Mum's stuff, or bad luck for Pete."

"Yeah, I saw the two black eyes you gave him. Do you go out of your way to beat people up?"

"Only arseholes. Besides, he told me it was Willy who sold him the jewelry. I take it that's more than you knew at the time."

A hint of pink crept across the top of Luca's cheekbones. "You should've told the police and they would've retrieved the jewelry and booked Pete."

"A lot of unnecessary paperwork for a bottom feeder."

Luca sighed and rubbed his hands across his face. His hair was tied back, accentuating a pronounced forehead that curved down to thin eyebrows. The smooth sweep of his nose ended in slightly flared nostrils and, from this angle, she could hardly see the scar above his lip. But it was his eyes that drew her in. Cool grey in this light, with feathered lines at the outer corners.

"You can't honestly tell me you think Willy is organizing all this," she said.

"You're right, but I need to use him to find out who *is*, which means I need you to back off."

She didn't like being told what to do, especially by a lying cop. Without another word she headed for her bedroom.

"Mya, you don't know how crazy he might be. If you push him—The things I see in this job—"

With her back still to him, she said, "I'm going to bed. You can let yourself out."

"Sure." He sounded defeated. "I'll be back in the morning for Natalie."

Chapter 23

Luca spooned the last of five milk-soaked Weetbix into his mouth and washed the bowl and spoon while still chewing. He didn't get much sleep last night. It was nearly two in the morning when he left Mya's house, and he kept imagining noises in the street. He saw Willy Mason slink home around three, which prompted him to keep a vigil from his second-story bedroom window until daylight.

It was imperative that he interview Natalie as soon as possible. She was flighty last night. After sleeping on it, she might've changed her mind about testifying against Willy. But he didn't want to knock on Mya's door too early. He looked at his black and red dive watch—seven thirty—and dialed Kate's number.

"Sorry it's so early, but I need you to accompany a patrol car to Willy Mason's house and arrest his arse."

"Wow. What happened?"

"I'll meet you at the station in an hour and explain. I'm bringing a witness."

"What are the charges?"

"Jewelry theft, forgery, battery."

"Okay. See you in an hour."

He tucked his uniform shirt into his slacks, shoved his feet into black sandshoes, and tied the laces—comfort and style. As he walked along the footpath to Mya's house, Willy's connection to Kevin Barnes, Melanie Lane, and Mya were swirling through his brain. His gut instinct told him that his sassy, long-haired neighbour wasn't involved, but ten years on the force meant he knew better than to assume anything.

"Morning, Luca."

He balked as the neighbour who lived between his and Mya's houses appeared from behind a standard rose bush: a thin, old man wearing a pressed white shirt, grey shorts, and long socks .

"Bert."

"Calling on Mya, are you?" A slight smile played at the corners of the old man's mouth and his eyes sparkled.

"Police business, Bert."

"Oh? She's not in trouble, is she?" Bert rested one hand on his hip and twirled secateurs in the other.

"Nothing to worry yourself about. I'm pretty sure Mya can handle trouble." Luca tried hard to keep the sarcasm out of his tone.

"I know she can, but—" Bert pursed his lips and glanced over his left shoulder at Mya's house. "She acts tough, that one," he flicked a thumb toward her house, "but only because she has to, you know? She's a good girl."

Luca blinked. Did he imagine Bert frowning at him, almost like a warning? He nodded goodbye and pushed Mya's front gate open. The curtains were still closed, so he knocked gently. After a minute, he raised his hand to knock again, but a floorboard inside the house creaked. He heard the bolts slide and the door cracked open. One hazel eye stared blankly at him.

"Hi. I'm here to take Natalie to the station."

Mya sighed and opened the door all the way. "You could've waited until a decent hour."

She looked pissed off, but that was nothing new.

"I didn't want to give Willy Mason an opportunity to flee, so I've sent a car to pick him up. I need to get Natalie's statement and find her somewhere safe to stay for a while."

He stepped across the threshold, but Mya didn't budge. Now there was only an arm's length between them. He scrutinized her long caramel hair, which was sticking up at all angles. His gaze lingered too long on the erect nipples under her cotton tank top, but he couldn't force it away. Warmth rose up his throat as he finally dragged his line of sight back to hers. The faint horizontal lines on her forehead had smoothed and green and gold flecks glittered in her irises. Her lips parted.

"Hi, Luca."

Natalie came into focus behind Mya and, in the time it took him to focus on her and back, Mya had turned away.

"Make yourself at home while I get dressed."

Luca refocused on the task at hand. "How are you feeling this morning, Natalie?" The teenager shuffled into the lounge room and sat on the edge of the farthest armchair. "Fine."

"Are you ready to come down to the station and give me your statement?"

"Didn't I do that last night?" The marks on her face were turning purple and black. He'd need to get photos of her injuries. Without all the makeup, she looked considerably younger.

"I need to get the whole story down on paper, and I've got a few questions for you."

"Oh."

"We also need to find you somewhere safe to stay for a while."

Her shoulders drooped. "Can't I stay here?"

His eyebrows shot up. He hadn't expected that. Then again, Mya was the person Natalie ran to last night. Perhaps they already knew each other. There was definitely some connection between the Masons, Natalie, and Mya.

He lowered his voice. "Can I ask why you came to Mya's house last night?"

Natalie chewed her bottom lip. "She protects people."

Now he was downright curious. He leaned forward on the couch. "Why do you say that?"

"I saw … some girls picking on a kid in the park the other day and she protected him. She knows how to handle herself."

"That she does."

Natalie pushed a collection of bracelets up and down her forearm.

"Do you want anything to eat before you go?" Mya stepped into the room wearing tight denim jeans. Soft curls fell over her shoulders and the lines were back on her forehead.

"Hey, are you a Linkin Park fan?" He nodded at the stellar LP symbol on the front of her black T-shirt.

"Huge." Her head cocked to one side as she studied him.

His gaze traced a line down the side of her soft throat. He didn't understand this woman at all and was worried by how much he wanted to.

"Nah, no breakfast," Natalie said.

"Okay, then I guess we should get going." Luca smiled at Mya. "Thanks for taking care of her last night."

"I didn't do it for *your* benefit."

"No, but thanks anyway. Do you mind if we go out the back way? So we can get into my car without being seen. And I'll need to talk to you again later, if that's all right."

"I'm going to visit Mum this morning and I'm working this afternoon, but you can get me on my mobile."

Luca took his phone from his pocket and navigated to the address book. "What's the number?"

She rattled it off. He followed her into the narrow back yard appreciating the way her rear end sashayed in the tight denim. Vegetables crowded along both fences. Huh. Mya gardened. Well, it made sense with her being a chef and all.

Stay focused.

Once he'd dealt with Natalie, he needed to have a serious chat with Mya about her involvement with the Masons and exactly how she fit into the jewelry and nursing home drama that was unfolding, not to mention why she had applied to Deed Poll to change her name again.

He tried to think of her as Lara Roach, but the image of a frightened little girl was all that came to mind. Hopefully she understood that becoming Sophie, or Jennifer, or whatever name she picked this time, wouldn't help her outrun her past. Neither would it change the woman inside either, and he wouldn't want it to. Mya Jensen was a whirlwind of fury and irritability, but she seemed to bring that same passion to everything she did, including making love. No, he wouldn't want to change her at all. If anything, it would be nice to acquaint her with the softer side of humanity.

Chapter 24

The humidity battled against a cool breeze. There had only been patchy clouds in the sky when Mya left home, but now dark swirls moved along the horizon and she could smell their dampness. Weather like this made her wish she had a car.

She planned on spending a couple of hours with her mum before catching up on chores at home. Her shift at the Croydon Hotel didn't start until four that afternoon.

Rich Haven's Victorian building looked ominous beneath the purple sky. Using her tiptoes for purchase, she waddled the motorbike backward into a parking space and kicked down the side stand. The moment she pulled her helmet off, a large blob of rain landed smack in the middle of her forehead.

Great.

The slate staircase darkened with moisture as she dashed up it and into the reception area. She pushed damp hair from her brow and swiped her hands down the back of her jeans while her eyes adjusted to the dull interior.

Beverly Aldridge wasn't behind the reception desk. Mya signed the register and took the western hallway. Footsteps approached fast and she stepped to one side just as Beverly trotted around the corner.

"Oh! Did someone call you?" Beverly reached out to take Mya's forearm.

An odd way to start a conversation. "No."

"I was just going to call you. Perhaps you should come with me."

Mya found herself being steered back to the reception. It felt a lot like being manhandled, so she snatched her arm back.

"If this is about Mum's jewelry, it can wait until after I visit her."

"Perhaps you should sit down for a minute, dear."

Dear? Her eyes travelled up Beverly's pastel-pink clad arm, across her ruffled bodice to sympathetic eyes. A knot formed in her stomach and she swallowed shallow breaths.

"Have a seat." Beverly waved a hand toward a row of carved chairs against the wall.

"I want to visit Mum first."

"I was just about to call you." Beverly reached for Mya.

Her pink fingernails patted the back of Mya's hand. Mya's mouth dried.

"Rosalie passed away this morning."

A grandfather clock chimed. Mya flinched as each peal reverberated through her bones. One, two, three, her knees faltered, four, five, six, a crushing weight pressed on her lungs, seven, eight, nine, her head spun from the lack of oxygen, ten, her mind went blank.

This time she let Beverly guide her to a chair.

"Are you all right, dear? I'm so sorry for your loss. Would you like a glass of water or something?"

It can't be true. Mum isn't even fifty. Beverly must've made a mistake. Someone else's mother died.

Bitter saliva flooded Mya's mouth and nausea twisted her stomach.

•••

Luca reclined against the wall of the interview room, his narrowed eyes locked on Willy Mason—a silent battle of wills. He waited until Willy looked away and then pushed off the wall.

"Thanks to your overreaction last night, Willy, Natalie Andrews is cooperating fully with the police. I have photographs of the injuries you inflicted on her, and she explained exactly how your little scam operates. By the end of the day, I'm going to have enough evidence to put you away for a long time. I even know who two of your acc—"

"That little tart doesn't know shit!"

"Does Kevin Walker sound familiar?"

Willy sat straight and crossed his thick arms, hands clenched. Luca imagined the man would like to wrap them around his throat. They glared at one another.

"What I don't know is who is running the show. I want Ev's full name."

"Now you're just clutching at straws. Besides, I don't know any Kevin Walker."

Luca shook his head, as though pitying Willy. "Maybe Kevin Barnes didn't tell you he was operating under an alias."

Willy swallowed and his left eye twitched minutely.

"Do you think they're going to help you out? You know as well as I do they'll hang you out to dry."

"Look, I just move the goods. I don't steal the stuff and I don't replace it with the fakes."

"Well, unless you start telling me exactly how the operation works, I've got more productive things to be doing. So what's your final answer?"

"Bite me."

"Bite me it is."

Luca strode from the room and locked the door behind him. Negotiating with criminals was like a waltz; one step forward, one to the side and back. It wasn't until you reached the twirl of new information that you got forward motion.

Kate stood in the hallway. "I've been waiting for you. Any luck with Willy?" She fell into step beside Luca.

"Not yet. Did you get Natalie's statement? I was afraid she was going to spook."

"Yes. I think it was wise for me to talk to her. She's a bit man-shy after her run-in with Willy."

Luca lowered his voice as they entered the lunch room. "Any information I can use?" He grabbed a mug from the overhead cupboard, dangled an English breakfast teabag in it, and poured water from the urn to two-thirds full.

"She can list most of the items she made and approximate time frames, but she doesn't appear to have knowledge about the other members of the scam. I tell you, she's talented. There's no way I'd pick the stuff she makes as fake.

"Anyway, I explained she might face charges for her part in the scam, but her cooperation was in her favour. She doesn't care. Her main concern is that Willy won't get his hands on her again."

"I understand." Luca splashed milk into his mug and jiggled the tea bag. "Natalie wants to stay with Mya—the neighbour whose house she ran to last night—but I'm worried it's not far enough away from the Mason family. I guess I can put her there for another night, until we sort out something more permanent."

"This is the same woman who helped you beat up Willy Mason and gave Pete from the pawn shop two black eyes?" Kate asked warily.

"Well, yeah."

She shook her head. "You really can pick 'em."

"Speaking of which, did you ask Natalie what I wanted you to?"

"She swears Mya isn't involved with Willy," Kate mumbled begrudgingly. "Hey, before I forget, a Beverly Aldridge left a message on the landline late yesterday, so I only just got it. She has collated the statistics about deaths at Rich Haven during the past nine months. Do you want me to pick them up?"

"Thanks, but I want to pay another visit to Pete's Pawn Shop, so I'll drop in on the way. Can you keep Natalie safe for a few hours and keep trying to track down Melanie Lane's real identity?"

"Sure thing. And I looked into that Balhannah address you gave me. The property is owned by Evan Smith, runs an accounting firm, clean record."

"Not much to work on, but thanks."

•••

The rain on the roof of Luca's old Toyota Corolla sounded like static on a radio. He squeezed between a Bentley and a Jaguar at the far end of the Rich Haven parking lot. If these rich bastards learned how to park their cars between the lines, he wouldn't need a can opener to get his in.

With a black jacket pulled over his head, he ran for the building, past Mya's red motorbike. He'd forgotten she was coming here today.

Great, another reason for her to think I'm stalking her.

He'd have to make more of an effort to keep his distance. This morning in her entrance hall, his self-control had been close to nonexistent. The woman's soft floral scent and supple skin were irresistible, and that long, luxurious hair …

If Natalie hadn't appeared, there might have been an unwise repeat of tangled sheets. Mya certainly acted like that should be avoided. Then again, the way she looked at him gave her desire away, and now that he was sure she wasn't in on the jewelry scam, maybe he didn't have to keep his distance.

A rumble of thunder accompanied him through the front door. He shook moisture from his jacket and surveyed the room. The reception desk was unattended, and he heard a familiar sound. Grief. He recognized the efficient Beverly Aldridge bent over a woman who was sitting on the floor. The woman wailed and resisted Beverly's attempts to pull her up.

Although Luca was sure the Rich Haven staff was trained in grief counselling, he offered assistance anyway. "Is everything all right?"

Beverly straightened and turned a phony smile to him. Perspiration beaded on her upper lip and her pencilled brows were pulled out of shape with worry. He smiled reassuringly and looked down at the stricken woman. His inhalation stopped mid-breath as he recognised the caramel waves of Mya's long hair. Her face was buried in her hands and her whole body shuddered.

"What the hell happened?"

Her head jerked up at his familiar voice, her eyes pained. Tears streamed down her cheeks and stuck hair to the edges of her face. Something wrenched inside him and he lurched forward. He understood that look. He'd felt it.

He knelt beside her. "What happened, Mya?"

"Oh, you know one another?" Beverly sounded relieved.

Mya buried her face in her hands again and wailed loudly.

Beverly put a hand on his shoulder. "Mya's mother passed away this morning. Usually I'd call a relative to be with her, but there isn't anyone else listed in Rosalie's file."

"It's all right. I'll stay with her," he offered.

He noticed a family make a wide berth around them, as though grief was contagious. Who cared what they thought? He sunk to the floor and moved within a centimetre of Mya, so she could feel his presence. Beverly handed him a box of tissues and returned to her desk.

For a few minutes he just watched Mya's body tremble. It looked like she had hypothermia, but it was just a sign of her suffering. Nauseating gurgles emanated from beneath a veil of hair as she struggled to breathe through a torrent of tears.

Eventually he whispered in her ear, "I'm really sorry about your mother, Mya. Have you been to see her yet?"

Her head whipped sideways. The horrified expression made him recoil. Perhaps that wasn't the right thing to suggest.

She shook her head infinitesimally. "They won't let me."

"Do you want to?"

A slow nod. He pushed onto his knees and then feet and offered her a hand. She stared at it blankly and then at his face. Tentatively she placed her hand in his. Once she was on her feet, she teetered, so he wrapped an arm around her waist. With her head down and body silently trembling, he guided her forward.

"Do you think that's a good idea?" Beverly called.

"Yes." He sounded decisive. If there was one thing he was familiar with, it was grief, and Mya needed to say goodbye on her own terms.

Beverly considered for a moment before pointing toward the left hallway. "Number thirty-two."

Was this a good idea? They'd shuffled past the door with a brass twenty on it; too late now. He should've checked on the state of Rosalie's body before he brought Mya to see it.

Shadows moved back and forth across the strip of light on the carpet, and he attempted to put himself between Mya and the room. Not a chance. She struggled past him, ran to the bed, and threw herself over her mother. Mercifully, Rosalie had been laid on the made bed. She wore a floral nightie and her hair was neat. Her face looked peaceful.

He breathed a sigh of relief.

Chapter 25

A doctor, who'd been scribbling on a clipboard chart in Rosalie's room, eyed Mya and Luca.

"I'll give you some privacy. Beverly at reception can contact me if you have any questions."

Luca slumped into the floral armchair by the window. Mya gathered Rosalie's head and shoulders into her arms and wept into her hair. Guilt told him to look away, but he wasn't looking at Mya and Rosalie—he was seeing himself draped over his wife. His throat constricted and his eyes stung. He blinked, but tears spilt onto his cheeks and he dragged in a juddering breath that didn't satisfy his lungs.

An insidious growth had lodged in Olivia's beautiful breast, right beside the heart he loved. Her once-velvet voice became rough, and eyes that used to sparkle and mock him became dull. She had apologized in advance for dying and leaving him. *She* apologized to *him*. He was the one who needed to apologize, for doing overtime instead of going home to her, for working on his laptop when he could have been making love to her.

Eventually, Mya sat and stroked Rosalie's face. He knew exactly what she was doing. She was committing her mother's face to memory, because these last minutes would have to last a lifetime. He wouldn't hurry her.

The sound of his mobile phone was too loud in the solemn room. He jumped and clutched it to his chest, then raced from the room, tossing an apologetic look at Mya. She didn't appear to notice.

"Hello?"

"Luca? I was expecting to hear from you after you visited Pete." Kate sounded worried.

"I didn't. I haven't. There's been a death."

Kate's sharp intake of air was her only question.

"When I got to Rich Haven, Mya's mother had just passed away. She was distraught, so I stayed."

"Luca, that's very nice of you, but you shouldn't be getting involved with this girl."

"She doesn't have any family," he whispered.

There was a long silence at the end of the phone. "Okay, I'll leave you to finish up there and wait to hear from you."

"Thanks, Kate."

The line went dead, but Luca pressed his cheek against the cool wall for several minutes. Finally, his ears tuned into muttering. He stuck his head through the doorway.

Mya's hand fluttered over Rosalie's body. "Tell me what happened to you, Mum. I know it was Rhonda. What did she do?"

She whimpered.

"What are you doing?" He grabbed Mya's wrists, and held tightly when she struggled.

Her eyes blazed with anger. He'd seen what she was capable of, but wasn't afraid. She needed human contact now, even if she didn't want it.

Mya sniffed. "Rhonda murdered Mum and I'm going to find out how."

"What are you talking about?" He knew he should be telling her that people in aged care facilities died of natural causes all the time, but he was the one who'd been trying to prove otherwise for more than a year. Then again, Rosalie Jensen didn't fit the victim profile; she had family.

Mya stood rigid. In a loud voice she declared, "My mother was murdered. I want an autopsy."

"And you're entitled to one. I'll make sure it happens. But why do you think she was murdered?"

"Rhonda did it, I know she did. She's been sending letters and I saw her red hair. Now Mum's dead and she wasn't old or sick." She sucked short, quick breaths and swayed.

She wasn't making sense. It must be a coping mechanism. He grabbed her elbows, expecting her to pull away, but she sunk lower, so he scooped her up and carried her to the armchair. Gently he set her down and knelt in front of her. He looked her in the eye.

"Mya, I don't know what happened to your mum, but I'm going to help you find the truth. I promise."

This time he surveyed the room with a critical eye. It looked tidy, maybe too tidy. No sign of a struggle or ransacking of drawers. Nothing appeared out of place.

He picked up the phone and dialed reception. "Can you call the doctor back to Rosalie Jensen's room, please?"

Within a few minutes, the grey-haired doctor arrived in the doorway. He tucked a clipboard under one arm. "Detective Patterson, how can I be of assistance?"

"Can you tell me who found Miss Jensen's body?"

"Of course." He flipped a page on the clipboard. "Nurse Anne Purdy found the body and called me immediately."

"Could I speak to the nurse?"

"Certainly."

After the doctor hung up the phone on the bedside table, he flicked his head in the direction of the door. Luca followed him into the hall.

"Are you a family member?"

"No, a family friend." It didn't sound like a lie, although Luca doubted Mya had any real friends. "In your opinion, doctor, is Rosalie's death suspicious?"

The man frowned and adjusted his bifocals to the end of his nose. "Why do you ask?"

"Force of habit."

"Well, I examined the body at nine fifteen this morning and found no vital signs, so I pronounced her. I suspect the cause of death is cardiac arrest, but I'm not confident enough to declare it on a certificate of death."

"So it will go to the coroner." Luca nodded and rubbed the stubble on his chin. "What makes you unsure, doctor?"

"Well, Miss Jensen wasn't as elderly as most of the patients at Rich Haven, but in her condition her life expectancy is reduced. However, I examined her at the beginning of the week and found her to be in good health. I'm not sure about suspicious, but her death is unexpected."

They both turned as a young brunette wearing a pale blue shirt and navy skirt approached.

Luca shook the doctor's withered hand. "Thanks for your help." He offered the same hand to the nurse.

Her eyes were downcast.

"Ms. Purdy, I believe you discovered Miss Jensen's body—" He caught himself and shot a glance at Mya.

She had slumped so her head was on the arm of the chair as she stared blankly at Rosalie.

He moved so his back was to her and lowered his voice. "I wonder if you can tell me how you found her."

Anne peeked from under thick black lashes. Presumably taking Luca's lead, she kept her voice low. "I was doing my morning rounds and said hello to Rosalie. Of course, she didn't answer because she didn't speak, but we like to stimulate the patients with conversation. Tell them what we're doing and why. Her eyes were closed, so I thought she might be dozing, but when I checked her more closely, I found her to be unresponsive. I immediately called the doctor on duty."

"Was she lying on the bed like this?"

"Pretty much. Of course, I tidied her up a little." Anne twirled a strand of hair around her finger.

"Can you describe exactly how Miss Jensen's body was arranged?"

A frown fluttered across the nurse's brow. "Um, sure. She was on her back and one leg was bent. Come to think of it, that was a bit strange. Rosalie can't move her legs, so whoever put her on the bed didn't straighten her out properly. Her arms were by her sides, I think her head was turned to the right as though she was looking out the window, and her hair was a bit mussed. So I just tidied her up."

"Is it usual for the staff to put her on the bed during the day?"

"No, not really. We usually put immobile patients in their armchair or wheelchair. It helps prevent bedsores, keeps up circulation, and gives us an opportunity to change the bed linen, et cetera. But there might have been a reason someone put her on the bed," she added quickly.

When he looked up from his notes, the nurse was wringing her hands. He smiled to put her at ease.

"Did you touch her clothing?"

"Let me see … she was wearing exactly what she has on now. I did straighten her cardigan. It was pulled to one side, but that's all."

"You are being a great help, and I won't keep you from your job much longer. Can you tell me if anything in the room was moved or is missing?"

She studied the room with a pucker of concentration between her brows. "No, I don't see anything missing. Oh, the orderly took her breakfast dishes away while I was here."

"Okay, thanks for your time. I've got one more thing for you to do. Please see if you can find those breakfast dishes and bring them back to the room. Don't touch them more than you have to and don't wash them. Do you understand?"

"Yes, sir. Is something wrong with Rosalie?" She peered around him.

"I'm not sure, but I do really need those dishes."

"Oh, yes. They might still be on the orderly's trolley." She flicked him a poor excuse for a smile and trotted down the hall.

Mya didn't look like she was moving any time soon, so he stepped into the hall, and dialed his boss.

"Sir, it's Luca. I'm at Rich Haven Aged Care Facility and I've got a suspicious death I'd like to investigate."

There was a pause. A long one. "Patterson, tell me you've got evidence this time."

"Not exactly, sir. I came here to pick up some information and found out a woman died this morning. The doctor won't sign the death certificate. I asked a few questions, and it looks a bit suspicious. I'd like to interview the staff and process the room."

"You're on holidays." The inspector sounded less than impressed.

"I'll get a team in and I won't hang around."

"Okay, you can call a small team in, but don't go making a production out of this unless you find some *evidence*. Got it?" Moss growled down the phone.

"Yes, sir."

How long would he have to pay for one stinking incident two years ago? He made the call to go in without knowing for sure what they were going to find inside. A cop was shot, but they saved the kidnapped child, for God's sake. He dialed Kate.

"Can you get a team over to Rich Haven? I want someone to interview the staff, a couple of officers to process the room, a photographer, and a guard put on the door until we know the extent of what we're dealing with." More silence at the end of the phone.

If everyone didn't let up with this attitude, he was going to see red. Yes, a police officer needed evidence, but every decent detective knew you had to trust your gut instincts, too.

"Look, I've just spoken to the inspector and he okayed it," he said through clenched teeth.

"Oh, sure. I'll come down with Constables Callum and Old. Will you be there to fill me in?"

"I'm going to take Mya home, because she's too distraught to drive."

"Do you think that's a good idea? I could organize—"

"Will you just go with me on this one, Kate?"

"Sure."

"Thanks. There's a doctor here you can talk to. He's going to send the body to the coroner's pathologist. Order a full tox-screen and find out when they're doing the autopsy."

Luca stood in the hall and scrubbed his hands across his face. As soon as the guard arrived he'd take Mya home, and he wasn't looking forward to prising her out of there at all.

This had been a long day already and he had a bad feeling tomorrow was only going to be worse. But he wouldn't jump to conclusions before the room was processed. To tell the truth, he hoped he was wrong. Being right about the depraved things people were willing to do to one another sucked.

Chapter 26

"Watch your head." Luca put his hand on Mya's crown as he helped her out of his car.

When he'd insisted on driving her home, she argued at first, but eventually succumbed to logic—she couldn't ride a motorbike in her state. Besides, her half-coherent version of events worried him. If someone murdered Rosalie and had tried to run Mya off the road, then he needed to look out for her.

He parked right in front of her house. It had stopped raining, but large puddles of dirty water pooled on the footpath and he guided her around them.

"That's weird," she said.

"What?" He followed her line of sight to the front porch.

"That pot has moved."

Strictly speaking, pots didn't move, people moved them. While she fished keys from the pocket of her leather jacket, he stared at a brown, circular stain on the porch. A stain the size of the pot thirty centimetres away.

"Did you move this pot when you watered it or something?"

"No. I can't remember doing that."

She slid a key into the deadbolt and turned. It clicked and her arm extended as she pushed the door inward. Something metallic caught Luca's eye.

"No!"

He grabbed her wrist with one hand and wrapped his other arm around her waist. She was lifted off her feet as he threw them from the porch.

Mya screamed.

They thudded onto the wet lawn, Mya face down and Luca on top of her.

"What the fuck are you doing?" She thrashed her arms and legs.

A gust of wind whipped hair into his eyes as he rolled off her, hands in front of his face in a defensive posture. "I'm sorry, I thought—"

A deep boom triggered an automatic response. He pushed her head into the grass and arched his body over hers.

A surge of wood splinters hit his back and legs like a thousand needles. In the seconds that followed he could hear only the ringing in his ears. Gradually other sounds penetrated. Laboured breathing, someone shouting from what seemed like a great distance.

The ruined front door of Mya's house was charred. Small flames tried to assert themselves into the fire-retardant paint around the shattered frame, where dark ribbons of smoke were caught by the gusting wind.

Mya squirmed, so he rolled off her. They sat on the wet ground, staring at the debris strewn across the porch, stairs, and lawn. He pulled his mobile out and dialed the emergency services.

"A fire unit is on the way," he told Mya.

Fast footsteps made them both turn. Bert Reiner ran up the path with a small red fire extinguisher in his hands, passed them, and leapt onto the porch.

"Wait!"

Luca jumped to his feet, but the old man already had the pin out, squeezing the trigger to sweep white foam up and down the door frame. It sounded like someone trying to hock up a ten-second loogey. Then it was over.

Bert stepped back as white goo dripped down the wall.

A crowd of neighbours formed across the road, and there was a smaller group further down—the Mason family—who were laughing.

Bert helped Mya to her feet and she dusted at the wet patches on her T-shirt and jeans. Luca's training and methodical nature kicked in. It was the best way he knew how to deal with situations outside of his control, and this was a raging bull waiting to charge. When he'd put Mya in his car to drive her home, it had been out of compassion, but when he saw her lying on the lawn, surrounded by debris and with terror in her eyes, well, he was damned sure not going to let anything else happen to her.

No matter whether his feelings were reciprocated, he would protect her and make her safe again.

He felt pinpricks of discomfort on his back, but he was standing, so all that mattered now was making sure the bastard— or bitch—who did this paid. He jotted down details of the timeline and scene: the names of individuals he could see and knew, and the sequence of events. This was what he was good at, gathering information from any and every source; sifting through it; looking for patterns, mistakes, clues. He would find the culprit; all that remained was to see how long it would take him.

Two fire appliances screamed up the road. One parked behind Luca's car, the other pulled in front of it at an angle. The station officer was the first yellow-suited firefighter to alight from the front of the cab.

"Clear the property." He issued the order with a wave of his arm in the direction of Luca, Mya, and Bert.

More firefighters spilled from the second appliance.

"Run out the hose and prepare to enter the house," the station officer instructed.

"No! The door was rigged," Luca yelled.

Curls of smoke weaved under the eaves and dispersed over the gutter, leaving the air with an acrid heat-bead smell.

The lead firefighter stepped in front of Luca. "Please stand aside until the house is clear, sir."

"Detective Patterson." Luca pulled out his badge.

"Nice to meet you, but you're still going to have to wait on the footpath until the house is clear. Thanks for the tip. We'll keep our eyes peeled for secondary devices."

Luca huffed and flipped open his mobile. It rang only once.

"Hi, Kate. I need you to come to Mya's house. Everything is going to shit here."

"What happ—"

"Just get here." He pressed the end button and turned to find Mya.

She was propped against the fence, staring at what used to be her front door. The strange expression on her face didn't look like the blank void of denial or the bitter aftertaste of grief. He'd seen fear on plenty of other faces before, but it looked out of place on Mya. Tears gathered along the rims of her eyes and her chin quivered, but even after everything that had happened to her today, she wouldn't give into her demons. He wanted to wrap his arms around her and protect her from the evil that lurked in her home.

A police car arrived and the leathery driver waved at Luca and swaggered over.

"Patterson." The officer looked like an old Charles Bronson, with grey flecks in his thick moustache and darkly tanned skin. "This your place?"

A stinging sensation on Luca's back was demanding attention. He shrugged his shoulders to reposition his jacket. "Afternoon, Davey. No, I was just dropping a neighbour home and her front door exploded."

"Shit! You're lucky neither of you were hurt." He gave Mya a cursory glance.

"I thought I saw a wire as she opened the door, so I threw us off the porch." He demonstrated with his arms. Stretching his back hurt.

"Really?" Davey rubbed his knobbly chin between thumb and forefinger. "It's very observant of you to be looking for trip wires when you drop a friend home."

This line of questioning was predictable, and he needed to head it off before he was bogged down by an interrogation he didn't have time for. Time was critical in finding Mya's stalker, and Davey could handle this scene without Luca.

"Look, I'm in the middle of an investigation and this woman might be linked, so I was on my guard. Derman will be here in a minute, and I want her to take Miss Jensen to a safe location."

Davey frowned as though digesting this version of events.

"You can clear it with Inspector Moss, if you like," Luca added. Reaching behind, he rubbed a finger over a sore spot on his back and flinched.

"That won't be necessary, but I'll need you to stay and give a statement."

"Sure thing. The fireys have called the bomb squad to check for secondary devices."

"Hey, are you hurt?"

Luca followed Davey's gaze down to his own hand. The fingers that had touched his back were smeared red. "I don't know. My back's hurting like stink."

He removed his jacket and turned to let Davey take a look.

"Shrapnel. You'd better let the ambos take a look. I'll get a team out here to process the house."

"Make sure your people interview every person at number eleven. I arrested one this morning and this may be a retaliation bombing."

Kate's unmarked sedan coasted between the fire appliance and the growing crowd of spectators and stopped at an angle. She leaped out and strode over to the police contingent.

"What's going on?"

Luca flicked his head sideways and they walked a few paces. He gave her a brief outline of the day's events, from finding Mya collapsed at Rich Haven to the explosion.

"Are you hurt?" Her gaze travelled over his body.

"Just some shrapnel from the explosion. I'll get it looked at in a minute. Right now I need you to get Mya out of here."

"I dropped Natalie at my place. She was supposed to stay with Mya tonight, but obviously that isn't possible. I don't think it's appropriate for them to stay with me, but I don't see a lot of options at present."

Luca nodded. "I don't think Mya should be left alone right now. You could take her to the station for a while."

Kate eyed Mya's drooping figure. "No, I'll take her home, but call me when you're done here, no matter what the time is."

"Thanks, Kate, you're a gem. There's a mess to clean up, but I'll find a motel or safe house for them tomorrow."

"And get your back seen to," she insisted in no uncertain terms.

• • •

Mya stared out the passenger window of Kate's gold Torana and wondered how it was that people still mowed lawns, read newspapers on park benches, and walked scruffy mutts. Surely something had changed in the world. *Her* world had certainly altered since this morning. The excruciating pain she'd felt after Bev told her about her mum … it was like her internal organs ruptured one by one and left a gelatinous pulp in their place.

At least the angry swirl of purple and grey clouds agreed with her mood. Thankfully, there was just numbness now, although the pain was bound to return.

Her only family was gone. Her one safe haven had been violated. A slender finger of pain moved through the pulp inside her and she shivered at the dull ache it left behind.

Twice she'd failed to protect her mum. Now they'd both paid the ultimate price.

Mya's heart felt like it had been replaced by a dark abyss. A murky place even she was afraid to enter, where the anger of injustice, abuse, and abandonment lurked, waiting to take revenge. Over the years she'd expended a lot of energy keeping this darkness at bay. She'd locked it into an internal vault and thrown away the key. She might not have the strength to hold the door shut anymore, and it scared the hell out of her.

Better to embrace the numbness.

Kate hadn't said a word during the drive from Croydon to Millswood, although she glanced sideways a few times. Mya had never had a boyfriend, but she was pretty sure the wariness on Kate's face was jealousy. The cop either fancied Luca, or had already had a piece of him. Maybe Kate was the doormat with whom Luca shared his conquests, or he was one of those wankers who liked to boast. Nah, that didn't sit right with what she'd seen of him so far. Either way, the woman wasn't keen on her guest.

Mya wasn't too keen either.

Kate turned into a red patterned cement driveway, marched to the front door, and started sifting through a large set of keys. Apparently this was Mya's cue to follow. Kate stepped aside and waved her across the threshold. The TV was muted and a guy with a short back-and-sides haircut reclined on a brown leather lounge suite with his socked feet on a salmon-pink cushion.

He narrowed his eyes at Kate. "Another one?"

Kate winced. Boyfriend or husband; either way Mya didn't like him already.

They continued through an arch, past a smoked-glass dining table with crushed velvet chairs, and into a spacious slate-tiled family room. A TV in here played a chick flick, and she recognized Natalie's colour-streaked hair.

"Take a seat. Can I get you a cup of tea or coffee?"

It took a moment to realise Kate was talking to her. "Tea, please. White, no sugar."

"Would you like something, Natalie?"

"Another Coke?"

"Certainly."

Natalie smiled by way of a greeting and returned her attention to the TV. Mya flopped onto the end of a maroon microfibre couch and pretended to watch the movie, but her eyes looked past the TV and unfocused as they tried to see through the wall.

The blissful numbness she'd clung to since Luca took her away from Rich Haven was melting. Something raw and bleak was being exposed. Her throat closed, so she swallowed hard several times. Her jaw ached as tears stung her already sore eyes. It was all she could do to stop from putting her head on her knees and rocking like a maniac.

It was as if Mya had been in that room. She could picture her mum's serene face as she lay on her bed, dressed in a nightie, and Rhonda sneaking into Rosalie's room, putting a pillow over her face and holding it there. Her mum trying to struggle, but she couldn't.

"Mya! Would you like to have your cuppa in the bedroom?" Kate was staring at her.

She had gripped the velour couch as though trying to wring a chicken's neck. Across the room, Natalie's eyes were wide.

Kate moved to stand in front of her, blocking Natalie's view. "I'll show you where you'll be sleeping," she said, holding an arm to the side to indicate the direction.

Mya didn't want to scare Natalie—the girl had been through enough—and she refused to have a meltdown in front of anyone, so she followed Kate down the hall to the third door on the left. Mya tumbled onto the bed, covering her face in the hope she'd be left alone.

"Do you want to talk about it?" Kate's voice was soft, the tense lines on her face gone and her mouth turned down at the corners.

"Go away." She tried to make it sound like a demand, but her voice cracked, so she pressed her lips tighter. It felt like shards of glass were being dragged through her intestines, up her chest, and out through her throat in a strangled cry.

Judging by the silence, Kate had returned to the kitchen.

The sound of paper being torn from a cardboard box shocked Mya upright.

"It's going to be all right." Kate held out a tissue and sat on the edge of the bed. "Luca told me what happened, and we're going to get to the bottom of this." She wrung her hands in her lap and her voice dropped to a whisper. "I'm sorry about your mum."

Even through moisture-blurred vision, Kate's short bob, plain face, and police uniform were severe. Still, Mya wanted to thank her for giving her a place to stay. Wanted to, but couldn't get the words out.

"I just want to be alone," she said instead.

Kate left the room quietly.

Chapter 27

Luca parked in front of police headquarters around mid-afternoon. It had taken a while to give his statement at Mya's house. He sidled out of the car with care, trying not to scrape the mosaic of bandages the ambos put on his back after they picked dozens of wood splinters out.

Now that there had been an attempt on Mya's life, he wanted to talk to Moss again. At this point it was speculation that the bombing was linked to the jewelry scam, and that Rosalie's death was suspicious. Theories were not going to convince the inspector, but his instinct told him he had to. Mya's life might depend on it.

He stepped through the automatic sliding doors and scanned the white glare of the palatial foyer.

"Luca." Moss waved a folded newspaper from his nook by Funk Café, in the foyer of the police station, a polystyrene cup resting on his knee.

He didn't get up from the couch, so Luca dropped onto the seat beside him.

Straight to the point, Moss placed the newspaper on a glass coffee table and angled his body toward Luca. "What's this house explosion got to do with the woman who died at the nursing home this morning?"

"Maybe nothing, but it was the deceased woman's daughter whose house was bombed. She claims her mother was murdered and—"

"Bombed?"

"I confirmed it onsite. Looked like an amateur device, but I won't know the details until the bomb squad has finished there."

Moss puckered his milk-foamed lips and nodded, as though he knew where Luca was going with this.

He held the old man's steady gaze. "There are a few seemingly unrelated anomalies that all seem to tie in to Rich Haven."

The inspector put his half cappuccino on the table and pushed his reading glasses further up his nose. "Like what?"

"First, the increased death rate since two Happy Vale staff moved there, then some jewelry was reported stolen and it turns out some kind of replica racket might be operating. Rosalie Jensen's death could be suspicious, especially now her daughter's house has been bombed, too. Something is going on at Rich Haven. I just have to figure out what exactly."

"I see. And what do you want from me, sergeant?"

"I want to head the operation, sir."

Moss did his staring thing, so Luca sat straighter and kept his gaze steady. He'd invested too much in this case to walk away. "I have a head start on this one, sir. I can tie these pieces together."

"I have no doubt you can get the job done." The inspector chewed his lip.

"I'm not taking unnecessary risks, sir." He paused for the length of a heartbeat—no need to confess to sneaking around Kevin Walker's house. "I want to suspend my leave and coordinate the teams already in place, with Constable Derman 2IC. I won't make a move without evidence, and you know I'll keep you in the loop."

The old man rubbed a hand over his face wearily. His skin fractured into a weathered landscape as he smiled. "What resources will you need?"

• • •

Mya woke with the pillow stuck to her face by a damp combination of drool and tears. The bedroom light was still on and her watch showed eleven fifty. Night, she guessed by the lack of light around the curtains. She sat and checked out the cramped room.

A single bed, full-length mirrored robes at one end, and a cane chair in the corner with a pile of folded clothes on it. Her clothes.

How the hell did they get there?

On the top of the pile was her red toiletries bag, which she assumed contained items from her bathroom. They must have been rescued from her ruined house.

Oh no, my house. Mum.

Her insides hollowed. She couldn't feel her heart beat or lungs expand as memories of her mum and the explosion rushed forward.

With a clumsy shuffle, she almost fell off the bed and crept into the dark hall. There were hushed voices in the kitchen and one belonged to a man. She stepped into the bright light and couldn't see a damned thing, so stood there blinking. Someone chuckled.

"Nice hair."

Luca's was the first face she'd seen after she'd been told about her mother. He was the one who protected her from the explosion. Usually she didn't need anyone, but tonight she wanted his warm arms wrapped around her, just to be close to another living being.

She was halfway across the room when she caught a glimpse of her hair in the wall oven. It looked like the mess of twigs and straw you'd find atop a telephone pole, with starling eggs in it. Not sure if she should make a run for the bathroom or stay, she tensed an arm in each direction.

"Hey, Mya." Luca came towards her, his powder-blue eyes intense. "I'm kidding. Come have a cuppa and I'll bring you up to speed."

He reached a hand in her direction, but she just stared at it. It was large and slightly callused, but she knew from experience it was gentle and warm.

Kate huffed and turned to fill the kettle. Luca took another step and Mya placed her hand on his upturned palm. Long fingers wrapped around it and a pleasant tingle flowed up her arm and neck.

He led her to the breakfast bar and pulled out a stool. When she was seated, he lifted himself to sit on the kitchen bench. "I stayed at your place until the fireys and bomb squad finished. They confirmed your door was rigged with explosives. I think the wind blew it open far enough to hit a wire across the back and pull a pin from the detonator. Apparently it was a fairly crude device, either set by an amateur or not intended to kill. It was never going to create enough of a blast to destroy the house. They searched the premises and confirmed there was only the one device. Anyway, it could've been a lot worse, so we were lucky."

"Lucky," she mumbled.

Kate pushed a mug of tea along the breakfast bar to Mya, and another to Luca.

"Only the door and a small portion of the entrance hall are damaged, but the smell of smoke might take a while to get out of the place," he added.

Honestly, she didn't care about the house, but he was just doing his job, so naturally he was more concerned about material stuff than the death of a disabled woman.

"I'm going to bed," Kate announced. "Oh, Luca, you'll need to deal with the Rich Haven director in the morning." She lowered her voice and moved closer to him, glancing at Mya. "I put a guard on Rosalie's room for the night, and the director's not happy about it. See yourself out."

"Yeah, thanks for everything."

Kate shuffled down the dark hall.

Mya sipped hot tea halfheartedly, watching an ant sneak along the join in the speckled kitchen laminate. She flinched when Luca jumped down from the bench. Maybe it was her imagination, but she thought the movement made him wince.

"You're hurt?" She reached a hand out and let it hang in midair.

"A few scratches on my back. Nothing too bad."

"Can I see?"

He shrugged. "Don't worry about it."

She returned her attention to the searching ant to give herself time to think. He was injured because he threw himself over her. No one had ever done that before.

Luca came closer, took the mug from her hand, and placed it on the bench. Her heart thumped a staccato beat. She could feel the heat from his body, but kept her gaze on the ant. When he smoothed her wild hair with the palm of his hand, she couldn't help but lean into it.

"How are you doing?"

She shrugged and blinked rapidly.

"You know you can ask me anything you want."

Her eyes snapped up and she said the first thing that popped into her mind. "How long will the autopsy take?" She expected him to look uncomfortable, or change the subject.

Instead, he held steady. "It will be done tomorrow. It'll take a few days to get the pathologist's report and longer still for test results, but I've put a hurry on them."

She nodded.

"I know you don't want to think about it at the moment, but can you remember anything about your mum's room that was out of place?"

Mya picked up her mug again to give her hands something to do and exhaled across the surface, closing her eyes as the warm air caressed them. Luca's hand was still on her shoulder and she focused on the warmth that permeated into her. Solace in a single hand.

"Her arm," she whispered.

"What about her arm?"

"It was straight by her side. Mum's left arm spasmed and she held it near her chin with the hand clenched." She put a hand up to show how.

"Anything else?"

"Thanks for … this morning, and at my house."

"You're welcome, Mya." He put a finger under her chin and lifted it so she had to look him in the eye. "I promise to figure this out and make you safe again."

"I've never been safe," she mumbled. *Crap, I didn't mean to say that aloud.*

He didn't say anything but moved closer. His thighs touched her knees, and his chest was centimetres from her face. She couldn't help it, she looked up. His eyes had changed to a glistening steel grey. He lowered his head slowly. One large hand cupped the side of her face and he pressed his soft lips to hers.

Her eyes closed as a soothing warmth spread down her throat and into her chest. The kiss was long and tender and, although it stirred desire, it didn't build into the uncontrollable craving it had last time they were together. It was more comforting.

When it was over, he held her head to his chest and she listened to his quick breaths. They stood like that for a while and the tension eased from her limbs.

"I'll see you tomorrow." He kissed the top of her head, grabbed his car keys, and headed for the back door. "Hope the clothes and toiletries are adequate. It was certainly an eye-opener selecting the underwear." He disappeared into the night, sporting a huge grin.

So he *was* the one who packed her stuff. What a cheek.

Chapter 28

Luca tucked his police shirt into black jeans and stuffed car keys into the back pocket—as formal as he planned to get on a Sunday. Hopefully it wasn't too early to turn up at Kate's house after the late hour last night. He pushed her side gate open and nearly tripped over a stack of empty black plastic pots.

At the rear of the house, he peered through the glass sliding door. Kate was in the bright kitchen, so he tapped lightly. She nearly dropped the bowl she was lifting from an overhead cupboard. Hand on heart, she waved him in. She tossed two Weetbix into a bowl, poured enough milk on to almost cover them, and then sprinkled sugar over the top. "So, did you make alternative arrangements for Mya and Natalie?"

"I've got a nice old couple on the outskirts of town who run a kind of halfway house-slash-bed and breakfast. They've agreed to help get Natalie on her feet, but she'll have to pay board."

"Sounds fair," Kate mumbled around a mouthful of pulped cereal.

"They can't take her until next week, but don't worry—I've got Callum organizing something for tonight," he added quickly. "Like I said on the phone last night, I want you on this taskforce as my right-hand man, or woman. I need you to link Kevin and Melanie to both the jewelry scam and the deaths at Rich Haven. Willy's confession isn't enough."

"We don't know for sure there *are* suspicious deaths at Rich Haven." She rinsed her bowl and slotted it into the dishwasher. "Could just be a coincidence."

Luca opened a buff folder on the bench top and flicked through the documents Beverly Aldridge had provided. "It may as well be, because there isn't any evidence to the contrary. More specifically, there isn't evidence, because no one was looking for it. Anyway, can you take this info about the recently deceased to the Fraud Investigation Squad so they can look for patterns? First thing Monday morning we'll need a magistrate to approve a Bankers Record form so we can access financial records. There has to be some way to link these deaths."

"You're clutching at straws. Coffee?"

"Yes, please. It's going to be *very* interesting to get the autopsy results for Rosalie."

"I know it's none of my business, but do you know anything about Mya? From what you and Natalie told me, she sounds suspicious." She held up a hand when he tried to interrupt. "I'm only asking because I'd hate to see you get dragged down with her."

"I appreciate your concern, Kate, but I did a background check and her bark is worse than her bite." He glanced down the hall and lowered his voice. "She's had a rough life." He ignored Kate's eye roll. "Her mother ended up in Rich Haven, because her father left the woman brain damaged. It's no wonder she's hostile and remote. As far as I can tell, she's done nothing but take care of her mother and work hard over the last decade."

"Natalie said she's got a reputation for being a lethal kickboxer."

"Yeah, she teaches it, but from what I've seen, she only fights when provoked." He rested his elbows on the bench and straightened quick smart. Damn those cuts on his back hurt. There wasn't any point getting frustrated with Kate; she was only laying out the facts and forcing him to think professionally—something he was finding increasingly difficult to do where Mya was concerned.

"Did you get your injuries seen to?" Kate rubbed sleep from her eyes.

"They're minor, so there's nothing to do but wait a few days until they scab over."

"So what's on the agenda today?"

"Well, you should take the day off. Don't feel like you have to babysit Mya and Natalie. I'm off to Rosalie Jensen's autopsy."

"Better you than me." Kate grimaced.

•••

Again, Mya woke in Kate's spare bedroom. An arm and leg hung over one side of the single bed. Staying in it all day seemed justifiable, but she couldn't. Too many questions needed to be answered, and the Rich Haven funeral director would want to confirm the funeral details, Luca would want a statement, and he'd probably want to know about Rhonda. If anyone could find out where Rhonda lived, surely it was him.

With new enthusiasm, Mya got out of bed—still wearing yesterday's undies and T-shirt, because Luca couldn't find pajamas where there weren't any—and checked out the pile of clean clothes on the cane chair. There were jeans, a couple of T-shirts, a blouse, tracksuit, and socks. She held a lacy bra-and-undie ensemble up. Trust a man to pick the skimpiest black lace she owned.

Grabbing the toiletries bag, she quietly opened the bedroom door, intending to sneak to the bathroom before anyone saw her. Halfway down the hall she heard voices and crept closer.

Kate's question was barely audible. "What's the Rich Haven director doing?"

Luca answered her. "I told him Rosalie Jensen's death is being treated as suspicious until such time as the autopsy proves otherwise, and, to get a jump on the situation, I expect him to cooperate with my team and let me know if he sees anything suspicious. Otherwise I'll send in a larger team, and they'll be a lot less discreet."

"Way to tread lightly. What about the jewelry?"

"I told the director we've arrested someone for the theft and duplication of Rosalie's jewelry but suspect a larger operation. He's being very cooperative and has offered to contact the families of all the residents and ask them to authenticate items kept by residents, even if they look genuine."

"Excellent," Kate said. "I need to blow dry my hair and get moving, because I've got a few chores to do today."

Mya jumped behind the nearest door, which happened to be the bathroom, and locked it. Standing barefoot on the cold tiles, she heard light footsteps halt and the handle rattle.

"Sorry," Kate called.

Inside the toiletries bag Mya found a comb, but it would have been better if Luca had packed a WeedWacker to tame the mess that was her hair today. There was a toothbrush, facial moisturizer, and deodorant, but no makeup. It would've been in the cabinet with the other items, although she rarely bothered with it. Was he, by chance, a rare breed of man who preferred the natural look? Brownie point to Luca.

Pinching a blob of Kate's toothpaste, she rushed through the basics, in a hurry to quiz Luca. Now that she was more lucid, she had heaps of questions. One thing she couldn't find in the bag was a hair band, and a search of the bathroom cabinet was fruitless, so she left her hair down.

She tossed the bag under the sink and headed for the kitchen, calling, "Bathroom's free" as she passed the master bedroom.

Luca turned at the sound and smiled. "Good morning, sleepyhead."

"Nine o'clock is *not* late on a Sunday, you freak."

He chuckled and busied himself filling the kettle and putting teabags into mugs. "I like your hair down."

That caught her off guard. She didn't do pleasantries as a rule, but attempted to return the compliment. "I like the jeans/cop combo." Okay, it sounded more sarcastic than complimentary.

Through the thin fabric of his pale blue police shirt, she could see a higgledy-piggledy arrangement of bandages.

A few scratches my arse. Did they hurt?

Something red on the floor caught her eye. Her motorbike helmet was in front of the heater, visor up. "How did that get here?"

"Oh, I had your motorbike transported back to your house, but the helmet was sitting in the rain, so the lining's wet."

"You stuck my bike on the back of a truck?" Her jaw dropped at the thought of her pride and joy being manhandled by a courier.

He laughed. "I rode it, actually."

"Oh." She hadn't picked him for a motorcyclist. That was thoughtful of him. "Can you give me a lift home today?"

His smile disappeared. "I don't think that's a good idea."

"I'm not asking your permission. I just want a lift."

"Mya, someone tried to kill you yesterday."

Her breath caught at the harsh reality.

"I'm organizing a motel room for a few days. Just until we figure this out."

With tight lips and narrow eyes, she squared her shoulders. "I'm *not* going to be intimidated."

Luca's chest strained against his shirt as he straightened. "It's not about running away. It's about keeping you alive. Besides, the door might be getting replaced today, but the place still stinks of smoke and needs repainting."

As much as she hated to admit it, he was right. It wasn't smart to sit where Rhonda could find her. His face was stern, so she changed the subject.

"Hey, do you know what happened at the pub last night? I was rostered on and didn't phone them. In fact, I haven't seen my mobile since yesterday."

"Don't worry, here it is." He pulled it from his back pocket and placed it on the bench. "I called the Croydon Hotel and let them know there'd been a death in the family"—he averted his eyes—"and said you won't be in for at least a week. Then I figured you could do with some peace, so I held onto it. Besides, I thought the bomber might try to contact you."

"Did she?"

He left the lid off the sugar and turned around. "Why do you say 'she'?"

"I told you yesterday I've been receiving threats and then a woman tried to run me off the road."

"You recognized the driver?"

"Well, no, but I saw frizzy red hair. It's got to be Rhonda."

"I'm sure you think so, but I'm going to need a little more to go on. What kind of threats?" He took a pen from an assortment in a purple plastic holder beside the phone. The jet engine sound of a hair dryer started in the bathroom.

"So far there have been notes and the four-wheel drive."

"Okay, so why don't you explain who this woman is and why you think she's making these threats to you specifically."

"After Cockroach died—"

"Cockroach?"

"Oh, I mean Jack Roach, my father. Anyway, this woman turned up about a year later, saying he was her father, too. She wanted to know all kinds of stuff about him and me."

"And that's when you changed your name." He grimaced and shrugged, looking suitably sheepish.

So, he'd done a background check. Not surprising for a detective, but what other little secrets had he discovered? The last thing she needed was him thinking he knew her, or worse, throwing a pity party for her lousy childhood. It had taken sheer willpower to create her new life, and no crazy stalker bitch or nosy cop was going to take it away.

He put the pen down, grabbed milk from the door of the fridge, and left it open while he poured. He squeezed the teabags between the teaspoon and his thumb and stirred slowly, thoughtfully, then slid a mug to Mya.

"Why do you think Rhonda wants to kill you?"

Nice subject change, Luca.

"I'm not sure, but she was irate when she turned up the first time. If she thinks Cockroach was her father, then maybe she thinks I owe her something. I guess I don't need to explain what he did to Mum, or how I inherited his estate." *Yeah, you ought to look guilty, buddy.*

"And you never heard Jack mention a previous wife, or children?"

Mya shook her head.

"I'll look into it. The probate office would have checked for and notified any living family, so I don't see how Rhonda's claim could be true. She might just have found out that you were coming into an inheritance and thought an eighteen-year-old was an easy target. Still, I can't see that as motivation enough to … do anything to Rosalie."

Luca tapped a finger on the kitchen counter. "There was something else I wanted to talk to you about. Are you planning on leaving Adelaide?"

Her whole body tensed. "You know I've applied to Deed Poll, don't you?"

One small nod confirmed the extent of his prying. "Mya, you're part of my investigation now and I need to know that you're not going to disappear. Tell me what you're running from."

"Nothing now, you idiot. I obviously didn't vanish fast enough for Mum. So sorry to inconvenience your investigation."

"That's not what I meant and you know it. I need to know where you are so I can keep you safe."

She slumped onto a barstool and stared into her tea. There was nothing in the world she wanted to do more than visit her mum today. Take her for a walk around the lake and brush her hair, but she wouldn't be able to visit her again. Ever. It felt like she'd lost her twice.

The numbness and shock had worn off. Now there was white-hot pain deep inside her. Everything dear to her had been stripped away, and it felt like her skin had been flayed from her body one agonizing sliver at a time.

She wrapped her arms around her body to hold it together. Tears prickled her eyes and she blinked them back. Luca had seen enough yesterday. The last thing she wanted was to have to run to the bedroom and hide.

"I need you to give me all the information you can about Rhon—"

She looked up to see why he'd stopped speaking. A traitor tear rolled down one cheek and she swiped it away with the back of her hand.

"I'm sorry if I'm talking about this in a matter-of-fact way. Mya—" He waited until she looked at him again. "I want to get to the bottom of this, but I understand if you can't tell me everything today."

"You do?"

"Of course. I know what it's like to lose someone you care about. We'll talk again this evening."

Her shoulders sagged with relief and she felt him move closer. Warmth radiated from his body with an aroma that made her feel safe and excited at the same time.

"Who did you lose?" she whispered.

His face turned away minutely. "It was my wife, seven years ago."

She counted backward. That would put him in his mid-twenties. So young to have been married and lost someone, but she knew all about losing everything when you were young. "I'm sorry. What happened?"

Luca sighed deeply. "We were married for a couple of years when Olivia discovered a lump in her breast."

"Oh." There really wasn't much more to say.

A finger touched gently under her chin, raising her gaze. There was something almost pained in Luca's eyes and his gaze slid down to her lips. *Kiss me already. No, that won't help clear my mind.*

Whoa, it was getting a bit serious here. Time for a subject change. "How did you get the scar on your lip?"

His arm dropped to his side. "I stepped between a bully and my seven-year-old cousin on the way home from school one day."

A born protector.

"How old were you?"

"Ten. As you can see, I had more attitude than brawn. The bully hit me in the face. Split my lip right open. I know it's ugly." He shrugged back from her.

She reached to trace the faint line and rested the tip of her finger on his lips. "No, it makes you look authentic. Anyway, you have the brawn to match the attitude now."

"Maybe."

Without another word, he picked up his file and headed for the back door. As the sliding door clicked shut, Mya noticed his mug of tea on the bench, still full.

Chapter 29

Luca knocked on the mortuary door and looked through the glass insert at shaggy, walnut-coloured hair. The forensic pathologist looked up from his reading and waved Luca in.

The air inside was cool, and Rosalie Jensen's naked body was face up on the gleaming steel table, which rested on a central support column. She looked peaceful, except for the telltale tag on her big toe. The pathologist and his assistant wore stern expressions, so Luca dropped the polite smile and switched to studying the slip-resistant PVC floor. Random black spots made it look like someone had spilled paint. He hadn't worked with this particular pathology team before, so wasn't sure what to expect. Most were casual, but some liked to assert their authority.

He offered a hand to the forensic pathologist, who reciprocated with a firm grasp. The skin on the man's hand was smooth, his nails clean and trimmed, but his face looked like it had been parched in the sun too long and developed tiny fissures in the surface.

"Patterson, I'm Milton Eggles." His voice was as rough as gravel underfoot. He didn't bother introducing his assistant, but the man nodded at Luca.

"Have you had time to go over my notes, doctor?" Luca tried hard not to wrinkle his nose against the overpowering smell of stale tobacco that emanated from the pathologist.

Eggles opened a buff manila folder and resumed reading. "There didn't appear to be anything suspicious in the room where the deceased was found … but the next of kin insisted on a post-mortem. Correct?"

"Yes. My—um, the next of kin recently received threats and believes her mother was murdered, but there was no obvious sign of a struggle and I didn't find anything that looked out of place in the room."

"Hmm." Eggles swapped the folder for a bound booklet of photographs with Central Crime Scene printed on the front, along with the case number. "The body looks posed." He glanced up. "Nursing home staff?"

"Yes. The nurse who found the body repositioned it slightly for the next of kin to view. However, she did say Rosalie's head was tilted to the right, arms by her side, one leg bent."

"And the deceased had an existing TBI?"

Yep, Jack Roach had given her a traumatic brain injury, all right. "Despite the fact that the next of kin's suspicions are currently unsupported, I'd like as much evidence as possible preserved, because the body will be cremated."

Eggles pulled a metal glove over the latex one on his left hand and then added another layer of blue latex over the top. He reached up to switch on a sound-recording device that hung from the ceiling.

"Shall we get started?"

Luca stepped to the foot end of the table so he could watch the post-mortem without getting in the way. Although he'd never actually met Rosalie Jensen, knowing she was someone Mya cared about made it feel almost like watching someone he knew. His stomach roiled.

It also made him more determined to find out what had happened.

With hawk-like eyes and nimble fingers, Eggles inspected between each toe and methodically moved up the front of the body, swabbing orifices, taking scrapings from under nails, peering in the crooks of elbows and between fingers. The technician took photographs and handed equipment to Eggles as evidence needed collecting.

Luca turned his face as the pathologist examined the labia.

Throughout, the pathologist commented on his findings. When he reached Rosalie's face, he bent closer to study something.

Luca lifted onto his toes. "What is it?"

"There are three faint marks on her left cheek. Could be hematomas, but it's too early to tell. I'll need to view the body again tomorrow. Let's see if there is anything else on the head, shall we?"

Eggles opened the mouth and took various samples, including what appeared to be skin from between her teeth. Finally the team turned Rosalie over, and then Eggles combed her hair to release trace evidence. He made a fastidious search of her scalp and, as he scrutinized the area behind Rosalie's left ear, his head drew back sharply.

Luca moved to the pathologist's side again.

"Can you see this tiny red dot?" Eggles held hair out of the way so Luca could see.

"Yes. Needle mark?"

"Looks like it."

"That's not a usual injection site." A hundred possibilities, yet he'd have to wait for the report to be sure. Time wasted. Time enough for perpetrators to get away with murder.

"No, it's not. I'll order a full toxicology work-up, but I'll need a list of medications being administered at the nursing home."

"I'll speak to the director as soon as we're done here," Luca promised.

He stood to one side as the men turned Rosalie onto her back again for the internal examination. No matter how many post-mortems he attended, his stomach never failed to churn as the first incision was made from the right shoulder to the sternum and then down to the pubic bone.

Rosalie Jensen might actually be a murder victim. Everyone had to sign in and out of Rich Haven, so her attacker should be traceable—theoretically. Every employee just became a suspect, but he didn't get to be a good detective without going the extra mile. It was the people who came and went on a more casual basis who would be harder to track.

• • •

Luca locked the door to the interview room and dropped into a plastic chair opposite Willy Mason. He couldn't get an appointment with the Rich Haven director for an hour, so putting pressure on the only suspect he had in custody seemed like the best use of his time.

Even sitting, Willy was considerably taller than Luca. With his thick arms crossed in front of his chest, he was the epitome of cavalier, but the skin around his eyes was taut. Luca had left Willy in a police cell overnight to give him time to reflect on how alone he was in this mess.

Of course, he didn't have a scrap of evidence to link Melanie and Kevin to the jewelry scam, so he couldn't bring them in for questioning, but instinct told him they were connected to Willy somehow. Now all he had to do was prove it.

He pushed his chair back and paced the blue linoleum floor of the interview room, waiting for Willy to make the first move. It didn't take long.

"You can't keep me here forever."

"Oh, I don't intend to." With hands flat on the table, he leaned over Willy. "I'm just deciding whether or not to bump the charges up to murder."

"What the—" Willy jumped to his feet.

"Sit down," Luca spat. He straightened to his full height and held his hands tense at his side.

Willy grunted and flopped back into the chair. "This is bullshit."

"A resident at Rich Haven was murdered yesterday." He bluffed, because there was no way to be sure until the toxicology results came back, but it was the only leverage he had at this point.

"I don't know anything about anyone getting murdered. I told you, I just move the goods." Willy propped his elbows on the table, looking Luca in the eye.

It certainly *seemed* like he was telling the truth.

"Well, you'd better give me some information that leads to your accomplices real soon, because I'm getting sick of going around in circles with you, Willy."

The big man swallowed loudly. "Look, I went to Kevin's house once, but that's it."

"What was the address?"

"Um … it was in Holden Hill. List Street, I think."

At least Willy wasn't pulling his chain. "I've been there. You're going to have to tell me something I don't know."

"Bloody hell. I told you, I got my instructions from the mobile phone they gave me."

"The phone's been disconnected. What do you know about Melanie Lane?"

"She was at Kevin's house, but she stayed in another room. I didn't talk to her."

"That's a real shame, Willy, because you just made yourself worthless to me." Luca turned for the door.

"Wait!"

He looked over his shoulder.

Willy's voice went up an octave. "I don't know anything else."

Luca stepped over the threshold and locked the door behind him. He instructed the desk sergeant to charge Willy with forgery, theft, and battery. There was no way to make any other charges stick.

Yet.

•••

"Thanks for bringing me along. I didn't fancy sitting in the house all day." Mya picked up a wedge of seedless watermelon from the supermarket fruit bin and sniffed to appraise the sweetness.

"You're welcome," Kate assured her, putting brown field mushrooms into a paper bag.

She was pretty sure Kate didn't want to be stuck in the house with her either, but at least shopping was an opportunity to get them all out and Natalie away from the television.

Natalie wandered ahead of the trolley, more interested in the makeup and glittered coin purses that hung from hooks above the shelves than groceries. Mya felt sorry for her, having all this on her plate at nineteen, but she'd get over it. You could move on from inadvertently being involved in theft. What you couldn't move on from was the only person you'd ever cared for sitting in a floral armchair drooling for the rest of her life.

And now Mya didn't even have that.

Kate looked less severe out of her cop garb, wearing three-quarter pants and a turquoise T-shirt with *Little Miss Helpful* written in glitter across the chest.

"I take it you know Luca pretty well." Mya tried to appear barely interested in the conversation as she bagged fuzzy peaches.

"Well enough."

"He seems a bit arrogant, but he was attempting to sympathize with me this morning and mentioned his wife. Does he use the widower story a lot?"

Kate stopped in the middle of the aisle and turned, her lips pulled tight. Great, if she pissed off her ride, she might be stranded at the supermarket.

"Luca doesn't say anything unless he means it, and I think he's well qualified to understand what it's like to lose someone. At the end of Olivia's illness he gave up a lot." She turned her back and continued down the aisle.

Maybe she should stop talking, but she wanted to know what Kate meant. "Because he lost someone?" Plenty of people lost loved ones.

With a pronounced huff, Kate said, "Not that it's any of your business, but Luca nursed Olivia on her deathbed, and he refused to leave her side. It put a considerable dent in his career."

Wow. I never would have guessed that.

Kate's fingertips were several centimetres shy of a packet of breadcrumbs on the top shelf, so Mya grabbed it.

Now it made sense, why Luca took her to see her mum yesterday. He knew how important it would be to have that time with her. But seven years was a long time to play the field, which made him either a philanderer or damaged goods—despite what she'd seen of him, she had a hard time believing there was such a thing as a guy who'd be so devastated by losing his wife that he wouldn't move on in seven years.

It took her until the checkout line to get the next question out. "He didn't find someone else?"

Kate shrugged as she fed cans onto the conveyor belt. "Work is his life now."

Something to think on for sure, but she'd be watching for the real man underneath. The one who might show after a beer or two, or when the going got tough.

Chapter 30

The Rich Haven director showed Luca into his office, toddled around to his side of the big mahogany desk, and laboured to squeeze his sizeable frame into an executive chair. Sweat trickled down his temples and his suspenders heaved in and out in time with his breathing.

Luca sat in a leather tub chair and waited for him to settle.

Mr. Pratt took a sip of water. "Detective Patterson, my most trusted staff have been following your orders to a T, but I just don't think there's anything to find here."

"And I appreciate that, but I can be more specific now. I attended the post-mortem on Rosalie Jensen this morning. There was evidence of foul play."

The director shifted in his seat and dabbed a white handkerchief along his brow.

About time the smarmy bastard felt uncomfortable. Letting this sort of thing happen in his establishment was walking the line of negligence.

"There are a couple of constables in reception waiting to look at your drugs register, specifically anything that can be injected."

"Detective, I assume you realize what it means for Rich Haven if it turns out that a drug has been administered inappropriately and the information is made public?"

"I assume you understand what it means if one of your staff has committed murder?" He glared at the fidgeting man, and then took pity. "Of course, no information will be made public unless absolutely necessary."

"I appreciate your discretion. When can the guard be dismissed from Ms. Jensen's room? It's making some families nervous."

"I'll dismiss him when I'm finished here."

Outside the office, Old and Callum were shifting their weight uncomfortably from foot to foot. They were the same team that processed Rosalie's room yesterday, so they had an advantage on this search.

Luca spoke in a low voice. "We need to reconcile the drugs on hand with the register, look for anomalies, make sure the paper trail is airtight."

Ten minutes later, a young brunette nurse walked them through the dispensary.

"This is the register of controlled drugs on the premises," she said, handing Luca a red folder. "Only registered nurses can administer them and each transaction is recorded."

"Where are the drugs stored?"

"In this locked cabinet." She tapped on a metal cupboard with double doors.

"We're going to need access to that."

"Certainly, but I will need to stay in the room while it's open."

"That's fine. Constable Old will take stock of the cabinet contents while Senior Constable Callum takes a look at your purchasing records."

"I can show you electronic versions," the nurse said, "but if you want to see hard copies, you'll need to see Beverly. She does all the filing."

"I'll leave you boys to it." Luca nodded at the constables. "I need to step outside to make a few phone calls."

Twenty minutes later he arrived back in the medical supply room to glum faces. "What is it?"

Old shut the controlled drugs cabinet and shook his head. "Sir, there are two vials of something called succinylcholine missing. Callum checked the purchasing records and, during the past nine months, there is a deficit of six vials. He's gone to reception to get hard copy documents."

"Hell."

The nurse's head was bowed and her fists clenched in her lap.

"Can you explain how or where these vials have gone?" he asked gently.

She turned watery chocolate eyes on him, her bottom lip quivering. "I don't know. I really don't know. It's my responsibility, but I always sign the register."

"Who else has access to this cabinet?"

"There's a registered nurse rostered on for each shift, four of us in total, plus the director, of course. I don't understand how this could happen. We reconcile the stock regularly."

"How often?"

"Biannually. Oh! I was on holidays the last time an audit was due, so someone else would have done it. Beverly can tell you who." A tear trickled down her rosy cheek.

"Can you tell me what you use succini—whatever that drug is called, for?"

"It's a neuromuscular blocking agent used for anaesthesia. We call it Sux for short and it's a Schedule-8 poison, so only a registered nurse can administer it. We keep it on hand for when we occasionally have to intubate patients." Her voice caught.

Luca kept his voice as low as possible. "You've been a great help. Why don't you lock the cabinet and take a break? The constables and I will visit Beverly."

The nurse bobbed her head up and down, turned the key in the cabinet, and shuffled out the door.

Old flicked through the pages of the register as they walked back to reception. "It seems one nurse made entries in the register more often than the others. Mightn't be anything, but I'll check it out."

Callum was at the photocopier behind the reception desk and waved his colleagues over. "Found some interesting stuff in the purchasing records. It seems the drug that went missing is rarely used, but four were ordered two months ago and another four two months before that. Adding those to the last *confirmed* number from an audit twelve months ago—there are a total of six vials unaccounted for."

The hairs on Luca's arms and scalp stood up. Six vials could mean six victims. Maybe Mya's suspicions had some basis after all. Good for the case, bad for her.

"I asked Beverly to show me the audit done six months ago." Callum shook his head. "Nothing. It seems each person thought someone else was doing it."

Luca looked at his watch. "You two stick at it. Get copies of anything and everything you think will be helpful, send samples of handwriting to forensics for comparison, and talk to the other three registered nurses. I'll brief the rest of the team if you can't get back to the station by four."

He wouldn't have time to get back to Kate's house and check on Mya, although he desperately wanted to. It had been a challenge to stay focused all day with visions of her hunting down Rhonda on her own plaguing him. With any luck she had taken his advice and stayed put. Whether she was coping, he was less confident about.

• • •

Mya turned metal skewers under the grill and pulled warm plates from the oven.

"You didn't have to do this," Kate said for the hundredth time.

"I know, and you didn't have to let me stay here. I want to say thanks and food is how I do it best."

Kate hovered by the sink.

"You can tip the rice into the colander and give it a rinse, if you like," Mya said as she stirred a caramel-coloured brew in a saucepan and turned off the gas flame under the wok.

She spread four warm plates across the bench and spooned a line of rice onto each, arranged two chicken skewers on top, and drizzled satay sauce over them, pouring the remainder into a gravy boat. Then she piled stir-fried vegetables on the side. "Grub's up," she called as she carried plates to the table.

Everyone took their seats and dug in. Kate's husband was as aloof as he'd been since they arrived.

They turned to the sound of a knock on the glass sliding door. Luca waved from the other side, making Mya's heart flutter. She turned her attention back to serving the food, trying to suppress the unwelcome excitement at seeing him. It must be because he'd have more information about her mum. That was it.

Kate let Luca in. "You're in time for dinner," she said.

"Thanks." He slid into a chair beside Natalie.

Mya reached for another plate and served a meal for Luca. Luckily, she'd made extra. With a plate balanced on her forearm and one in each hand, she carried them to the table.

"That's tricky," Natalie commented.

"Years in hospitality." Mya chose the empty chair opposite Luca in preference to sitting beside him. More chance to look at him and less of inadvertently brushing against him.

"Looks good," Luca said.

The meal was mostly undertaken in silence. Natalie kept her eyes on her plate, occasionally spinning a costume ring around her finger. Luca picked up a skewer with his finger and pulled chicken off the end with his teeth. It was probably her imagination, but his face looked different today. Softer. Kinder. What would it be like to have someone care so deeply about you that he'd nurse you on your deathbed?

"These veggies are delicious." Kate nodded her approval. "Nice and crisp. What flavour's on them?"

Mya smiled her appreciation. "Ginger, garlic, and oyster sauce." At the Croydon Hotel, she didn't get to see the pleasure her food brought to people. It was nice to watch their faces.

Luca put his cutlery down. "So, Natalie, a couple of families at Rich Haven came forth to report fake jewelry. I'd like to take you to the station tomorrow and see if they are pieces you made. The more evidence we have against Willy, the more firmly we can make the charges stick."

Natalie nodded and fingered her crisp, white collar. "Sure, that's good." It sounded like she was asking.

"It would help if you could remember any visitors to the Mason house, or conversations you overheard. I need to find Willy's partners fast."

"I've been thinking, but I don't remember nothing."

"Even the smallest detail can help." Luca pressed for more.

Natalie's mouth turned down and a pattern formed on her rigid chin. "Luca, do I have to go to the old people's house next week?"

He chewed his tongue as he scrutinized her. "No. No you don't. You can live wherever you like, but I didn't think you had any other options."

"I don't." Natalie slumped.

The young woman had a lot of grown-up decisions ahead of her and no one to help her make them. Mya's heart gave a little squeeze.

"I can understand your trepidation, but this really is a good opportunity," Luca told her. "These folks are very nice, and they'll make sure you're well looked after. They'll help you find a job, and when you're on your feet they'll help you find more suitable accommodation. It's not a detention centre."

"Will Willy know where I'm staying?"

"Definitely not. Although you won't be officially protected, the folks who run the place are very discreet. And I'll give you my mobile number, so if you ever feel threatened, you can call me."

That was very generous of him.

"Shall we adjourn to the family room?" Kate stood to clear the plates.

Natalie took up residence in front of the TV, while Mya turned off the oven and served sticky date pudding with blobs of ice-cream. Conversation died for a few minutes as everyone savoured the rich dessert.

Once he'd finished, Luca extracted a folder from his backpack. "Kate, can we speak in private for a minute?"

Mya narrowed her eyes as the two headed out the back door and sat at a plastic table. They huddled around papers, brows furrowed. A couple of times they glanced at her, which she took as confirmation they were talking about her. Well, he wasn't the only one who could keep secrets.

When they came back inside, Luca announced, "Well, it's time to catch some shuteye. Are you ladies ready to head to the motel?"

"Thanks for everything, Kate." Mya had no doubt her hostess was glad to see the back of her and Natalie.

There was an instant sinking feeling in her gut as Luca picked up their bags and headed outside. She should be glad to get out of Kate's place, but she didn't know how safe she'd feel without two cops coming and going. And if Rhonda had located her house, then who was to say she couldn't find the motel?

Chapter 31

Mya rode shotgun in Luca's Corolla, so Natalie got the back seat. There were things she wanted to ask him, but not with the teenager within earshot. Instead, she rested her temple on the cold window and watched the night slide past. The black background was washed with colours from the streetlights and shop windows, running into one another in the glistening puddles. The windscreen started to fog with three people in the car, so Luca turned the air-conditioner on low.

"Sorry, the air's too warm. It'll only take a few minutes."

Mya shrugged. His distinctive woody, cinnamon fragrance circulated through the confined space and wreaked havoc with her already fragile emotions. When she was around him, she had an overwhelming urge to touch. She'd preserved the memory of his warm, silky flesh under her fingers and drew on it now. Let it affect each of her senses.

As a distraction, she turned on the CD player and a familiar song blared from the speakers.

"Meteora. No way." Luca had her all-time favourite band in his CD player.

"Only the best."

The Vale Apartments were at the edge of suburbia, on the corner of a rural road, with tall Alexandra palms along the driveway. Luca maneuvered through a brick arch and stopped in the visitors' park. Mya's gaze followed him into the glass-walled reception, where he hit the bell on the counter. A woman appeared.

"He's nice, huh?"

Mya turned in her seat to look at Natalie, who absent-mindedly spun a rainbow of metal bangles around her arm. "Yeah, he's pretty hot."

Natalie giggled. "You fancy him, don't you?"

Inside the reception area, Luca pulled a wallet from his shirt pocket and passed a plastic card to the woman behind the counter. The man sure looked fine in those tight jeans and crisp shirt.

"What makes you say that?" Mya asked.

"The way you look at him."

"Mmm."

"He fancies you, too."

Mya snorted. "Yeah, like he fancies anything in a skirt."

"Nah. He's gentle with you."

Her mouth opened, but there was no smartarse remark on the tip of her tongue, so she shut it again. Gentle. It wasn't a word she usually associated with men. Why would a man be gentle with a woman? She had no experience to draw on.

Her mum had told her Cockroach had been charming when they first met. Apparently he was *gentle* when he courted her, but he changed. Men couldn't be trusted.

Luca got back into the car. "Number thirteen. Hope no one's superstitious."

"I'll pay you for the room," Mya said, turning her attention back to the nightscape.

"Yeah, sure. No hurry."

The three-bedroom apartment had a small lounge room with a plaid couch and old box TV, a four-seater pine table and pristine white kitchenette. Not bad. It might be like a holiday; she'd never had one of those. A vacation with a bunch of people she hardly knew and someone trying to kill her. Yeah, sounded like a hoot.

Luca pushed open the first bedroom door.

"Do you want to choose a room?" he asked.

She shrugged. He deposited Natalie's bag on the bed and took Mya's to the next room.

Back in the lounge room, Natalie had already installed herself on the couch, kicked off her shoes, and turned on the TV.

"Okay, ladies, I'll leave you to it. Make sure you keep your mobile phones on you at all times, in case I need to get hold of you, and lock the door behind me."

Mya followed him outside and shut the door so Natalie couldn't hear them. "I have a couple of questions."

"Sure." Luca leaned against the building and pulled the band from his hair, releasing long, blond waves.

It softened his face and distracted Mya from her train of thought.

"What do you want to talk about?"

"How did the autopsy go today?"

"Oh." He stared at his hands as they twisted back and forth. "Fine. We found a couple of unusual marks, but nothing conclusive yet. I'll let you know when I have more information."

He pushed the cuticles back on his left hand using his right thumbnail, but he wouldn't look at her. All the signs of a liar.

"Did you find out anything about Rhonda?"

"I've got Kate working on it and she found records for a Rhonda Morten who lived in Murray Bridge a decade ago. There are no records of her ever having lived with your fath—"

"Cockroach," she corrected. "The bastard was never any kind of father."

"Jack," he amended. "But the trail dead-ends a couple of years later. I'm assuming she married, but Kate hasn't picked up the trail yet."

She traced a finger along the rough mortar between the bricks. "Do you have a photo of her? I can't remember what she looks like."

Luca crossed his arms and fixed her with a hard glare. For several minutes he just stared, as though trying to extract information straight from her brain. "Mya, I know you want revenge, but you need to be patient. There isn't any evidence this woman killed Rosalie, and I don't want you going on some vigilante mission."

"I don't need evidence to know it's her."

Luca's jaw clenched.

She took a deep breath. "But I can understand it's needed. It would help if I knew what she looked like these days, in case she follows me or something."

"Sure. I'll see if Kate has a picture. I could speak to the inspector about putting a guard on this place if it'll make you feel safer."

"No. It's not a matter of feeling safe." She lied. "When do you think I'll be able to cremate Mum?"

Luca's voice was so soft it drew her attention. "The coroner's office should release her in the next few days. They'll let Rich Haven know as soon as they do. Do you want me to go with you to make the arrangements?"

The crow's feet at the edges of his eyes were gone, his eyebrows raised in question. It was nice of him to offer, but she shook her head. Goosebumps ran up her arms, so she wrapped them around herself.

"You're cold." He stepped forward and rubbed his palms up and down her bare arms. "You should go inside."

He said it but didn't move. His warm touch instantly simmered her blood right to her core. She studied the faint line of stubble along his cheek to the corner of his mouth, over the curve of his lip to the top of the Cupid's bow. When she looked up, his steely gaze flicked between her eyes and mouth in silent question.

She lifted onto her toes and pressed her lips to his. Her eyes closed, lips parted, and her hands slid around to his firm butt. After a moment of hesitation, his hands moved to the small of her back. Looks like he remembered their lust-filled morning, too.

Suddenly he pulled back. His hands rested lightly on her hips, but there was cold space between them. "I'm sorry. I shouldn't. You're still grieving."

She pursed her lips and, with two fingers in his belt loops, dragged him closer. With her hands clasped firmly behind his neck, she kissed him again. His lips were warm and pliable against hers. She deftly pushed him against his car and put her knees on the bonnet to straddle him.

He rested his head against her cheek, and hot breath trickled down her neck, making her shiver with delight. Soft lips trailed damp kisses behind her ear and down her neck as she untucked his shirt and stroked the silky warmth of his waist, the curves of his chest, and down his flat stomach. The muscles there twitched.

Their lips brushed lightly, tongues skated across teeth and then twisted together. Right now she wanted him to throw her on the hood of his car and screw her until she forgot everything wrong in her life, but the kiss was becoming less urgent.

"Mya," he whispered into her hair, holding her tight. "You have no idea how much I want to do this, but I can't."

She felt a pang of something she'd never experienced before: self-consciousness perhaps. Here she was throwing herself at this man, for the second time—something else she'd never done before—and he wanted to stop. The rejection smarted and annoyance set in.

"Can't" had never stopped *her* from doing what she wanted, so she slid a hand between them and rested it on his erection. Luca retrieved it and kissed the palm. He grinned and tucked a wisp of hair behind her ear.

"You're a very beautiful and sexy woman, but this isn't the right time. It wouldn't be professional."

"Bloody cops." She grunted her disproval and slid off his lap, wrapping her arms around her body again.

Luca sighed and pulled her into his embrace. "Mya, I want you." He kissed her forehead. "Maybe, if you still want to once this mess is over ..." He left the suggestion hanging, brushed his lips across hers once more, and got into his car.

With her back now against the warm brick wall of the apartment, she watched him leave, and stood there for a long time after he'd gone.

Chapter 32

With a milky coffee pressed between his palms, Luca sat on his back doorstep. Only wispy white remnants of yesterday's storm clouds remained in the sky. A vivid blue wren and its dull brown mate flitted in and out of a flowering grevillea, with a neighbour's cat watching from beneath a wheelbarrow.

The whir of a pushbike's tires whizzed down the back alley, and its rider trailed a stick along the corrugated fence. *Click clack, click clack.* The cat fled across the lawn and over the fence, leaving the wrens panting silently in the bush.

Luca closed his eyes and soaked up the sun's warmth. How Mya was coping worried him. She was just the type to want to right perceived wrongs. Violently. And he just kept complicating things. What the hell was he thinking, kissing her last night? She'd looked so vulnerable, he'd wanted to comfort her, that's what; and a whole lot more, but it wouldn't be professional to take it any further while she was under his protection. It didn't matter what *he* wanted, only what she needed.

This case was really messing with his head, not to mention his vacation. As the second hand on his watch ticked nine o'clock, Luca headed inside to boot up his laptop. He dialed the mortuary and patiently negotiated his way past the receptionist. Finally a voice like stones going down a ceramic pipe came on the line.

"Good morning, Patterson. Like I told you yesterday, I will do my best to get Rosalie Jensen's report to you by Tuesday, and phoning me every day isn't going to help."

The forensic pathologist coughed so hard, Luca had to wait until he finished to be heard.

"I appreciate your assistance, Eggles, but I'm not phoning to hassle you. New information has come to light, and I want to request a test for succinyl—Crap, I can't say it. The nurse called it Sux."

"Succinylcholine?"

"Yes, that's it."

"Well, that's going to take more time. Plasma was sent to Central Crime Scene with the other samples, so I'll order the test as a matter of urgency. Are you coming to look at those marks on Rosalie Jensen's face later this morning?"

"I'll be there, thank you."

Luca opened Internet Explorer on his laptop and typed *succinylcholine* into the search window. The forensic results could take many days. Time enough for the killer to hide his or her tracks. If he was more familiar with the drug, he might figure out why someone chose it. Was it merely convenient, or did the murderer have another purpose that was yet to be exposed? Finding the reason would put him a step closer to solving this case, and getting retribution for Mya.

• • •

A deafening electronic wind chime sounded and Mya cringed into the floral couch.

"Hang on a minute, dear. I'll just see who that is." Doreen Ballinger waddled out of the lounge room, dusting scone crumbs from her lips.

Mya had spent the morning knocking on doors in Railway Terrace, asking her neighbours if they'd seen anything unusual on Saturday before the bomb went off. The cops had already done the rounds, but she had doubts that investigations in Croydon got a lot of their time.

Doreen's whole home seemed to have yellowed with age, from the custard-coloured wallpaper to the ochre carpet. Even the wood furniture looked tea-stained in the dim light. A low but familiar voice resounded from down the hall. She put her plate of scones on the doilied side table.

What the hell was Luca doing here? He must've seen Kate's Torana outside.

Damn, I should've waited until after I'd been to Rich Haven.

"If you don't mind, I'll have a quick word with her." Luca appeared in the doorway with a crimson face and clenched fists.

She stood and met him halfway across the room.

"What the hell are you doing?" He growled.

There was no call for that savage undertone. Her hands went to her hips uninvited. "Doing your job, I guess."

The grinding of his teeth was almost humourous.

"Davey already interviewed everyone on this street. You are not supposed to be gallivanting around, when there's a target on your back—"

"I can go wherever—"

"—and sticking your nose into the investigation isn't going to help things move any faster."

"Is everything all right, dear?" Doreen materialized from behind Luca's shoulder.

He stepped aside and took a deep breath. Ha, couldn't let the civilians see him losing control.

"How about we take this outside, Mya?"

"I haven't finished my scone," she said petulantly. "Besides, Doreen was just telling me a very interesting story about a car parked out front of my house the morning of the explosion."

Luca did a double take.

"I think Luca has just changed his mind about having a cup of tea and a scone," Mya told Doreen.

The old lady busied herself serving Luca, while he rocked from foot to foot uncomfortably.

"Why don't you take a seat, detective?" Doreen handed him a cup and saucer. "Now where was I? Oh yes, there was a white car parked in front of Mya's house at about 11 o'clock in the morning."

Predictably, Luca went into cop mode. Mya smiled. Now she had his attention.

"Did you notice what make of car it was?" he asked.

"Oh, I'm not very good with those kinds of things, dear, but I did notice some of the numbers on the registration plate."

"That's excellent news." He shot Mya an apologetic look but ruined it by narrowing his eyes afterward, as though he'd just remembered he was angry with her.

"Yes, that's what young Mya said." Doreen sat back down and arranged her pleated skirt tidily. "The hood of the car was up and it was making an awful racket for about five minutes."

"Sounds like a fanbelt slipping," Mya offered.

Luca nodded. "Could be a deliberate diversion."

"Do you mind me asking why you didn't tell Constable Davey this when he knocked on your door?"

Doreen chewed her bottom lip. "I didn't want to make trouble for young Mya, and I really didn't think it was related to the explosion. Will I be in trouble?"

"No, of course not. I'm just glad you've come forward now. Did you see the driver at all?"

"Oh yes, dear. It was a redheaded woman, but I thought it was odd, because she didn't seem interested in fixing the car. At first I assumed she was waiting for a roadside service, but after a while she just shut the hood and took off."

"She wasn't trying to hide at all?"

"No, but I didn't get a good look at her face. I didn't want to be too nosy and go outside."

He took note of the partial plate number. "I'll have someone check this out. Did you hear a window break at all? That's how the perps gained entry to the house."

"I'm afraid not, dear."

Doreen saw Mya and Luca to the front door, forcing packages of wrapped scones into their hands. They waved goodbye and Mya made for the Torana. No such luck.

"Wait a minute," Luca called from the footpath.

Just what she needed, another lecture from the sexy detective.

"I can't concentrate on solving these crimes if I'm worried about you running around town unprotected."

She ignored him and got in the car. It was nice to know that he thought about her when she wasn't with him, but it wasn't going to stop a lifetime of looking out for number one.

He knocked on the window and she wound it down.

"Thanks for sharing the information. I'll get Davey to chase it down."

"You're welcome," she said.

"Are you going back to the apartment now?"

"No." The prompt rise of colour up his throat made her smirk. "I have an appointment at Rich Haven, remember?"

"Oh, with the funeral director, that's right. Are you sure you don't want me to come along for moral support?"

A short shake of the head, and she turned the engine over. End of conversation.

• • •

As soon as Mya was out of sight, Luca dialed Davey to relay the partial plate number. Damn, Mya was infuriating, but there was no denying that she'd just outmaneuvered him. Her redhead theory was looking more likely. Kate needed to work double-time on finding out where Rhonda Roach was.

This mess was getting stickier by the minute. Every fact he acquired made the resolution seem further away instead of closer. What he was sure of was that he needed to put all of these elements together before another body turned up—like Mya's. But rudimentary bombs and childish threats still didn't seem to fit with stealth murders.

•••

The car on the side road rolled forward and Mya swerved to avoid being knocked off her motorbike. She immediately felt silly, because she wasn't on the Triumph, but behind the wheel of Kate's gold Torana. The tires squealed and the driver of the other vehicle gave her a funny look.

Driving a car felt strange. At least it was a manual, which made her feel more at home. Luca had warned her to go straight to Rich Haven and back, no side trips.

Bossy cop.

She squinted into the morning sun as the car banged over speed humps. Dozens of people walked in the manicured gardens with their elderly relatives in wheelchairs and walking frames. A lump stuck in her throat. On a day like today, she would've taken her mum to the lake for sure.

She'd let Rosalie down in the worst way. The least she could do was face the consequences.

Her feet dragged across the pavement of the car park, as though conspiring with her resolve, to keep her from the task ahead. An undertaking that would make her worst nightmare real.

The colours of the building were vivid in the bright light—tabby-cat stone walls, black filigree, and white-washed quoins. Too cheerful for today's mission. A lump momentarily choked her.

No, she could do this.

The smile evaporated from Beverly Aldridge's face when she looked up. Mya's cheeks burned with the memory of her vociferous collapse and accusations two days ago. Hell, it felt like forever ago.

"Hi, Bev. I'm here to see the funeral director."

The older woman tilted her head and offered a sympathetic smile. "I'll call her down."

"Do I need to sign in?" It felt weird asking, but she didn't know what the protocol was now that …

"If you don't mind." Bev dialed the phone.

Mya signed the register and took a seat, hands clasped on her lap. It was stupid to feel self-conscious. She'd been coming here for nearly a decade. A few minutes later a fifty-something woman in a navy skirt-suit appeared from the eastern hallway. She beamed with a set of too-perfect teeth, like she was having the time of her life. Her perky, Jane Fonda hairstyle had wedding quantities of hairspray holding every crunchy piece in place.

"Miss Jensen, I'm Penny Oliver, the resident funeral director. I'm sorry for your loss. Why don't we go into the boardroom, so we can have some privacy?"

Penny's steps were quick and short as she laboured against her tight skirt and ten-centimetre heels. Mya followed in jeans and sandshoes.

"You really are lucky that Rosalie had the forethought to pre-arrange her funeral."

Mya didn't bother correcting her. She'd arranged it herself, after some prompting from Bev. Never did she have the chance to ask her mum what she wanted.

Penny continued to chatter. "It's not something people want to think about when they're healthy, but it's inevitable. Believe me, it saves family members a lot of heartache when the time comes."

What she wouldn't give to stick her toe in front of Penny's stilettos and watch the perky woman sprawl on the carpet. Instead Mya pressed her lips tighter together.

The boardroom was almost bigger than her house, with a dark wood table and twenty-two high-backed chairs around it. Penny held out a chair at the end, where there was a silver tray with water glasses on it. Then she angled into her own seat, uncomfortably close to Mya. She produced a crisp sheet of paper from a leather compendium.

"Now, I need to check the information compiled eight years ago." Penny droned on about the chapel, music, readings, flowers, and the cremation.

None of it would bring her mum back. It was all Mya could do to stop herself from covering her ears and screaming. Her gaze drifted to the window and the manicured gardens. A decade of memories, yet she hoped she'd never set foot in the place again after the funeral.

"Are you sure you don't want a priest to say a few words?"

With her attention focused on the slender canes of a willow tree swaying in the breeze, Mya said, "What's the point? No God ever watched over her while she was alive."

"Or a wake?"

"Mum's gone. No amount of wasting money will bring her back."

"It's a good way to say goodbye. You don't have to have an open casket or anything."

"There's no one to come but me."

The funeral director sighed and offered Mya a tissue.

She hadn't realized she was crying. "I'll say goodbye to her, but no wake."

"And I believe we're waiting on the coroner's office to release the body."

Mya flinched. "Yes."

"Okay, there's nothing more I need. I can assure you, your mother's funeral will be dignified and tranquil."

They shook hands, and Mya hurried to get the hell out of there.

Chapter 33

Luca watched the pathology technician open a stainless steel door on the mortuary refrigerator and slide Rosalie Jensen's body halfway out. Eggles bent to study her face through a lighted magnifying glass.

"There are three faint peri-mortem bruises on her left cheek, vaguely oval in shape. Ruler, please."

The assistant handed it over.

"Evenly spaced, approximately two centimetres apart, but not in a straight line. Detective, would you like to take a closer look?"

Luca stepped forward to examine the bruises. The centre mark was closer to the nose and the right mark the farthest away. "What do you think caused them?"

"Hmm." The pathologist moved the magnifying glass over the area again. "I'm not sure." He tilted Rosalie's head to the right. "There's another bruise here." He pointed to a butterfly-shaped mark halfway down the side of her neck.

"Looks like an ink blot. It's not like any weapon mark I've seen before." Luca imagined what would make this configuration of bruises.

Eggles photographed it.

"Wait!" Luca gasped. "May I try something?"

"Be my guest."

Luca slipped on a pair of blue latex gloves. He forgot to breathe through his mouth and the persistent scent of decay stuck between his teeth. He huffed it back out. With his head tilting from one side to the other, he still couldn't piece together the situation that might have unfolded in Rosalie's bedroom. He spread the fingers of his left hand and touched her cheek. The oval bruises almost exactly matched his fingertips.

"Yes, you're right," Eggles agreed, "but what about the neck?"

Luca positioned his left hand and arm in various directions, but nothing aligned.

"What about this?" Eggles stood beside Rosalie's head. "If I were going to inject someone behind the ear, I would ..." He touched fingertips to her left cheek and lowered his palm over the butterfly bruise. "That's it."

They exchanged a knowing look. Rosalie resisted, so her assailant had to hold her face. Without being asked, the assistant handed over a measuring tape and his boss measured the distance between the palm and fingerprints.

"This will give us an idea of the size of the assailant's hand."

"Looks short enough to be a woman," Luca speculated.

Hell, Mya might just be right about Rosalie being murdered. In that case, he needed to keep an even closer eye on her. It was reasonable to assume the perp would want to finish off what the bombing didn't accomplish.

...

The apartment was empty when Mya returned from Rich Haven. She flopped face first onto the too-hard bed. There were decades of memories of her mum, and they were all she had now. So many events had machinated to bring her to this point in her life, but she couldn't regret them all. Without the pain and tears and degradation, she wouldn't have had this much time with her mum.

She'd once felt sorry for Cockroach after his mother died from a burst appendix. No one found her until it was too late. An appendix seemed too small and insignificant an organ to cause such a catastrophe in their lives.

Mya had been too young to really understand his grief, but now she owned it. The clogged feeling between her ears, the hollowness in her chest, the gut-wrenching pain of losing the most important person in her life. It was no wonder Jack had been unable to love the people who were still in his life. Self-preservation was a powerful thing.

Rosalie had wanted to live. Mya had seen it in her eyes. If only she could be sure her mum hadn't known what was happening to her in the end, and hadn't suffered.

The stench of disinfectant from Rich Haven lingered on her skin, and the pillow beneath her face smelled of an unfamiliar detergent. She used it to muffle a scream.

After the funeral she was going home, no matter what Luca said. She wouldn't live in fear. Rhonda could go to hell. There was nothing more the bitch could take from her anyway. Better still, she'd hunt her down and make sure the redhead never hurt anyone ever again.

She must have lain on the bed for a long time, because by the time her eyes and mind came back into focus, the sun was low enough to blind her through the window. A flock of pink and grey galahs fossicked on the lawn for insects. They took flight in a swirl of hoarse squawks as a car pulled up.

Car doors shut and the front door of the apartment opened. Luca, Kate, and Natalie were talking in the kitchen. A kettle boiled and then the bedroom door opened.

"Would you like a cuppa, Mya?" Kate asked.

For a moment she seriously considered pretending to be asleep. "No, thanks."

"I picked up some dinner. Thought it'd be good to eat together, so we can go over what we found today."

"I don't want dinner. I don't want anything."

The door closed with a soft click and footsteps retreated down the hall.

• • •

"Is Mya all right?" Luca asked as Kate reappeared.

"Hard to tell. She wants to be alone and doesn't want dinner."

"I knew someone should've gone with her to Rich Haven." He shook his head.

"She's independent, Luca. There has never been anyone else to rely on."

Kate pulled Indian food from a plastic bag and dumped it in the middle of the dining table while Luca searched the cupboards for plates and cutlery.

Natalie pointed the remote control at the TV and flopped onto the couch. Had she always watched this much TV? It couldn't be healthy. He sniffed his hands. The stench of powder-coated latex gloves lingered, so he washed them yet again.

Kate sidled up to him and whispered, "How did Natalie go today?"

"Good. She recognized quite a few pieces of jewelry that Rich Haven families turned in, so we have plenty of evidence on that front. Unfortunately, she didn't have any new information about how the operation worked or the other members. Did you dig up anything interesting?"

Luca poured Coke into four glasses and Kate dished out pappadams.

"As a matter of fact, I did." She flashed him a sly smile. "I found a property owned by Rhonda Morten."

"You mean before the trail dead-ends?"

"No, I mean she still owns it."

His heart rate quickened, but he didn't want to hope.

"She bought a property in Birdwood and there is no record of its sale. I dug deeper and the rates and utilities are being paid regularly, but it doesn't look like anyone lives there."

"You drove out there? Today?" He tore four squares from a roll of paper towel in lieu of serviettes.

"Yep. I only got back at five. I've got the Fraud Squad tracing the bank account where payments are coming from."

"Good work." He high-fived her.

"Do you want to turn that thing off and have some dinner?" Kate frowned at Natalie before returning to their conversation. "Did you get any new information from Willy?"

"I'm keeping up the pressure, but he's not talking. I-I've got some bad news, though." He concentrated on a hangnail but felt Kate's gaze on him. "The Rich Haven director phoned this afternoon. Kevin and Melanie didn't show for work today. I put a car on Kevin's and Evan's houses, but no luck."

"Damn! They've done a runner." Kate banged her fist on the table.

"There's nothing we can do about it. There just isn't any concrete evidence of their involvement." He pulled his hair band out and dragged fingers through to separate the strands.

"Oh, I almost forgot that Davey wanted me to pass on a message. He traced the car parked out front of Mya's house. It was a rental and the ID used to hire it was fake," Kate said.

"Of course it was. You know, I was thinking earlier that the whole stalking thing didn't fit with the scam at Rich Haven. Now I'm not so sure. Going to the trouble of having a fake ID and hiring a car so it can't be traced shows significant planning. Not what I'd expect from your average stalker."

Natalie slid silently into a seat, and he watched her play with her food.

"What about Mya?" Natalie asked.

He sighed. "I'll see if I can get her to come eat something."

He tapped on her bedroom door and, after a moment of silence, opened it. Mya lay facing the window, so he took her still-packed bag off a vinyl chair and sat so he could see her face. Her hair was flayed like a halo on the pillow and, despite her puffy face, she looked beautiful. Seeing her vulnerable like this was disarming. It would be nice to hold her tight and make her feel safe, but she might be too fragile for even that after today.

It was comical how much his perception of her had changed. A week ago he was sure she was involved in a scam, a belief that was intensified by her prickly personality. Now he appreciated where she was coming from. She'd fought for everything she had and was let down—by her father, the law—and still she had the spirit to empower other downtrodden women. There was something deeply attractive about a person who could rise above so much crap.

"Did you get everything organized today?" he asked her.

She nodded, but her eyes remained focused somewhere outside the window. He was intimately familiar with the stages of grieving. She was still in shock and he was worried about what she'd do when she reached the anger stage. For that reason, he wouldn't tell her about the Sux yet. Poison going missing was likely to explode the pressure cooker.

"I should've moved Mum as soon as I got the first letter from Rhonda," she whispered, eyes glistening.

Guilt.

"It's only natural to feel that way, but none of this is your fault. I know you're in pain right now, but I promise it'll get better."

"When?"

"Maybe a long time, but it will get better." He placed a hand on her forearm and their gazes met.

Mya sighed. "You think I should get up and have dinner with everyone."

"You need to do what feels right for you."

"Nothing feels right."

"Then live each moment as it comes. I know it's excruciating right now, but it'll get better, eventually."

Ha! Who was he to give advice? Olivia had been dead seven years and he'd only now made a real effort to move on. Ironically, it was Mya who'd stirred in him a desire to find love again. The one woman in Australia who was least likely to want him; after all, he embodied everything she hated—authority figures, men, and he'd lied to her about who he was when they'd first met. It would be just his luck to find a hot chick he actually liked, living two doors from him, and not be able to be with her. Not to mention she could well spend seven years doing her own mourning.

But she was the most resilient person he'd ever met, so there was hope.

Chapter 34

Luca pulled an A4 pad of lined paper from under a pile of manila folders on his work desk, and flipped it over to a fresh page. With a scrawling hand, he jotted key points about his case, hoping to make some sense of it, or see a link where he hadn't before.

There was a knock at the door and Old appeared.

"Good morning. What can I do for you?" Luca waved a hand at the spare chair in his office and watched all seven feet of the man fold awkwardly onto it. Old ran two fingers along a short ginger moustache and opened the folder he held.

"Casual day?" He nodded at Luca's jeans.

"I don't intend staying long."

"Half your luck. Fraud Squad examined the estates of the deceased women, as you requested."

"Already? Great. What did they find?"

As Old bowed his head, the polished skin on either side of his deep widow's peak gleamed. "Six women bequeathed money to Spurious Enterprises shortly before they died. At first glance it looks like a legitimate charity."

"But?" Luca was on the edge of his seat, biting hard on the end of his pen.

"But the function of the charity is listed differently on each bequest. So we dug a little deeper. In one instance Spurious Enterprises is listed as supporting cancer research. The husband of the woman making the bequest died of lung cancer."

"No shit?" Luca pushed his chair back and paced the room. Surely this was the break he'd been waiting for.

"In another instance Spurious Enterprises was an animal welfare organisation. Guess who the woman making the bequest lived with before going into Rich Haven?" Old didn't wait for a response. "Twenty-seven cats."

"Wow."

"You see where I'm going with this."

"Did you link this bogus charity to Melanie Lane or Kevin Walker?"

"That's where the good news ends. The director of Spurious Enterprises is Evan Smith We're still working on an address."

"I can tell you that," Luca said. "I've seen Evan Smith's house. Good work, Old."

The constable levered himself out of the chair and passed the file over. He ducked under the doorframe on his way out.

Luca put his office phone on loudspeaker and rested the handset on the desk as he sorted mail. There was hardly any desk visible under the mound of paperwork.

"Your call is important to us. Please hold and the next available operator will be with you shortly."

Luca shook his head. How could forensics be backlogged first thing in the morning? Hopefully it meant they'd found a match to the handwriting on the Sux order dockets.

While he waited, he made three piles of mail: urgent, vaguely interesting, handball, and the rest slid over the edge of the desktop into a bin. An invitation to the upcoming long service awards dinner went into the second pile.

Luca's mobile chirped and he retrieved it from his top pocket with two fingers. "Patterson."

"Eggles here. I have your toxicology results."

"Good timing. I'm on the other line to your office. You could have faxed the information." With the mobile pressed to his ear, Luca hung up the office phone.

"The results are being faxed as we speak, so you can look through them at your leisure, but I thought you might have some questions."

Luca's office chair squeaked as he sat forward. "What did you find?"

Eggles muffled the handset as he coughed violently. When he finally recovered, his voice was even rougher. "Sorry. Rosalie Jensen tested positive for succinylcholine and I could find no reason for it to be administered to her. Given the hidden injection site, I have to conclude that the elevated reading indicates intentional poisoning."

"Shit!" Luca gulped the bitter saliva that pooled in his mouth. The hairs on his forearm stood on end. "Can you tell me exactly how this drug works?"

"Succinylcholine is difficult to detect, because it metabolizes quickly. In fact, reliable testing was only developed during the last decade and requires advanced high-pressure liquid chromatography equipment.

"It's a powerful paralytic drug and a large enough dose will cease respiration. It doesn't cross the blood-brain barrier, so there is no alteration to consciousness or pain perception. The victim is unable to move or speak and is likely to experience extreme panic. Full paralysis occurs within thirty seconds, and then the heart races to keep the brain functioning, but fails within minutes."

"The murderer would have time to torment the victim without them being able to respond," Luca whispered.

"Yes. It's *not* a nice way to die." The pathologist paused. "If you have any more questions, feel free to call me."

"I will. Thanks."

Luca stared at a blob of red on a white canvas with a single yellow line running through it, hanging on the wall. He hated modern art and this piece reminded him of something piercing a heart. There was no way he was going to tell Mya what Rosalie went through during her last minutes.

Kate knocked lightly on the door, making him start. She had her mouth open, ready to tell him something, but he cut her off.

"We're going to see Willy Mason right now." He slapped the desktop with one palm.

•••

Mya grabbed a towel and bottle of water as she eyed Natalie. The girl fidgeted on the couch.

"You know, it's a good idea for women to learn how to protect themselves," Mya started tentatively.

Natalie kept her eyes on the screen, but picked at the stitching on her jeans.

"I'm going to the gym if you want to join me."

Natalie did a double take. "Um, Luca said we should stay here."

She knew Natalie felt intimidated by her, but still, she ought to get brownie points for saving her from Willy Mason. "Sure. I just thought you might want to get out of the house for a while."

With her head down, Natalie touched the almost healed wound above her eye and whispered, "I don't know how to fight people."

Mya perched on the arm of the couch. "It's not so much about fighting as protecting. I can teach you. It won't cost anything."

Natalie smiled shyly and turned off the TV. "Sure."

Kate had generously left her car for Mya to use again, and she contemplated swinging by her house on the way to the gym. Luca would think it was a lousy idea. The explosion was three days ago, but it felt like an eternity. She still saw the ragged door frame and small flames licking the ceiling in her nightmares. The same nightmares Rhonda starred in. The cops didn't seem any closer to finding her, which was no surprise.

Damn, she felt so helpless.

Maybe she wasn't ready to face the house just yet. Today she wanted to punch the shit out of something.

As she travelled along the main road, a black four-by-four pulled out of a side street and followed them. At the next intersection it ran the lights. Mya revved the Torana to 4,000 RPM, changed gears, and accelerated. The black vehicle kept pace. Holy shit. She didn't have to find Rhonda; the redhead had found her. This was her chance to do what the cops were too incompetent to do, but not with Natalie in the car. The girl had gone through enough trauma.

Natalie had a white-knuckled grip on the door handle, so Mya eased off the accelerator. Still, there might not be another opportunity to find out for sure who was behind the wheel.

At the next side street she turned suddenly. The four-by-four continued on the main road. False alarm. Mya took a calming breath.

"This is my local stomping ground." She pulled into the gym car park. "Every girl should know how to defend herself."

Natalie nodded.

They stepped through the glass front door and Mya yelled, "Oi! Tommy."

"MJ, you decided to grace us with your presence." He strutted over and wrapped her in a death grip until she threatened to knee him in the nuts. "I didn't expect to see you so soon after your mum … "

"I've just come to hit something." Now wasn't the time to have a heart-to-heart with her old buddy. Besides, he'd make a big deal if he knew Rhonda might have something to do with her mum's death. Later.

He took a step back and put his palms forward in surrender. "Who's your sidekick?" He shook Natalie's hand, and then flicked his eyebrows up and down suggestively at Mya. "Wanna go a few rounds?"

"Nope. I'm flying solo today, but you can give Natalie a starter lesson."

Natalie's eyelids flipped up to her brows and she squirmed in her tennis shoes.

Tommy turned off the charm and went into professional mode. "Come on, let's get you kitted up and I'll show you the basics."

Mya waved to Natalie as she followed him.

It felt good to pull the boxing gloves on, familiar. She steadied the punching bag before landing her first blow. It barely moved.

"Crap, I'm outta shape."

She closed her eyes and took a few deep breaths, but it didn't clear the image of her mum's lifeless body laid out on the bed. Anger seeped from the vault.

Thud. Thud. Thwack. Two punches followed by the top of her foot, and it felt great. Keeping her eyes on the swinging bag, she got into a rhythm. Punch, punch, kick. Punch, punch, kick.

"You want me to hold that still for you?"

The leather bag creaked as Mya's rhythm broke. One of her regular sparring buddies slid behind the bag and grabbed it with two hands.

"Thanks."

His mess of brown hair blurred as she focused on the bag. She put more force behind her next hit, letting the air grunt out of her lungs with every blow. Sweat trickled down her spine, out of her hair, and into her eyes. She wiped a forearm across her face and kept going. Punch, punch, kick. Punch, punch, kick.

After a while Mya swapped places with the bag holder, and then back again. She was soaked with sweat and puffing by the time she heard Natalie's voice behind her.

"I guess I oughta be glad that ain't me."

She turned to see Natalie giggling. "How'd your first lesson go?"

Tommy tossed Mya a towel to swipe over her flushed face, neck, and arms.

"Tommy was cool." Natalie blushed and stared at the worn blue carpet. "I can't kickbox like you, but he showed me a few moves."

"Great. We can come back tomorrow, if you like."

"Sure." Natalie's eyes were alight with self-worth.

"Wet T-shirt competition?" Tommy stood at a distance as he pointed at Mya's chest, smirk in place.

She looked down to see her nipples straining against the damp fabric, and lunged forward to plant a kick on Tommy's knee. It buckled.

"And creeps like you are why girls like us learn to kick arse." She grinned at Natalie.

"Hey, hey. It's nothing I haven't seen before. Lord knows you'd take my arm off if I tried to touch." He shouldered her playfully. "See you tomorrow and, let me know if you need anything."

A gentle nudge with her shoulder was all that was needed. Tommy wouldn't push her for information, but he'd be there for her. He was better than any big brother she could have dreamed up for herself.

Come to think of it, he'd make a great bodyguard. Maybe she should have Natalie hang out here more, until things settled down.

Chapter 35

Luca dropped his personal effects and gun into a metal box and Kate followed suit. The guard on the other side of the bulletproof glass at the Adelaide Remand Centre, turned a critical gaze their way, checked their IDs, and then pulled the box to his side of the barrier. He put their belongings into a holding container and pressed a button.

A buzzer sounded and Luca pushed the door open.

There were black scuff marks along the lower half of the wall. Not everyone came willingly. Including Willy Mason, or so he'd heard from Davey.

Kate smoothed the front of her shirt. "Got a call from forensics. They matched the falsified purchase orders to Melanie Lane's handwriting."

Luca stopped walking. "He's positive?"

"Not 100 percent, of course, but confident."

"Finally, a link. When we've finished here I want you to order an APB and have her picked up. We've got enough to hold her for a few hours while we put this all together. I suspect Willy will be feeling a lot more compliant after a night in here."

They went into the viewing room where they could watch Willy through the one-way glass. He balanced on a plastic chair in the interview room, making it look inadequate. Even the shapeless prison-issue orange jumpsuit did nothing to hide his size. The way he was studying the cream walls of the six-by-four interrogation room, you would have thought they were covered in graffiti art instead of scuffed paint.

"We need this," Luca said.

"Good luck." Kate switched on the microphone so she'd be able to hear the conversation.

Luca moved from the dark room into the bright hall. One deep breath to gather himself, and then he turned the handle to the interview room. He burst in and slammed the door shut. Keeping momentum, he stepped around the table and bent over Willy. The big man automatically sat back as Luca got in his face.

"I've got evidence now, Willy. They murdered someone with a family, and the autopsy confirmed it."

"What the hell are you talking about?" The man crossed his arms in front of his chest.

Good, he was on the defensive.

"The same buddies who cut you loose over this jewelry scam have murdered an old lady at Rich Haven. They're going to leave you rotting in here, Willy. They're going to let you do the time for this, too."

"Hey, hey. I don't know nothin' about murdering anyone—"

"Then you'd better start giving me something I can use to find your buddies." Spittle sprayed from between Luca's lips as he shouted, inches from Willy's stubbled face.

The man's eye twitched at the corner and his shoulders slumped the tiniest bit.

"If you've got nothing to say to me, the guard can take you back to your cell." Luca rotated, the rubber heel of his black sandshoe squeaking against the linoleum.

"Wait!"

He paused, one hand on the handle, his back to Willy.

"I heard Melanie talking to Kevin once. They were in another room, and I heard her moan about some chick she wanted dead."

Luca held his breath and turned around. "And?"

"I dunno. She was talking about tormenting some woman and how she was gonna get what she deserved."

Rosalie Jensen. Did the murderer know her? Is that why her profile broke from the others?

"Did she use a name, suburb, any detail that's going to make this useful to me?"

"I told you they didn't tell me nothin' about who was running the show, or how they got the old ladies to sign over their wills—Shit."

"Yeah, shit. You knew they were knocking off old ladies, didn't you, Willy?"

"I'm not stupid." He curled his fingers into fists on the wood-laminate table. "The only way you get money from a will is when the person dies, but I didn't have nothin' to do with it."

Luca stood with his feet apart, hands unnaturally straight by his sides as he tried to keep his temper reined in. "We're going around in circles here. Are you going to tell me anything useful, or are you just pissing in my ear?"

"I heard Melanie say the letters were working and the bitch was shittin' herself."

"We're done." Luca threw the door open, stepped through, and locked it before Willy had a chance to wrap those pancake-sized hands around his neck.

His heart was racing as he stood in the hall, edgy, trying to put one and four together to get two.

Kate stuck her head out of the observation room. "What was that?"

"Mya told me she was getting threatening letters."

"That makes sense. Maybe they send letters before they kill the old ladies."

"No, it doesn't make sense. Before—at Happy Vale Nursing Home—they only selected women with no surviving family. Rosalie Jensen had Mya. Besides, Mya told me it was someone called Rhonda sending the letters."

"She was mistaken."

"I'm going to her house to get a look at one of those letters. See if it matches any of the handwriting samples from Rich Haven personnel."

"What am *I* supposed to do?" Kate rested tight fists on her hips.

"Throw Willy back in the lock-up." He strode down the fluoro-lit hall. "And tell Mya I'm coming to see her in the next hour."

• • •

Mya wasn't answering her mobile phone. If she was doing it deliberately, he'd—

Luca took a deep breath and turned the key in her new front door. It was only fitted yesterday, and he forgot to hand over the keys when she was upset last night. He'd better tell her soon, or she'd accuse him of trying to con her out of a house—or worse, trying to move in.

He screwed up his nose at the lingering stale smoke smell—better leave the door open to let some fresh air in. It looked like grey and black cloud patterns had been airbrushed across the top of the walls and ceiling. She'd need to get a painter in.

Luca smiled at the rickety hall table, bare since he'd stashed the bowl of weapons in her wardrobe while his colleague inspected the damage. No point in bringing something to their attention that had nothing to do with the case.

The lounge room looked the same as it did when he last sat in it, with bills and promotional material on the dining table, but no sign of Rhonda's letters. He checked the bin, but it was almost empty. There were a few sheets of paper on the side table by the recliner chair, so he flicked through them. Jotted words, phrases, and page numbers from the book she'd been reading. She sure was an enigma.

On the coffee table, he lifted a couple of books, a bowl of mints, and a menu for the local fish-and-chip shop. He found a flattened mint wrapper and flopped onto the faded red leather lounge to think. He dialed her mobile again, but it went to voicemail.

With hands behind his head, he scanned the room. Where would he stash a threatening letter if he were Mya? The crammed-full bookshelf looked orderly and he wasn't keen on going in her bedroom, but where else could he look?

As he pushed off the couch, his foot slipped. A piece of paper protruded from under it and he reached to slide it out with one finger. It had been torn from a spiral notepad. Probably more book annotations. He turned it over and read.

As he did, the hairs on his arms stood higher with each word.

> Did you miss me, Mya? Living it up in that nice house, with that big motorbike you ride. I'll bet it cost a small fortune.
>
> Can you feel me breathing down your neck yet? It won't be long before it's time to pay up.

He put the sample of Melanie's handwriting next to it and his throat constricted. The backward-slanting script was the same. A tingle crawled up his nostrils, as though he was about to sneeze, but he wasn't. It continued across his scalp and down the back of his neck.

He had it all wrong. Melanie Lane and Rhonda Morten weren't in cahoots. Melanie *was* Rhonda, and she'd been watching Mya.

"Shit!"

Two paces and he was across the lounge room. He stuffed the letter into his back pocket and stepped onto the front porch. He locked the door and dialed Kate as he crossed the yard.

"Const—"

"Kate. Did you reach Mya?"

"And hello to you, too. I tried the apartment several times and no one answered. I guess she's not back from the gym y—"

"Can you go there and check?" He sidled into his car and screeched the wheels as he put his foot to the floor. He hadn't decided where he was going yet, but knew he needed to get there fast.

"Luca, what's going on?"

He ignored Kate's question. "What gym was Mya was going to?"

"She didn't say. Wh—"

"Try her mobile. And Natalie's. Then phone dispatch and find out if a car is still on Kevin's house. I'll call you shortly." He hung up and, with one hand on the steering wheel, searched the business directory on his phone with the other. There were two gyms near Mya's house. The closest was three kilometres away. He pressed his foot harder on the accelerator.

Chapter 36

The gym was on the other side of the railway track, in the industrial area of Croydon. Luca passed Jenny's Snack Bar and parked in front of All Car Motors. Railway Fitness Centre was the third shop in a long, besser-block building with pigeon poo streaked gutters. He pushed the door and an electronic beeper sounded, causing several sweaty heads to turn his way.

He scanned the room: blue threadbare carpet, old gym equipment with chipped white paint, a boxing ring with sagging ropes, and a punching bag with a dark stain from years of abuse. Definitely Mya's kind of place.

"Can I help you?" A muscle-bound guy with cropped hair and one of those singlets that gaped to the waist held out a hand.

"Do you have a member by the name of Mya Jensen?" Luca sidestepped the guy's swollen bicep to continue his visual search.

"Who's asking?"

He pulled his badge. "Detective Patterson. Do you know her or not?"

"Yeah, MJ's a member. She was in this morning."

He recoiled from the pet name. Why the hell did this guy get to call her MJ? "What's your name?"

"Tommy. I own this place. Hey, is MJ in some kind of trouble?"

"She might be in danger. I need to find her right away. What time did she leave?"

"About ten, maybe a bit before. She was with a chick called Natalie, who I've never seen before. I gave her a self-defense lesson on the house."

Luca tipped his head to the side in confusion.

"Me and MJ go *way* back," Tommy explained.

Luca narrowed his eyes and reassessed Tommy's bloated body, from the trapezius attached halfway up his neck to the waist-thick thighs sticking out of his silk shorts. Not that he had the least idea what Mya's "type" was, but he couldn't picture her with this pumped-up poser. When he caught up with her, he'd quiz her about how Tommy fit into her life.

"Did she seem upset at all?"

"MJ usually works out a couple of times a week. Seemed okay this morning. Gave the bag a beating it won't forget." Tommy laughed.

"I'll bet she did. Did you see her leave with anyone?"

"Just Natalie."

Where the hell was she? "Did she say where they were going?"

"Nah, MJ's pretty private. I've known her for a decade, and I've never seen her bring a friend in before."

Good, Mya didn't share everything with this guy. Luca pulled a business card from his wallet and handed it over. "Call me if you see her."

He scanned the gym once more and then headed back to his car. If the girls left at ten, they should be at the apartment. It was eleven thirty now and only a ten-minute drive. Chester Bennington started singing in his pocket, signalling a call from Kate.

"Luca, I've tried Mya and Natalie's mobiles and they ring out. No one's at the apartment or my house and neither is my car."

He rotated on the spot, searching the car park. The sun glinted off a gold roof at the far end. His Adam's apple lodged in the back of his throat. Kate's Torana. He jogged through the car park, scanning the ground and other cars for clues—of what he didn't know.

Thank God the Torana looked intact, door closed, but—

He stepped around to the boot and crouched. The left rear tire was flat, with the sidewall slashed. Okay, so maybe the girls walked to a garage to get help. But it was only next door so he would have seen them by now.

"Luca? Luca, are you still there?" Kate called from the phone dangling in his hand.

"Hang on."

Mya and Natalie would have come out of the gym and walked to the car, but Mya noticed the flat. She'd be machine savvy enough to know it wasn't a road puncture, so would be on alert. Someone must've jumped her from behind and incapacitated her with a single blow, because if she saw them coming, she'd be swinging and kicking before they knew what hit them.

Of course, if Melanie/Rhonda had been watching her, *she* would know enough not to give Mya that chance. But where was Natalie when this happened? Melanie must've had help. Maybe Kevin or Evan.

He raised the phone to his ear again. "Get over to Kevin's house and check it again."

"Where are you going?"

He heard the resignation in her voice. Once this was all over, he'd have to shout Kate dinner or something, to apologize for being such a tyrant. "Your car is at the gym, but Mya and Natalie seem to be missing. I'm going out to rural Balhannah again and take a look at Evan Smith's house."

The two women must have been taken against their will. Rage burned through his veins. Something glinted in the sun and he bent to pick it up. A hair tie. Mya's? An image of luxuriant caramel hair spread like a halo around her face stopped his lungs from expanding. His fist clenched around the rubber band until his short nails dug into his palm.

They'd had only one morning together, and a couple of kisses. Hardly any time, but something wrenched inside him at the idea that he'd failed to protect her.

Just like he'd failed Olivia.

Not again. He couldn't lose another person he cared about. It wasn't fair. He'd barely lived through it the first time.

The force of his emotions took him by surprise. Did he care about Mya? Enough to need to see her again. At least to have the chance to tell her how he felt.

"I have to find her."

Chapter 37

Mya drew a long breath in through her nose and huffed it out. The air smelled funny, like two-stroke fuel, dust, and rubber. The side of her head felt damp, and when she tried to open her mouth to take a deeper breath, she couldn't.

Her stomach lurched as her whole body rocked from side to side.

I don't remember getting on a boat.

A steady crunching sound grated at her nerve endings. Carrots in a blender? Sand and shells under a boogie board as it slid into the shallows? No, it was tires on gravel. Her body rolled again and something hard dug into her back. She groaned and opened one eye.

"The skank is back with us," a female voice said. "You didn't hit her hard enough."

"Don't worry, I will next time," a deeper voice replied.

A blond Ken-doll was driving the car, so Mya figured she was in the back. A woman with frizzy ginger hair sat beside him, then turned half around, smiling. There was something familiar about that malicious smile and those faded hazel eyes.

The woman limping by the lake, a black four-by-four driving straight at her, frizzy red hair.

Fuck!

"It's payback time, Lara. Or should I call you Mya? You did a nice job of disappearing, but karma's a bitch. Imagine my surprise when I started working at Rich Haven and recognized Jean Roach. But she didn't go by that name either, did she? I was tempted to hold a pillow over her face there and then, but I'm too clever to get caught, so I started planning my revenge.

"And boy, is it going to be sweet. You know, it was a newspaper clipping my mum kept about Jack's death that tipped me off. It mentioned Jean Roach, which is how I made the connection. Little Lara Roach is all grown up now, and you're well off too, with a house and a nice job. I've seen that hunky cop coming and going from your place, but he won't be able to help you anymore." Rhonda faced forward again, giggling like a schoolgirl.

Mya shivered against the dirty corrugated floor in the back of the vehicle. Her lips wouldn't come apart and there was a rubber and glue smell under her nose. Her arms were bound behind, making her shoulders ache. What was the last thing she remembered? Leaving the gym with Natalie.

Natalie!

With wild eyes, she searched within her limited field of vision; a small red jerry-can in one corner and a pair of white sandshoes with blue stripes down the side. The thin legs rose to Natalie's tear-streaked face. The teenager sat atop a metal toolbox, her hands behind her back and silver duct tape across her mouth. Her eyes were bright red and there were clean tear trails down her dusty cheeks.

Mya stared into Natalie's terror-stricken eyes. It was the same look on her mum's face the last day Cockroach beat her. All Mya wanted to do that day was get out of the house and ride trains, so she wouldn't have to listen to the yelling, but she couldn't leave without trying to get her mum out, too. In the kitchen her mum sat on the floor with a bright red welt on her pale cheek. Cockroach towered over her with a clenched fist.

"Mum and I were going to the supermarket to get steak for dinner," she lied.

Cockroach was partial to steak, and his arm dropped to his side as he glared. Lara hid her shaking hands behind her back and walked past him. She tried to help her mum up, but he swatted her out of the way and she crashed into the cupboards shoulder first. The thin, metal handle dug into her flesh, but she straightened defiantly. She was as tall as him, but he was a damned sight meaner.

He turned his attention back to Jean.

Crazy as it was, she couldn't give up.

"Get out of my way," she yelled. Anything to make him stop.

He did. His eyes narrowed and his hairy knuckles connected with the top of her cheekbone, ramming her head into the cupboards and splitting the skin above her temple. She crumpled onto the floor, struggling to right her blurred vision. Gasping for breath.

Needed to get back up.

Now that she was on the floor, too, she was on the same level as her mum. They looked into one another's eyes. Desperation, fear, hopelessness—it was all there, reflecting back at her.

Natalie snivelled, bringing Mya out of the daymare. She squeezed her eyes shut to stop the images. Her stomach lurched as the vehicle slowed and then stopped.

Rhonda and the bloke got out, and she heard the tailgate open behind her. Natalie's eyes widened and she cringed against the side of the car, her scream muffled by the duct-tape. Two big hands grabbed Mya's biceps and dragged her backward.

When her feet hit the ground, she was spun around. A wave of vertigo made her surroundings rock, but the hands kept her upright, so she tried to focus on the man in front of her. His male-model face was unfamiliar. She turned her head toward the creak of a car boot, just in time to cop a slap across her cheek.

"You've got a lifetime of payback coming, Lara," Rhonda sneered. "All I wanted to do was talk to you all those years ago, but you wouldn't give me the time of day. Thought you were so much better than me. Look at you now." She took a step back. "Lay into her, Kev."

Kev's face was beautiful but blank. He let go of one bicep and she watched his arm draw back. It rocketed forward, fist connecting with her jaw, and a shard of pain exploded in her skull. Her head lolled sideways and she dangled from his iron grip. Rhonda's laugh echoed in her ears. No doubt the groggy nausea felt similar to being drunk.

There was a dark red pattern on the knuckles of Kev's left hand. Warm fluid trickled down the side of her head. She wondered what the bastard had hit her with in the gym car park. Everything hurt.

Natalie whimpered in the car.

Kev's arm drew back again, and this time she tried desperately to track its trajectory. At the last minute she dodged, still catching a glancing blow. With her hands bound behind her, she used the only weapon available. She lifted her right knee as high as it would go and thrust it into Kev's gut. He stumbled back a few steps, losing his grip on her arm. She followed up with a side kick to his ribs and delighted in the dull thud.

Rhonda squealed and kicked Mya in the shins. "You bitch!"

She turned to face Rhonda and—

One cheek exploded with flaming pain. The side of her face scraped along rocks and dirt and spots danced in front of her eyes. How the hell did she get on the ground again? Her cheekbone felt shattered where Kev hit her. He rolled her onto her back with one foot. Then he knelt on her, his knees pinning both arms, his hands around her throat, squeezing.

Kev's face morphed into Cockroach's ugly mug, and Mya's anger gushed out of the coffer. There was no way to tell if her sight was red from blood dripping into her eyes or anger, but she wanted to kick and bite and maim.

Someone screamed. Rhonda was bent over Mya, dangling a strip of duct tape between two fingers.

"Hope that hurt, you tramp."

At least she could finally open her mouth, but the scream died on her lips. Kev's grip on her throat wasn't letting any air into her lungs. The spots in front of her eyes got bigger. Her brain grew foggy. Cockroach would have the last laugh after all.

Chapter 38

It took Luca thirty-five minutes to reach the rural township of Balhannah. Time during which Mya could be getting further away from him, or suffering. He turned left onto a potholed dirt road. In the daylight the letterbox was easy to find, and this time he boldly followed the deeply rutted driveway to Evan Smith's house. No need for stealth. He parked in the shade of a pine tree, beside the olive-green garage. There were no cars in the driveway.

He strode up the paved path to the panelled front door and banged his fist against it. No sound from within. Swiftly he circled the long house, peering into and tapping on windows. He jumped back from the laundry window when a fluffy white face materialized. Just a cat.

The garage was unlocked, but there was no one hiding inside and no secret trap door in the floor. The sound of his mobile phone made him grab at his pistol, heart racing.

Damn! "Kate?"

"I'm at Kevin's place and it's quiet as a library. What do you want me to do next?" She sounded terse.

"Sit tight for the moment."

"An unmarked car is parked out front. I don't need to be here. What's going on?"

"Hang on. Give me a minute to think."

He paced in the driveway, sending up little puffs of talcum-powder fine soil with each revolution. Rhonda had to be the key to this mess—to the deaths in the nursing homes, the jewelry thefts, Mya and Natalie's disappearance—but where the hell would she take them?

Across the valley Luca spotted a quaint cottage nestled amongst a copse of trees. He stopped pacing. "Where did you say Rhonda's property was?"

"Birdwood. Luca, what's so urgent?"

"I have a hunch that Rhonda and Kevin have kidnapped Mya and Natalie."

"Rhonda? Melanie is the one working with Kevin—"

Luca jogged back to his car. "Melanie *is* Rhonda. This morning forensics confirmed that Rosalie was poisoned. If Rhonda has Mya and Natalie … I need you to email the address of her property to my phone."

"I'll do it right away."

Luca relaxed minutely. At least he had something to focus on. "Thanks, Kate. Can you tell the squad at Kevin's house to stay put and call me if anyone turns up?"

"Sure. I'll meet you at Rhonda's."

He waited for Kate's email—a Google map pinpointing Rhonda's property—studied it, and then stuffed his mobile into his shirt pocket. He threw the car into reverse the second it started. The gear box crunched in protest and a shower of gravel hit the garage as the tires spun.

"Don't let me be too late. *Please* don't let me be too late."

•••

Muffled screams startled Mya. She dragged in a grating breath. Her throat was as rough as steel wool, and cold stones poked into one hip. There was a whimper to the right and she turned her head, but couldn't focus. A big blur dragged a smaller blur with white sandshoes.

Natalie!

Mya wiggled her hands in a see-saw motion. Whoever put the tape around her wrists was in a hurry, because it had some give.

"I can't get her in the boot by myself," Rhonda sniped.

Mya's heart pounded, her breathing shallowed. She was lightheaded, but that wasn't the only reason panic was taking hold.

They're going to put me in a metal box, just like Cockroach used to. No! I'm not going in there again. I cried and pleaded, struggled in the dark, and claw until my nails broke, but he only laughed.

Mya pulled hard with her left hand and pushed with the right one. The glue from the tape felt like it was tearing off the top layer of her skin, but she kept going. Every time she lifted her head to see what Kev and Rhonda were doing, the world whirled and her stomach lurched. Bile surfed her throat, so she rested her head on the ground again.

"Don't worry, honey, everything is going to plan," Kev purred. "I'll put Mya in the boot of the rental car, then stash jewelry girl somewhere she won't be any trouble. Hold this."

Natalie fell as Kev let go of her arm.

He bent and grabbed Mya, throwing her over his shoulder as easily as a sack of flour. She wiggled her wrists harder. Loose, but not loose enough. Her feet dangled in front of Kev; could she kick him in the groin? No good if he hit her again, broke her other cheek, and then she couldn't fight back. He grunted as he dropped her into the car boot.

The effort of trying to make her limp body move was making her sweat. She started to hyperventilate. Sure, her chest expanded, but no air was being sucked into her paralyzed lungs. She'd scream if she thought anyone would hear, but Kev wouldn't be lugging her about in view of the public.

If she could get out of the boot, get her feet on the ground, she'd run. Run and never stop. Ah, but there was Natalie—she couldn't leave the girl to fend for herself. If Mya couldn't make her body move, they would both be dead.

"You drive the rental and I'll follow in the Land Cruiser," Kev said. "When we get to Blanche Point at Port Willunga, I'll put her in the front seat and we'll roll it off the cliff."

Rhonda clapped her hands. "With any luck she'll wake up just before she hits the bottom."

A wet smooching sound was followed by Natalie's half cry, half scream through the duct tape. Then there was the sound of something being dragged across the gravel driveway. Mya shivered. She couldn't let Natalie down. Couldn't let her end up like her mum.

Natalie's cries came from further away. It was time to move, right now, before it was too late.

"Let's get this show on the road," Rhonda mumbled.

If Kev had taken Natalie, then it was just Rhonda now. Those odds Mya could handle; besides, there was no way the lid of the boot was going down with her in it. *Face your fears head on,* Ned had taught her when she first walked into his gym, and that's what she'd been doing since.

Her right hand was almost free when a shadow fell across her face. She kicked up with both legs. The boot popped up; Rhonda stumbled back and squealed. Mya swung her calves over the dip in the boot, wiggled her bottom forward, and rocked until both feet were on the ground.

Rhonda's nostrils flared like the fire-breathing dragon she was. She stooped to pick up a long stick and stood with feet planted wide, her teeth bared.

Mya was tense and ready for a fight. Still, it was worth trying to explain the disconnect between what Rhonda had said and what Mya knew to be true. Maybe she could talk the woman around.

"I didn't believe you when you said Jack was your father. If I had, I would have helped you. I didn't take off to do you out of any inheritance. I did it to get away from a life with him."

"Rubbish! He never sent us any money. I never even got a Christmas present. I bet you got all kinds of presents."

"No, I didn't. I needed that money to look after my mum." Mya ducked under the swipe of the stick. The horizon pitched and she couldn't regain her equilibrium fast enough to avoid its backstroke. The stick connected with her shoulder and sharp barbs along the wood drew pricks of blood.

"Jack pissed off as soon as my mother got pregnant, so she didn't even put his name on the birth certificate." Rhonda slapped the stick against the palm of her hand. "That's why nobody contacted me when he died. How do you think it feels to have a 'father unknown'?"

"At least you didn't have to live with him," Mya shouted.

There was no reasoning with Rhonda. She'd spent more than a decade believing Mya had done her out of an inheritance, and if she'd killed Rosalie, then she deserved what was coming to her.

Stop messing around.

Anger flowed through Mya's veins like molten lava, and this time she had no intention of trying to stop it. This was the moment she'd been waiting for. The time for payback. Her teeth were clamped together so hard they grated, but her gaze stayed locked on target.

At last her right hand peeled from the tape. She brought her arms up in a protective boxing stance. Rhonda gasped and jumped back.

"You know what I can do, and Kev's not here to back you up now. I was just a teenager when you showed up." Mya sidestepped.

Rhonda mirrored the movement. "You don't want to know the kinds of things I had to do to make ends meet after my mum died. You know, your retarded mother couldn't even scream when I killed her, but I could see in her eyes she knew she was dying."

Mya's shriek of rage ripped away any thoughts of danger or civility. She launched fists first and landed a blow squarely on Rhonda's chin.

She followed quickly with a gut punch. The redhead doubled over, clutching her stomach and gasping for air. Without a pause, Mya lined her up again and sent a push kick into her shoulder.

Rhonda hit the dirt with a thud and, hands splayed behind, tried to squirm away.

Not going to happen.

Natalie's piercing scream sounded from behind a tall hedge. It crawled up Mya's arms, under her skin, and into her brain. The physical force of the hate she had carried around for so long—Cockroach's boot raised above her mum's head, the metal lid of a toolbox coming down, Rosalie struggling for breath—swelled in her tensed muscles. This was the moment to finish Rhonda.

Another bloodcurdling scream.

God, he's going to kill her.

There wasn't time to put her revenge first.

A sly smile crossed Rhonda's face. If she thought Mya had given up, she was going to be sadly disappointed. There was a metal rod in the boot, close enough to reach. She spun around. The tire iron connected with Rhonda's head with a dull thump. The silly cow frowned, a startled look in her eyes. Then she crumpled to the ground like a rag doll.

The world was still cockeyed from her concussion, but Mya ran toward the glossy pittosporum hedge. She edged around it and caught a glimpse of Kev dragging Natalie by the hair. They were headed toward a huge wooden barn with boarded windows and peeling paint. Duct tape hung half off the teen's red mouth and a bruise blossomed across one eye.

Five long strides and Mya launched. Her boot connected with the back of Kev's knees, which made a satisfying thud when they hit the ground. His grip on Natalie relaxed. Her pretty blue eyes stared over his shoulder.

Mya didn't wait for him to get back up. She spun to deliver a roundhouse kick to the side of his head. Kev grunted and fell sideways but rolled and grabbed Mya's ankle. One quick pull upended her and her shoulder crunched onto the coarse gravel.

Pain ricocheted up her neck and into her skull. All strength drained from the injured arm, but she kept moving.

Scissoring her legs to free them, she scrambled to her haunches.

Whack. The force of Kev's kick lifted her clear off the ground and dumped her on her side again. She gasped, wrapped arms around her stomach. Precious little air got into her lungs, making her lightheaded again. She was lying on the ground like a pathetic victim.

Every centimetre of her body throbbed with pain, but every millilitre of her blood boiled with rage.

Kev must've taken her for beat, because he delivered Natalie an open-handed slap. Her cheek instantly pinked. He followed with a boot to the girl's ribs.

Mya met Natalie's terrified gaze. Unlike the rocky ground she was on now, the linoleum had been cool as Mya lay staring at her mum, the day Cockroach struck his final blow. She had lain on the floor, unable to catch her breath, and watched Rosalie's blood spray from between her swollen lips.

Mya had screamed for him to stop, but his big boot came down on her mum's head, and she heard a crack. She was looking into her mum's eyes at the exact moment when awareness went out of them. A moment of inaction she would never forgive herself for.

She refused to watch, while Natalie was brutalized too. Drawing the last skerrick of strength from her sapped body, she flattened palms on the rough ground, pushed onto her knees and then feet. For a moment she stood there, swaying. Kev must've heard the movement, because he slowly turned around.

Natalie was on the ground, alive, but she looked like she'd been run over by a tractor.

"Run," Mya yelled. "Run!"

The teenager moved her legs and arms crab style, propelling herself backward. Kev hesitated, as though unsure who to throttle first. Natalie clambered to her feet and, with one last panicked look, ran for the barn. The big brute lunged in her direction but stopped short when a fistful of gravel hit his face.

Mya didn't give him time to react but sprung forward and delivered a swift kick to his gut. His mouth gaped, eyes widened. She shifted her weight and drove the thick sole of her boot into his kneecap.

"Shit!" He bent to the injury. An arm went up to defend against her next strike.

Too late; she kept on coming. When he was on his back, she leapt onto his chest, her knees pinning his shoulders, and felt the soft flesh on his cheeks give under her knuckles. Blood streamed down his face. He tore one arm free and pulled her off sideways but wasn't quick enough to his feet.

Mya grabbed the nearest fist-sized rock and brought it down hard.

Chapter 39

Luca's Corolla fishtailed as he tried to read the tiny map on his phone and drive with one hand. The tires slid from the dirt verge back to the tarmac. Golden wheat stretched as far as he could see, dotted with the occasional farmhouse. Swaggering gnarly gums followed unseen watercourses. The property should be just around the corner.

I can't lose her now.

Mya might be troubled, even abrasive, but there was more to her—the intelligence, resilience, and passion he'd come to appreciate. Oh, the passion. There was something primal about the way she made love, something desperate about the intensity of her kisses, but what frightened him most was how much he wanted to be the one to soothe her. *He* wanted to be the one to unravel her mysteries and show her she didn't have to do everything on her own.

His mobile started singing and he eased off the accelerator while he answered. A toot behind made him flinch. A police Commodore was in his rear view mirror.

"I'm right behind you," Kate said and then the line went dead.

He pulled to the roadside, jogged to the passenger door of the police car, and got in. Kate accelerated before the door was even closed.

"No lights or siren," he told her.

She wrenched the steering wheel around the corner and then slowed to fifty kilometres an hour—fast enough not to look suspicious, but slow enough to see well as they passed Rhonda's property.

A black four-wheel drive was parked by a garage.

"That's Rhonda's vehicle and reasonable cause," he said.

Further along the driveway there was a white sedan with its boot up, and behind that a tall hedge and barn with boarded windows. Along the front of the property, narrow horse yards were fenced with white-washed wood, a rusted metal-plate on the gate read *Agistment and stabling—enquire within*, but there were no horses. At the back of the property he spotted a sandy arena with faded letter-boards and what looked like a house concealed by a copse of trees.

He couldn't see any movement but wasn't about to make them a target by coming up the driveway. Instead he pointed to a dirt track a few hundred metres down the road. Kate followed it until it started to curve in the wrong direction, and then parked on the soft verge.

"Phones to vibrate," Luca said, dropping his into his breast pocket.

She nodded. "Shouldn't we wait for back-up?"

That was supposedly the right answer the last time he was in this type of situation, but if he hadn't gone in, would the little girl have survived? He'd stormed the house and the young constable in tow was shot; not fatally, but Moss called it an unnecessary risk.

What level of risk was acceptable when someone's life was on the line?

"If you want to wait here, be my guest. We can't be positive Natalie and Mya are on the property, so at the moment we're acting on just cause."

He patted both firearms—one on his ankle and one in a shoulder holster—ducked between strands of a wire fence, and jogged toward the house. Kate's quick footfalls trailed behind. The nearest house was at least a kilometre away, and he felt exposed in the paddock, dodging cowpats and trying not to roll his ankle in ruts.

At the property's white fence, he paused. Quiet.

He climbed the rails and sprinted to the back veranda. With a flick of his head, he indicated to Kate the direction he planned to go. She nodded, hand hovering over the pistol in her waist holster.

Luca moved quickly along the back wall and peered through each window. No furniture except in the lounge room, where a few mismatched chairs crowded a folding card table. Not a permanent residence. He tried the handle of the back door, but it was locked.

At the edge of the void between the house and barn, he paused to scan for movement or sound, and then made a dash. He landed back first against the barn wall. A soft bump indicated Kate's arrival beside him.

Planks of wood had been nailed roughly across the windows. Not good. It usually meant there was something to hide, and the planks were too close together to see anything inside. He sidled along the wall, listening for the faintest sound, his eyes wide. If only he'd see or hear something, to let him know the girls were still alive.

The fist of dread in his stomach was clenched so tight he could barely walk straight.

Tap.

He jumped at the faint sound, right hand resting on his pistol and popping the press stud on the strap to release it. A trail of footprints pointed the way to the corner of the barn, where he stuck just his face around the corner.

A side door was ajar. His heartbeat was faster than the click-clack of a train on tracks, as he wrapped a hand around the knob. Two quick pants and he pulled it open and slipped inside.

Light from the doorway only reached partway across the room, so he crouched by the wall and waited for his eyes to adjust to the dim interior. The smell of dusty hay and long-dried manure clung to the wood, but there was no sign of life.

When his sight improved, he eased into the large, open area, which was divided into rows of stalls. At the back was an enclosed room, probably an office or tack room, with stairs beside it.

Thud. Luca stilled and waited to hear the dull sound again, so he could tell where it came from.

Thud. Someone was breathing nearby.

Salty sweat stung his eyes and he swiped the back of his hand across them. Slowly, he drew his pistol and released the safety catch. Glancing at Kate over his shoulder, he pointed in the direction of the sound. She nodded, gun still holstered, but hand hovering over it. Probably didn't want to do the paperwork if he was wrong. They crept forward.

Hay was packed under the windows; a horse rug draped over a low partition had matted hair stuck to the lining and the scent of stale sweat clung to it. Luca peered over the divider at dust-covered tack.

There was another bump, followed by a whimper.

He swallowed hard, adjusted his grip on the pistol, and inched forward. At the end of the wood partition he swung the handgun in the direction of a squeal.

"Natalie!"

Tears rolled from the girl's bloodshot eyes. He pulled the dangling tape from the side of her face and Kate freed the girl's hands.

"Do you know how many people are here?" he asked.

"A man and woman, but"—Natalie's voice caught—"they have Mya."

Luca's gut twisted. "I know, but I'm going to find her. Get her out of here, Kate, and call for backup."

"Will do."

"Natalie, where was the last place you saw Mya?"

She wobbled her head. "Out front."

He placed a hand on each of her shoulders and looked her in the eye. "I need you to go with Kate. She'll keep you safe."

Kate waved the girl forward.

He was surprised when Natalie moved without hesitation. She was obviously traumatized, but not hysterical. Mya must be rubbing off on her. He followed the women outside and watched them jog along the back of the barn, past the house, and climb over the fence.

A maniacal scream from the front of the property sounded like a war cry. Luca's gut did a somersault. What if he was too late? Gun pointed at the ground in front of him, he crept along the wall of the barn.

He listened. There were rhythmic grunts and the unmistakeable sound of soft flesh being beaten.

Mya!

He peered around the corner, his eyes scanning from side to side, and gasped.

A still male figure was on the ground, with blood-soaked blond hair and Mya straddling him. Her hand lifted high and he saw the red rock. Down it came. Over and over.

"Mya, stop!" He sprinted, tucking his pistol into its holster as he went.

She didn't turn or stop the onslaught.

Luca grabbed her wrist. She pulled against his grip, let out a feral squeal, and dropped the rock. With her free hand, she continued to hit the motionless man beneath her.

"Stop. It's Luca. You're safe now."

He grabbed both arms and lifted her off the prone man. She struggled, limbs flailing wildly, until he managed to pin her in a bear hug. He held tightly and she went from squirming to limp. A violent shudder sent a shockwave through both of them.

Taking baby steps, he moved her a few metres away from the gore and gradually relaxed his arms, expecting her to run. Instead, she slumped to the ground, pulled her knees to her chest, and wrapped her arms around them. Her vacant stare sent a chill through him.

The male body was probably Kevin Walker, although it was difficult to tell from the soft pulp of the face. He knelt and found a faint pulse at the carotid artery.

"Hell, he's still alive." Luca dialed triple zero to request an ambulance.

Stupid as it seemed, he followed procedure and slipped handcuffs on the man.

Piow.

The whip-crack of a pistol exploded to Luca's left and the sound ricocheted off the barn. Ears ringing, he whirled around, drawing his weapon. There wasn't time to check himself for bullet wounds. Not feeling any could be a good sign, or he could be a dead man walking.

A redheaded woman stood beside the hedge, trying to steady herself from the kickback of the gun she held. She raised it again. Hell, the barrel was pointed off to the side. No, not Mya!

With his gun still raised, he chanced a sideways glance, expecting to see a neat bullet hole in Mya's forehead. She didn't look any worse than before. If she wasn't dead, she would be in a few seconds.

He refocused on the redhead and took aim, then squeezed the trigger again and again. With feet braced shoulder width apart, and temporarily deaf from the report, he stared at Rhonda and she at him. Then she frowned and looked down at her chest, where a dark stain spread above her left breast. The pistol dropped from her hand, her eyes rolled up into her head, and her body folded into a disorderly pile.

The rise and fall of multiple police sirens neared. He continued to train his gun on her, but she didn't move again.

The carnage in the courtyard turned his stomach. Mya rocked back and forth, traumatized either from what she'd done, or what had been done to her.

Kevin would be dead if Luca hadn't stopped her—the perp still might not make it—but did that make her a killer? He knew better than most that every person had a point to which they could be pushed. Past that point, even a sane person could snap.

For the first time in his life, he was oddly unsure of what to do. When he looked into her dry eyes, he felt only the need to protect her.

"Luca."

Heart in his throat, he swung his pistol around.

Kate ducked and he quickly flicked the safety back on and holstered the weapon.

She grimaced at the sight of Kevin. "Are they both dead?"

"Kevin isn't yet, but the ambulance better hurry."

"I'll get the first aid kit from the car." Kate took off at a run.

Luca squatted to check the redhead's pulse, although the amount of blood leaking from her was a give away. Police sirens wailed, followed by blue and red lights that swirled across the property. The first vehicle braked abruptly as the driver realized he'd entered a crime scene.

Luca pulled his badge and held it in front of him as two officers leapt from the car, pistols drawn. They appraised the scene and aimed their pistols at Mya.

Luca stepped in front of her. "Hey, she's not the perp. She was kidnapped."

The officers looked unsure.

"You might want to keep an eye on this one." Luca nudged Kevin with his toe.

"What about her?" A dark-haired constable nodded at Mya, eyeing her blood-stained hands and vacant expression.

"I'll watch her. I don't think there's anyone else on the property, but I couldn't get into the house."

The other sergeant motioned for his constable to go check.

"And someone should pick up the second victim. She's on a side road over there with my partner."

Two more officers tumbled from a second car. They didn't bother drawing their weapons as they approached Rhonda. Blood stained the light-grey gravel. A young constable dry retched when he inspected what used to be Kevin's face.

Chapter 40

"They've been in there for an hour. I've been waiting all night. Why can't I go in?" Luca pulled at his hair and paced along the hallway at the Royal Adelaide Hospital.

"You are *not* speaking to her until after the debriefing. I'm not having this case compromised." Moss sighed and placed a hand on Luca's shoulder, stilling him. "I know you're worried, Patterson, but she's in good hands. Just be patient."

He felt himself physically sag. It sucked when the boss was right.

The door clicked and he spun around. A stout psychiatrist stepped into the hall.

She tucked a short, black bob behind one ear and glanced at Luca. "Inspector Moss, may I talk freely?"

"Yes."

The psychiatrist looked doubtful, but continued. "I've persisted for an hour, but I'm not getting anywhere. She's catatonic. It's her way of dealing with the trauma she's suffered."

"I need to get a man in there to interview her as soon as possible," the inspector insisted. "How long do think she'll be like this?"

"It could be quite a while before she's coherent again, but, I do have one idea. Perhaps you could bring a friend in to see her. It might make her feel safer."

Luca's heart lurched. Was he her friend? As close as anyone else seemed to be. If he played his cards right, he could be just what the doctor needed. Moss raised an eyebrow at Luca.

He shrugged. "She has work colleagues, but I don't think she spends time with them socially. The guy at the gym seemed to know her"—his lips tightened—"but Kate and I spent more time with her this week than anyone usually does."

"Hmm." The psychiatrist ran a critical eye over Luca. "You're the one who rescued her?"

He nodded.

"Perhaps you could talk to her."

Yes, this was what he needed; to see with his own eyes that she was okay. And a tiny part of him hoped she needed to see him as much.

The inspector chewed his bottom lip. "I don't want you talking about anything that happened when she was kidnapped. Nothing that compromises this case, or you'll be on suspension faster than lightning. Understand?"

Luca smiled hugely.

He let the psychiatrist enter the sparsely furnished office first. Mya was in a wide armchair, a blanket over her legs, her hands clasped so tightly that her knuckles had turned white. A wide bandage was wrapped around her head, a hydrogel second-skin on her grazed cheek, and her eyes were puffy.

She looked rather small in the big chair, staring at a spot on the blue carpet. She didn't give any sign that she'd noticed them enter the room.

The psychiatrist sat opposite Mya and raised a hand to her lips, to indicate Luca shouldn't speak. He dragged a plastic chair beside Mya and placed a hand on her knee, stroking her long, cold fingers with his pinkie. She didn't flinch.

He felt more anxious as each minute passed. This wasn't the robust, vibrant woman he'd come to love. After a while, she grasped his finger, like a child did when its hand was too small.

Mya turned tearful eyes to him. His pulse spiked and he shot a panicked look at the psychiatrist.

"That's good. She's becoming aware of her surroundings." She passed a box of tissues to Luca and he wiped tears from Mya's cheeks.

She was back. Only barely, but it was enough to hope. It didn't matter how long it took, he would stay with her until she didn't need him anymore. All that mattered was that she was whole again. And if there was any justice in life, Mya would see how besotted he was and give him a chance to prove that he wasn't like other men she'd had in her life.

•••

Mya felt cold and empty, unsure how she got here, or where here was. There was something warm clasped in her hand and the heat radiated slowly up one arm, through her shoulder, melting the ice in her chest, which had been making it difficult to breathe.

She turned her head and met cool blue eyes with faint lines on either side. They watched as she studied them. Above was Luca's pronounced brow, honey-blond hair parted in the middle, strong cheekbones, broad nose, the faint white line of a scar over tight lips.

He looks worried.

A gentle hand wiped a tissue under each of her eyes—oh! She drew in a quick breath and held it as the flash flood of memories threatened to drown her. Kev and Rhonda tied her up, hurt her. She tried to save Natalie, but—

He came. He came to save me.

The logical part of her brain reasoned that he had to come. It was a cop's job. He probably came for Natalie and just happened to save her too.

"Natalie?" The words scratched her throat, making them barely audible.

Luca leaned closer. "She's got a few bruises, but she's all right. *You* saved her, Mya."

She sagged into the armchair, suddenly exhausted. With her eyes closed, she felt strong arms lift and hold her against a warm chest that smelled like cinnamon body wash. Her head bobbed from the movement of being carried, and soon the arms placed her onto something soft but cool. A stream of warm breath ran down her neck.

"I'll let you get some sleep now, but I'll be back," the comforting voice said. "I'll always come back for you, Mya."

She couldn't open her eyes but felt her lips curve slightly. Her limbs were heavy.

He did come for me.

Maybe this was what it felt like when someone cared. Somewhere deep inside her chest, warmth blossomed.

Chapter 41

Luca watched two uniformed officers retreat down the hospital's white hallway. They had interviewed Mya for an hour and a half, so he assumed she was speaking this morning. Moss refused to allow him to spend the night by her hospital bed, but he was itching to talk to her now.

He needed to know she would be okay, so he could tell her he couldn't live without her.

Luca tried not to breathe too deeply, because the caustic stench of disinfectant made him queasy. His temples pounded like there was a jackhammer in his skull as memories he'd rather forget slide-showed behind his retinas. He would no doubt always associate this place with Olivia in a hospital bed, her emaciated arm on top of the sheet so he could hold her hand, pressing a tiny button every five minutes to release the morphine.

Why hadn't he realized what he had until it was lost? There was no way he would make the same mistake with Mya. He couldn't make her love him back, but he could be there for her. At least offer.

Through the glass pane in the door to her room, he watched a doctor write on a clipboard, place it in the wire basket at the end of the bed, and leave the room.

"Detective Patterson?"

Luca shook the doctor's hand. Despite knowing Mya wasn't in danger, a boa constrictor coiled in his stomach in anticipation of bad news.

"You don't look like you got much sleep last night," the doctor said, offering a soft smile of nicotine-stained teeth in his dark face.

"Huh. You need recliner chairs in the waiting room. How's the patient?"

"Still sedated, but I'll be able to release her this afternoon. Your investigative team was in there for quite a while, so I don't think more visitors are a good idea for a while."

"Oh, okay."

Through the glass door, Luca could see only the end of the bed protruding from behind a pale blue curtain. Mya's feet were a bulge under the hospital blanket, and they were twitching. Impatient. He smiled.

"What's her long-term prognosis?"

"She's suffering Post Traumatic Stress Disorder—probably has been since she was sixteen."

"What does that mean for her now?"

"PTSD affects the neurotransmitters and her ability to manage stress. It tends to manifest in one of three ways: episodes of reliving the event over and over, which can be quite debilitating; avoidance, where you will see a numbing of emotional reactions and remoteness; or irritation and difficulty concentrating."

"She exhibited remoteness *before* yesterday's event."

"I'm not surprised she was showing symptoms, even after so many years, because she didn't receive treatment in her teens. Witnessing her mother beaten to within an inch of her life must have caused significant trauma to such a young mind, but she's a resilient woman, and I believe, with intense therapy—maybe over several years—she'll be able to move past this event."

"Just therapy?"

"The best thing for her is a strong social support network."

Crap, where the hell was Mya going to find that? She'd spent her whole life keeping everyone at arm's length.

"Ongoing therapy is essential, but there's an increased risk of substance abuse, depression, stress-induced disorders. Does she have family to stay with?"

"No."

"I see. It's not a good idea for her to go home alone."

"I live two doors from her. I can check on her every day and make sure she goes to therapy."

"It's not ideal, but I guess it will suffice." The doctor reached for his pager. "Excuse me." He hurried down the hall.

Luca headed back to the waiting room.

••••

Luca's back had a painful indent from the plastic hospital chairs, so he stood and stared out the window. Local residents went about their business as though no one's life hung in the balance inside the hospital.

"Thought you might need a decent coffee." Kate squeezed her lips together in a poor attempt at a smile and pushed a lidded paper cup into his hand. She looked tired, too.

"Thanks, it's been a long couple of days." He rubbed sleep from the corner of his eye and inhaled the aromatic brew. "Mmm."

"How'd the debrief go?" Kate licked foam from inside the lid of her cappuccino.

"No charges were laid, so she can go home this afternoon. Any news on Kevin?"

"He's alive, but Mya messed his face up good and proper. Looks like he'll be spending his recovery time behind bars anyway. We found a fake ID in Rhonda's handbag and an empty Sux vial on the floor of her car, which we pulled fingerprints from. I measured her hands, like you asked, and the size matches the bruising the pathologist found on Rosalie. Good call."

Luca closed his eyes. Finally they had evidence, although it came too late for some. "At least we know why Rosalie's profile broke from the group's usual method of selecting women without living family."

"Yeah, because Rhonda made it personal."

"Contact evidence has been sent to the lab and I'm waiting on results, but it looks like we can attribute six deaths at Rich Haven to the group. Unfortunately, there isn't enough surviving evidence at Happy Vale Nursing Home to act on."

"I guess we'll never know for sure."

Kate tutted. "Oh, and Old wanted me to let you know that Evan Smith was picked up at an airport in Hawaii."

"And …"

"You're not going to be happy. Looks like he cleaned out the Spurious Enterprises accounts and sent the money offshore. They're having trouble following it."

"At least we've got enough to put Kevin and Willy away." It was a relief, but the law was never a sure thing.

Only the dregs of his coffee remained, so Luca tossed the paper cup into a bin before consulting his watch for the hundredth time. He ran a hand along his jaw and felt the bite of stubble.

"Maybe I should go home, shave, and change my clothes. The doctor said Mya needs to rest. It's going to be a long road to recovery, but if she can let go of the past, I think she'll be just fine."

Kate put a hand on his shoulder. "Are you going to take that advice yourself?"

She held his gaze until he had to look away.

"What do you mean?"

"You're an intelligent man. Surely you realize you love Mya. The question is what are you going to do about it?"

He took a deep breath. "In all honesty, I want to tell her how I feel, but I—she—she's made it pretty clear all along that she's not interested in a commitment. I can't do casual anymore."

"Just tell her, Luca."

Chapter 42

Mya stared at a blue fleck in the bottle-green carpet. She knew the funeral would be like this; just her standing beside a gleaming coffin that she couldn't look at. She wrung her hands together and sneaked a glance at the glossy oak box with its brass handles and wreath of native flowers on the top. They didn't mean anything, and she didn't want to think about who was inside.

Could all of this tragedy have been avoided if only she'd stood on the street and talked to Rhonda Morten all those years ago? Luca had confirmed that Jack had abandoned Rhonda and her mother. If Cockroach had treated them as badly as her and Rosalie, she should have helped them, but Rosalie had been her primary focus at the time.

She had spilled so many tears, there was nothing left. Her mum was at peace now, no longer tormented by Jack's mistakes. The shock was that it had taken more than a decade to figure out the same went for her. She didn't have to be tormented by him anymore either. He was part of her past; some good, most bad, but in the past nonetheless.

This was her life now. She'd chosen the name, the house, the location. With a little help from Tommy and his dad, Ned, she'd learned to protect herself and keep on the straight and narrow.

Surprisingly, Mya didn't feel as empty as she thought she would. Sure, there was an ache for the loss of her mother, but memories glowed deep inside her. They were untouchable and smouldered beside something unexpected: a warm feeling for Luca.

Discovering an emotional connection to him had been a surprise, but one she wouldn't trade for quids. He had seen what she was capable of and still he was the first face she recognized at the hospital. Twice a day he had dropped in to see her since she went home. Most evenings he stayed until late, and she knew he was trying to help her feel safe. She didn't yet, but his company helped. Each night, before he left, he switched on the nightlight beside her bed and waited on the porch until he heard the two bolts slide across.

The funeral director stuck her head through the door and flashed a half smile.

"Is everything okay in here?"

God, if only that woman would stop asking. She'd told her no hymns, no eulogy, or photos on the overhead projector. After all, this wasn't the first time she'd mourned her mother. Rosalie had been thirty-seven years old when Cockroach stole her life the first time and forty-nine when Rhonda finally took it.

Natalie had picked Mya's dress for the funeral—a black number with a faux white handkerchief protruding from a sealed breast pocket. Suitably conservative with a knee-length hem and three-quarter sleeves. Probably the last time it would see daylight.

Mya's arms hung by her side. Had she stood there long enough? How long was sufficient to pay respect to someone who lived inside her?

She flinched as a large hand wrapped around hers. Her gaze followed a suited arm up to Luca's powder-blue eyes. His face was solemn. He nodded to her other side and she turned to see a relaxed Natalie wearing a dazzling cubic zirconia resting on a velvet ribbon around her throat. An elderly couple hovered protectively behind her—the couple she boarded with, no doubt.

Beverly Aldridge gave a timid wave behind Natalie. Beside her, Tommy from the gym had gone all out in a shirt and slacks. Even old Bert Reiner had combed his hair to one side and put on a tie. His face crinkled into a smile when she made eye contact. Then the Croydon Hotel contingent arrived with a flurry: Flynn in an Irish-green suit and Jilly hanging onto his arm to balance in stiletto heels.

A lump stuck in her throat at the sight of all these people in her life. They'd been there all this time, but she hadn't realized how permanently they'd taken up residence.

Kate appeared with a single white rose in one hand. She placed the delicate bloom on top of the coffin, then kissed Mya on the cheek. Her embrace was unexpected, and Mya's throat constricted further. Tears pricked her eyes.

Luca squeezed her hand and she stepped back to get a good look at him. He was dashing in a navy suit, his hair pulled off his face. He looked like … family.

She wasn't alone anymore.

Chapter 43

Two months later

Luca straightened his shirt collar and adjusted the bunch of orange-spotted tiger lilies in front of him. Usually he'd bring wine to a dinner invitation, but Mya didn't drink. He'd been at her house every day during the past eight weeks, so it was ridiculous how nervous he felt. He knocked on the door and waited. This was the first time he'd actually been *invited* into her home.

She hadn't made it clear why this meal was different to any other—plenty of times he'd lobbed on her doorstep with a bag of groceries and started cooking—but it felt different. Almost like a date.

I shouldn't get too excited; she hasn't let me in yet. He chuckled.

The familiar sound of two bolts sliding across the back of the door brought a smart comment to his lips, but it died as the door opened.

Mya wore a lemon-yellow cotton dress. Mouth wide, his appraisal started at her bare feet and followed slender legs until they disappeared under folds of light material. A breeze pressed the cotton against her lean body so it clung to her curves. It took his breath away. When he finally dragged his gaze back to her face, her cheeks were pink.

"Natalie," she said by way of an explanation for the attire.

"You look beautiful." He presented the flowers.

She smiled demurely and headed for the kitchen.

Luca did his best to play it casual, like any other night. "Can I help?"

"Sure, we're dining al fresco." She poured tap water into a saucepan and settled the flowers in it. "You can take those outside."

She pointed to a pile of plates, serviettes and cutlery. "And there's a bottle of water in the fridge."

Luca followed her instructions and stepped onto the small, hardwood deck. Grape vines coiled up support posts and across overhead beams, providing lush shade. He set two places at the wood-slat table and folded the napkins. The muscles in his stomach trembled. The lunch was too civilized for the Mya the world saw, but he knew a different woman: sensual, intelligent, and resilient.

It thrilled him that he knew insignificant stuff about her, too, like the fact her favourite reading spot was the wrought iron seat by the shed, where she could hear bees hum in the vegetable garden.

The back door squeaked. Mya pushed through, carrying a plate of antipasto and cheeses.

"That looks delicious," he commented. They stood on opposite sides of the table in awkward silence.

Best to go with small talk until she settled in. "Hey, have you heard from Natalie lately?"

"Yeah, the old folks helped her get a jeweler's apprenticeship. She's stoked."

"She deserves it."

Mya cut a sliver of brie and pressed it onto a cracker. "Yep, she's really talented."

The sight of her in that yellow dress was more than Luca could resist. He walked around the table and took her hand in his, ignoring how her body stiffened at the touch. As he stared into her hazel eyes, her throat tensed and she swallowed. Full lips shone with a smear of pink gloss and he couldn't resist their magnetic pull.

Lightly, he brushed his mouth across hers.

They stood cheek to cheek and he savoured the familiar lavender scent on her skin, her warm breath on his neck. He needed to take this slowly. With the tip of one finger, he traced her spine between her shoulder blades, down the small of her back, and pulled her hips closer. With his other hand, he stroked her cheek and neck, thrilled when she leaned into his touch.

"Mya," he whispered.

He took her face between his hands and kissed her, deeply. Not frantic like the first time, more sensual. When they pulled apart, her cheeks were flushed. Hell was more likely to freeze over before she admitted actual feelings for him, but he needed to know. He was too old and worn out to do casual flings anymore.

"Is this what you want?"

He was prepared for resistance, but the sadness that shuttered her face crushed a tiny piece inside him. Of course, she'd spent a lifetime pushing people away. Too long to just give up her defenses.

"I'm not interested in occasional anymore, Mya. I know how great life can be when you share it with the right person, and I want that again. Olivia taught me so much about devotion to someone you can't live without. But it's taken seven years to learn her final lesson. I wouldn't listen at the end, when she promised I'd find someone worth risking my heart for again, but I did, and it's you. I don't have any preconceived ideas about how this will work. I just know I want it to. Do you?"

She tried to untangle herself from him, but he kept hold of one hand. A warm reminder of what he knew her heart desired.

"How can I ever live up to Olivia? She sounds perfect, not damaged like me."

"You're looking at this all wrong, Mya. Olivia is a part of my past I'll never forget or regret, but I'm not looking to relive what I felt with her. You are a completely different person and I couldn't help but fall in love with you, because I like that person. No one is flawless, not you and especially not me."

"I don't think I can give you what you want," she whispered.

He waited while she seemed to search for words.

"I haven't been in love like you, Luca. It's not worth it for me."

"But that's where you're wrong. It *is* worth it." He held a hand up against her protest. "I'm not saying it will magically erase your past, but it will give you strength. You don't have to do everything on your own."

Her head bowed, breathing became unsteady and, when she looked up, her eyes were moist. It tugged at his heart. He hated to see her in any kind of pain.

"I'm sorry. I didn't mean to—" With one finger he wiped a tear from the corner of her eye.

"You're right, I can't do it on my own," she said, "but I don't know how to do it any other way."

"I'm not asking you to move in with me or sell your house. I know you need to keep control. And I don't want to control your life, just share it."

"And what happens when you hurt me?" Her expression was suddenly ferocious.

"Look, we might argue, sure, but I will *never* hit you."

This time when she pulled away, he let her. With an internal sigh, and although it tugged at every fibre of his being, he turned his back. He cut a wedge of fruit cheese and slapped it on a biscuit.

She needed to make the decision.

By the time he was on his third serve of antipasto, it felt like gravel going down his constricted throat. That was when her slender arms slid around his waist. She pressed against his back and rested her head between his shoulder blades. Luca felt the tension drain from both of them. He smiled but didn't move.

She had to want it, say it.

Want me.

• • •

Mya was perfectly content to rest on Luca's broad back forever, but she knew she couldn't. He wanted more. Maybe more than she had to give.

The mystery of the toiletries he'd packed and brought to Kate's house after the explosion, had been something she'd thought a lot about. Today she finally understood why he left the makeup out. He liked her just the way she was.

The doctor had told her Luca didn't need to check on her twice a day anymore, but still he came. Not demanding anything, hardly even touching her, just being there. They did regular stuff, like play cards, tend the veggie garden, and sit in the sun with a book. Once he coaxed her out of the house to see a movie.

He had seen her at her worst, yet here he was, standing on her deck eating cheese and water crackers. With a deep breath for fortitude, she stepped back and pulled him around to face her. His expression was tentative.

"I want to try," she whispered.

"Really?" He sounded incredulous.

She nodded.

"Truly?"

She nodded again.

His eyes lit up as his shell-white teeth were exposed and he swooped her off her feet. With her arms around his neck, he turned full circle and crushed his lips against hers with a new intensity. It sent a jolt of raw energy through her body.

When he set her back onto her feet, she pressed against him. The thin fabric between them did nothing to hide the contours of his body, and her hands started to explore. She tugged the shirt out of his pants and her hands roamed across his warm back. Tiny raised bumps were scattered across it; scar tissue from the bomb shrapnel. She forced the thought away and focused on the dips and curves of his body. God she'd missed his touch.

The memory of their naked bodies in his bed ignited a white hot flame of desire that flared and engulfed her from heel to crown. Luca's lips skipped down her neck and she hooked a leg over his hip in an effort to get closer. His hot palm skimmed her thigh and went under the dress, exploring the tiny lace knickers.

She fumbled with shirt buttons and in frustration, pulled back suddenly.

His hands stilled.

She wrapped a hand around his. "Dinner can wait." A sly smile played on her lips.

There was a moment of confusion on his face when he realised where she was leading.

"In *your* bed?"

"Yes. Just so long as you remember I can kick your arse anytime."

His mouth pulled up in her favourite crooked smile.

"Then I'd better make sure I perform. No girlfriend of mine is going to miss out on orgasms."

Girlfriend—now there was a word she could get used to. And she didn't mind the sound of orgasm either.

About the Author

www.sandyvaile.com

I'm Sandy Vaile and my motto in life is *I'll try anything once*. To that end I take every opportunity that presents and have a wealth of life experiences to draw on when writing.

Home is a wine-producing region in South Australia. By day I'm a quality coordinator (that's code for list making word nerd), mother, and wife, shadowed by a rambunctious Hungarian Vizsla. But when I let my hair down, I'm a motorbike riding, tattoo wielding, daredevil.

Okay, I'm not that exciting all the time. I do the regular stuff, too, like pottering in the garden, preparing (mostly eating) decadent desserts, reading inspirational fiction, and listening to soul-nourishing music—from acoustic ensembles to hard rock.

I was captivated by creative writing from a young age, with a career in journalism mapped out at high school. Unfortunately, I received some early lessons in the unexpected nature of life, and was diverted from my true calling. It wasn't until I'd ~~settled down~~ had children, and matured that I rediscovered the joy of reading and writing.

I've dabbled in fantasy, sci-fi, and short stories, but my real love is suspense. (I can't imagine why when I love to jump out of planes, ride hot air balloons and get tattoos.) My accolades include publishing various short stories, competition placements, a short listing for Mya's story in the Valerie Parv Award, and judging romance writing contests.

My goal when writing is that other people will connect with my characters and their hardships as closely as I do. Enjoy!

To learn more about this author, visit *www.sandyvaile.com*, *Facebook*, or Twitter *@Sandy_Vaile*.

A Sneak Peek from Crimson Romance
(From *In the Shadow of Vengeance*
by Nancy C. Weeks)

This can't be happening again. It's too soon.

Elizabeth Williams caressed her lower abdomen. Of course it could happen this quickly; it was a simple fact of life. Women could get pregnant within weeks of giving birth.

On the upside, at least she didn't have to worry about stomach crunches for another nine months. But even that positive thought didn't erase the anxiety churning through her. The demands of the coveted nursing program weren't going to ease because she juggled the care of two infants. And then there was her dream to travel the globe with Spencer, providing medical aid to areas that needed it most. They could have managed with one child, but two would place that opportunity on the back burner for years.

She shifted her position in the driver seat and glanced at the entrance to the hospital as she dug the plastic pregnancy stick from her back pocket. All she had to do was get out of the car, walk across the parking lot, and find her husband. They would talk it out together and find a way to enjoy their growing family while keeping their dreams alive. At this hour, he was most likely in his office. He didn't have any surgeries scheduled on Saturday, but he did go in to make his rounds. That afternoon, they planned to drive to her parents' farm three hours east of Omaha for her father's birthday. Once her husband learned about the baby and they both had time to process it, this time away from the hospital would be refreshing.

Erin wasn't planned, but she brought such joy into their life. And although Elizabeth's and Spencer's relationship seemed a little strained lately, that was stress. Every couple went through low periods. He spent long hours making a name for himself as a surgical resident. Elizabeth's sister thought he was selfish with his attention, but she didn't understand him. Spencer dedicated himself completely to his patients, and they loved him for the time he gave to them. There wasn't a more compassionate surgeon than Elizabeth's husband.

Easing her grip on the steering wheel, she smiled at her beautiful daughter in the infant mirror above her dashboard. Erin was so tiny, only fourteen pounds, but right at her target weight for a four-month-old. "Your daddy loves you, sweet girl, and he's going to love your brother or sister, too. This is going to be a good thing."

Opening the door, she released her seatbelt and got out. The warmth of the midday sun brushed over her face, and a sense of calm settled her nerves. It would all work out because it had to. They were a family. Her parents must have had rough patches in their thirty years of marriage. That was all this was, a rough patch.

Lifting the sleeping infant out of the car carrier, she cradled her against her heart. The soft baby scent drove away any apprehension. "Well, Erin, my girl," Elizabeth whispered, glancing at her wrist watch, "Let's find your father and tell him the good news together. Seeing your sweet face will make it all okay."

At that moment, the automatic doors to the hospital entrance whooshed open and her husband raced out. She called out to him, but he must have not heard her. He didn't even pause at the crosswalk between the entrance and the parking lot. A stunning, dark-skinned woman Elizabeth had never seen before met him at his car only two rows away. He unlocked the passenger door of his Jaguar and moved aside so she could drop into the seat. He then ran around and got in. The familiar sound of the engine roared to life and he drove out of the lot, never once looking back.

Numbness settled deep into Elizabeth's bones. She knew what she had witnessed, but her heart hadn't caught up to her mind. A huge part of her wanted to ignore what she had seen and take her daughter home.

As she secured Erin back in the infant carrier, she kept an eye on Spencer's red Jaguar. Instead of turning right toward home or the clinic at the stop sign, he took a left. Elizabeth quickly got back behind the wheel of her Mazda and followed him, keeping several cars back. Midday traffic was heavy, making it easier to keep up with him.

As her mind came up with one excuse after another why he left the hospital with that woman, one stood out, taking on a life of its own.

Spencer was having an affair.

The sentence repeated itself over again as her heartbeats bounced against her ribcage. That was the reason he was so distant with her. Except for a brief moment of passion when they'd conceived the baby, it had been weeks since they made love.

When she caught up to him, it wasn't going to be a pleasant reunion. She believed every person had a nasty side, and hers was in high gear. If Spencer was cheating on her, she had to know the truth. If he wasn't, she would owe him a hell of an apology. At least it would open up communication between them.

A quick glance at Erin, and Elizabeth said a silent prayer that her daughter slept through what was slowly turning from a moment of madness into a full-blown bat-crazy. As much as she wanted to turn around and leave well enough alone, a gut feeling propelled her to continue.

Of course this was sheer madness. They had been in love for three years, almost inseparable—until she got pregnant with Erin. They'd met during her first week of nursing school at the University of Nebraska. After a whirlwind romance that lasted half the year, he asked her to move in with him. Since her parents would have had a conniption fit at the thought of their daughter living with a boyfriend, they married. And for the most part, they were very happy together. What made her jump down this rabbit hole?

Spencer's schedule.

He never left the surgical unit in the middle of the day. Everything in his life was planned out in advance and no one messed with that plan. He should be in his office, checking on lab results, going through the mountain of paperwork. You could set your clock by Spencer's schedule. So where the heck was he going?

After several blocks, Spencer zigzagged through an unfamiliar area of the city. This was the stupidest thing she'd ever done, and she needed to turn around. She hit her turn signal at the next light when the Jaguar shifted lanes and turned into an office complex. Elizabeth eased off the accelerator and followed him through several turns until he parked in front of a two-story building.

Shady Grove Outpatient Surgery Center. And to think she had expected a hotel.

Elizabeth pulled into the spot where she could see the entrance of the center and Spencer's Jaguar. He opened the car door for the woman and she placed a hand at his elbow as if he was hers to claim.

"The bitch," she whispered through clenched teeth.

They rushed up the sidewalk. Spencer drew her against him and kissed her neck as she tried to unlock the door. Elizabeth shut her eyes tightly and took in a shaky breath.

"Bastard! That low-life, cheating bastard." When she opened her eyes, they were gone. She choked back a sob and slammed her fist into the steering wheel.

What seemed like hours on her nerves were only a few minutes. She unclipped her belt and got out of the car. Gently unlatching Erin from the car seat, she hugged her to her chest. Bringing your daughter to confront your cheating husband had to be the lowest on any list. But she couldn't very well knock on the babysitter's door and ask her to keep an eye on her daughter while she followed her rat-bastard husband either.

Elizabeth wanted to stomp her foot and cuss up a storm. Instead, she placed one foot in front of the other until she reached the double glass entrance door to the facility. A thick heaviness settled over her. The large oak tree at the corner of the lot that separated parking between the Outpatient Surgery Center and the Shady Grove Imaging Center next door stood completely still. She searched the sky and spotted thick storm clouds south of the city. It was if her mood were affecting the weather.

With a shaky hand, she grabbed the door handle and it turned. Easing across the foyer into the plush, cool reception area, she moved around the nurse's station. A deep maternal instinct made her hold Erin close to her as she silently made her way toward the back of the building. The fact that her sweet baby could sleep through one of the worst moments in Elizabeth's life was a true blessing.

She struggled with how to handle this moment. Did she call out to the cheating pair before they had a chance to get naked and personal, or did she sneak around like an idiot and catch them in the act? How was this game played? There should be a rulebook on how to discover your spouse in the act of committing adultery. He was breaking every damn promise he'd ever made her.

A hum of voices caught her attention and she moved to the end of the long hallway. The doors to what looked like examination rooms were open except for the last one on the left. The voices grew angry, especially her husband's.

"Why did you bring him here? I told you I couldn't do this today."

"Even with a rush transport, we may still not make it in time. I didn't have a choice."

"There are always choices, Victor. One of them is to follow my orders to the letter."

She had never heard that tone of voice from Spencer, nor did she recognize the other man speaking. One thing was clear: the chill that sliced down her spine wasn't caused by seeing her husband with another woman. He might be having an affair, but that wasn't all that was going on here.

Well, crap, now what? Standing right outside the door, Elizabeth had two choices: walk away or make herself known. Her mother's famous saying slid across her mind. *If you're going to step in cow manure, better make it worth your while.*

Placing her hand on the door, she pushed it open midway. It took a moment for her mind to focus.

God, oh God.

She couldn't pull away from the gruesome scene in front of her. She had seen surgery performed before. This wasn't it. This was—

Blood. The migrant worker they treated at the clinic, unconscious. The ventilator. Spencer's surgical assistant with his hands covered in blood. The kicker, the one thing that slammed Elizabeth's heart into her gut, was the familiar white container with the international symbol for live organ donor plastered on all sides.

Spencer was harvesting organs.

Her arms went around Erin as she backed out of the room. Spencer's muffled angry voice called out to the others in the room, but all she could hear was her heart drumming between her ears.

Nothing in Elizabeth's world made sense. All she knew was she had to get out of there. If Spencer was capable of—whatever the hell this was, she had to protect Erin and the new baby.

Keeping an arm over Erin, she sprinted out the door and around the side of the building to her car. In record time, she had the infant in her car seat and was backing out of the space as Spencer, still in his surgical garb, raced out of the building. The man with him pulled out a handgun and aimed it at her car.

Spencer shoved his elbow into the man's gut before running to his own Jaguar.

Elizabeth didn't wait around for introductions but sped out of the lot onto the service road. Erin began to squirm. Any minute, she would let loose how she felt about being jarred awake from her nap, making this nightmare even more difficult. Since there was too much traffic coming toward her to return the way Elizabeth came, she turned south, pressed down hard on the accelerator, and drove.

Humming a tune that usually helped relax her daughter, she glared into the rearview mirror as Spencer's Jaguar pulled behind her. Not waiting for the light to change to green, she spun right again onto a four-lane road. She had no idea where she was going. Her strategy was to place as much distance between her and her husband as possible until she could figure out a better plan.

The car movement must have rocked Erin back to sleep. Thank God for small miracles. The four-lane road turned into two lanes on the outskirts of town and headed out of Omaha. Elizabeth couldn't decide if she should take the next turnoff and return the way she came, or keep driving.

Did she really see what she thought she saw? The man on the table had been seen at the clinic a couple of times for a sprained wrist. She remembered taking his vital signs and hearing about his wife and son. He worked the farms in the area, saving money to send back to his family. He couldn't be more than twenty-five years old.

She wiped the back of her hand across her eyes, clearing away the moisture so she could see. Shit, what was Spencer involved in? There had to be an explanation for the white organ donor case and the man with the gun.

She couldn't even remember the young immigrant worker's name. If they were harvesting his organs, that meant Spencer—the man she fell in love with, had two children with—was a monster.

She choked back a sob as she searched Erin's diaper bag in the seat next to her for her cell phone. Her father would know what to do. He and her mom were probably sitting down for lunch.

The last couple of cars turned off and Spencer pulled right behind her again. Bone-deep fear raced through her as she searched out the front window. Any hope of losing him failed. All signs of the city disappeared as the landscape turned to rolling hills and farmland. Neat rows of corn that seem to go on for miles grew on both sides of the road. While their stalk height obstructed her view from seeing any signs of a town in the distance, she couldn't miss the low threatening storm clouds right in front of her.

Spencer increased his speed until he was right on her back bumper. He signaled with his hand for her to pull over. When she ignored him, he tapped her bumper with his car, jerking her forward.

She shot him a glare and shook her head. "Not just no, you sick bastard, but no way in hell am I going to get stuck out here in the boonies alone with you and your hit man."

The expression on the face of the man who sat next to Spencer wasn't hard to read, even at the speed she was driving. If he had his way, she would have never left the parking lot of the outpatient surgery center.

She dug deeper into the bag but still couldn't feel her phone. A vivid list of cuss words slid across her tongue. Not knowing what else to do, she pressed down on the accelerator and hugged the middle of the road. If she couldn't hide from him or outrun him, she could keep him from passing and cutting her off.

As she searched above the corn stalks for signs of another town, the sky turned a grayish black, casting deep shadows over the landscape as a hard gust of wind whipped around her, making it difficult to control her car. She clutched the steering wheel with both hands. The jagged lightning bolts that seemed to strike the road ahead jolted her. When bulky stalks of corn hit her window, Elizabeth almost jumped out of her seat.

"Crap! Now what?" She screamed as more debris slammed into her car. An instant later, the sky ripped open and hail pounded down onto her roof.

Spencer blasted his horn at her several times. Her eyes scanned the horizon for the funnel cloud. Living in Tornado Alley all her life, she didn't ignore the signs.

The wind became so unyielding, she slowed her car and pulled over to the side of the road. With a possible madman behind her and a funnel cloud somewhere above, she had no place to run. But the one thing her father had drilled into his children was to never try to outrun a tornado nor find shelter in a car. Both options were death traps.

She swung Erin's diaper bag over her shoulder and got out of the car. Spencer pulled behind her. Covering her head with one arm to protect against the golf ball-sized hail, she opened the back door and reached for the infant Snugli, putting it on like a backpack with the pouch in front.

Spencer stepped out of his car. "Elizabeth, what the hell are you—"

The roar of the wind took the rest of the sentence. He ducked down as stalks of corn struck him. She settled Erin in the front pouch and removed the thickest blanket from her bag. Wrapping it around Erin's head, she raced toward a low-lying ditch across the road.

A new calm settled over her the instant she held her daughter against her. It didn't matter what Spencer had done or who the man with the gun was. All that mattered at that moment was protecting Erin from the storm that raged overhead. There was only one safety net and Elizabeth had to find it fast. If this field was anything like her father's, there would be a narrow dirt road.

And where that dirt road intersected the paved road, there should be a storm drain.

As if her very thoughts summoned it to her, her hand landed on a raised mound. She quickly turned and searched the road for Spencer, but the sky opened the floodgates and sheets of rain pounded down on top of her. She couldn't have seen her own hand in front of her face, and the howl of the wind was deafening. With one hand shielding Erin's head, she felt for the cemented half-circle opening, and crawled into the dark, wet drain. Settling her back against the side, she removed the soaked blanket and tried to calm her screaming infant.

She didn't have a clue how long she hid in the storm drain, but one minute, the heavens were raining terror down on her and the next, everything was completely calm. The wind died down and the rain turned to a drizzle. She hugged her daughter and slowly eased out of the drain.

She stumbled backward at her first glance at her surroundings. The road was so completely covered in debris, she couldn't see the asphalt. Rows of corn were flattened to the ground.

She climbed the wet slope to the road. Where was her car? Spencer and his gun-happy friend were nowhere in sight. Taking in a shaky breath, she wrapped both arms around Erin, who had finally stopped screaming.

She remembered every sickening event that led her to this place, but her mind couldn't focus on what she was supposed to do next. Placing one foot in front of the other, she headed down the center of the road.

This must be what shock feels like.

Time stilled as she cradled Erin. The closeness seemed to calm both of them. She followed the sounds of sirens that grew louder the closer she got to a small, one-road town. Wandering down the center of what had to be Main Street, she wanted to scream out to turn that damn siren off, but she couldn't muster up the energy.

The few people in the street had the same dazed look on their faces Elizabeth assumed was on hers. The tornado had done a number on the buildings. Very few stood upright. Fragments of the drywall, glass, twisted lumber, and trash covered the road and sidewalks.

A woman approached. "Dear, are you all right?"

She wasn't sure how she found her voice, but Elizabeth answered. "Yes, ma'am. My daughter and I are fine."

The woman glanced around her. "It came up out of nowhere. I was in my garden and barely had time to get into the basement."

She didn't know what to say to that. Instead, she asked the only question on her mind. "How close is the interstate from here?" She didn't care where she was, only how to get back home.

The stranger placed a hand on Elizabeth's arm. "It's about three miles down the road. I need to go check on my husband. He runs the boot shop there," she said, pointing across the street. Her voice cracked as she said, "You are welcome to wait on my porch. My home, by God's grace, wasn't hit."

Elizabeth nodded her thanks and watched as the woman made her way to her husband. Instead of settling on the porch, however, she headed toward the car in the driveway. It hadn't been touched either. Looking inside the driver's side window, she spotted the keys in the ignition. Before she could talk herself out of what would be the second stupidest thing she did that day, she opened the car door and got behind the wheel. Wrapping the seat belt around her and Erin, she pulled out of the driveway and drove back the way she had come. The words *just borrowing the car* seeped across her consciousness. She never glanced back as she headed toward the highway.

Even though the road was covered in cornstalks and wreckage, she made it to the interstate and headed toward Omaha. The closer she got to the city, the less storm damage there was.

Elizabeth had a choice to make. She could take the beltway around the city and head due east toward her childhood home. Her parents would know what to do, and she had never needed them more than at that moment. But at the turnoff, instead of taking the exit east, the fear of bringing this nightmare to her parents' door compelled her to take the exit for downtown instead. She drove several blocks and slowed when she reached a ten-story white building she had always been curious about but never had any reason to visit. Entering the short driveway, she drove up to the guarded gate. Behind the iron gates was a large insignia that hung on the side of the building: Federal Bureau of Investigation.

Elizabeth turned off the car and unbuckled her seatbelt. Glancing down at her soiled, wet clothing, she ran a hand over her hair and tried not to look like she felt: unbalanced. The guard approached her as she got out of the car.

"Ma'am, you need to stay in the car."

She cleared her throat as she zoomed in on the guard's hand moving toward the handgun at his side. "Tornado … not sure where," she blared out in a strained whisper. "I had to borrow this car. It's not mine. I don't know what happened to my car."

"Ma'am, are you hurt? The baby you're holding …?"

Elizabeth touched her lips to the top of her child's head. "Erin's my daughter. I need to talk to someone. There's been a murder." She sucked in a deep breath. "I think it's a murder, not sure … I'm not sure of anything."

In the mood for more Crimson Romance?
Check out *A Love Beyond* by Leslie P. García
at *CrimsonRomance.com*.